Where It All Began

SAPPHIRE HALE

All characters and events in this publication, other than those clearly in the public domain, are fictitious and any resemblance to real persons, living or dead, is purely coincidental.

ISBN: 9798390615898

DEDICATION

For my Mama and my Papa,
and for the readers who loved Where We Left Off.
You are the reason why I write.

CONTENTS

PLAYLISTS

KITTY

Knife Under My Pillow – Maggie Lindemann
Bring Me To Life – Evanescence
Lolita – Lana Del Rey
Mother's Daughter – Miley Cyrus
The Heart Wants What It Wants – Selena Gomez
Jet Black Heart – 5 Seconds of Summer
Make Your Own Kind Of Music – The Mamas and The Papas
Radio – Lana Del Rey

MADDEN

Out Of My Limit – 5 Seconds of Summer
I'm Not A Vampire – Falling in Reverse
Break Stuff – Limp Bizkit
Infra-Red – Three Days Grace
Make Up Sex – Machine Gun Kelly ft. blackbear
Bad Omens – 5 Seconds of Summer
Down – Blink-182
Bloody Valentine – Machine Gun Kelly

CHAPTER 1

Kitty

"Come here, Pumpkin."

My dad pulls me in for a hug as my mom shuts up the livestock transportation carrier box attached to the back of the truck. He's Scandinavian decent, his parents French Canadian, and being wrapped up in his arms is like Olympic wrestling with the Terminator. He's six-three, weighs more than some of our farming equipment, and, to top it all off, his name is Hardy.

A more appropriate name I cannot imagine.

On the other hand my mom, Marie Hanson Lu, is fairy-limbed and thimble-sized. Her parents emigrated to the States from China, and my dad was smitten from the second that he laid his eyes on her. With long onyx hair and big sparkly eyes, Mama is my own personal doppelganger.

When the final molecule of air is squeezed from my lungs Papa releases me and then gives me a smack on the back for good measure.

The gesture is meant to be comforting. It almost has me flying international.

"You'll be good whilst we're away?" My mom gives me a mock-concerned look and then clutches me into an embrace of her own. Although she's acting as if she's joking, I know that she also sort of isn't, so technically what she's giving me is a mock-mock-concerned look. It's meta as hell.

And it's not as if their worries are founded on any tangible evidence – I am the model child. I actively participated in high school. I got good grades. I only dropped out of college when they collectively decided that it would be more financially expedient for me to go straight into admin at the ranch, instead of paying for a qualification that a career working my parents' pastures didn't require. Compared to my brother Kaleb, whose family participation goes no further than a monthly text to confirm that he's still breathing, I am Saint Kitty.

Also unlike Kaleb, I am not on the road for ninety-nine percent of the year, touring with a tough sweaty rock band. I should get double points for that one.

"She's always good," my dad beams.

Thank you, Papa. I reward him with my most dimply smile.

"I know," my mom placates soothingly, "but it's dangerous out here is all."

End Of The Road Ranch, simultaneously our home and our livelihood, is located Far Far Away from basically everything. We live at the farthest point of Phoenix Falls, and my mom isn't kidding about the potential dangers out here. Located just before the thick forest that trickles its way up into the back mountains, this land is known to home all kinds of wild animals that you wouldn't want to come across, ever. Plus, there's the fact that we have a *lot* of land, and not every Average Joe is happy to accept that. Rural territory is a big deal here, and my parents aren't afraid to enforce that reminder by occasionally flexing their constitutional rights.

I glance into the passenger side of the truck. My Papa's pistol winks back at me.

"I'll check the locks every night," I reply. Which predator I'm keeping locked out, who the hell knows. At this point, there are too many to count.

"I know you will," my mom says, smiling, although there's another emotion that I can't quite put my finger on twinkling behind her pretty eyes.

Whilst my mom is making the most of the summer's American quarter horse competitions, it's all up to me to maintain our land and our livestock. I know that it's doable – I've spent every single summer feeding and rotating the animals, and priming the harvest – but to do it on your *own* is not exactly a sensible feat. Forget coyotes and rival ranch-hands, you can get chopped up by your own machines. Hurricanes, wild fires – if you can name it, it's out for blood.

Which is another reason why I'm side-eyeing my parents so suspiciously right now. They're really going to leave me – barely out of her teens, weighs-less-than-a-sack-of-grain Kitty – to protect the land all on my own? Personally, I love the idea of a female lone ranger – I mean, it's about time – but even *I'm* getting little nervous butterflies fluttering around in my belly. Originally my mom was going to be travelling solo but, at the last minute, my dad decided to accompany her, therefore entrusting me to watch over everything until they return.

It's all highly suspect.

"Stock up those cupboards as soon as we're outta here. Card's on the counter," my dad instructs as they give me a final parting compression, making me the filling in a squishy pumpkin sandwich.

Papa gives my cheek a pinch as my mom dips into the passenger side of the truck, and then he's hauling himself into the driver's seat, ready to chauffeur his prized cowgirl across the country.

"Call you later, Pumpkin!" he shouts over the rev of the engine, eyes on the gravel pathway up ahead but still waving to me with his free hand. The sound of my mom's favourite The Mamas and The Papas CD starts to infiltrate the air as they roll down their windows, but in seconds all that remains are the thick tire tracks in the dirt and the sandy particles that the wheels kicked up, twinkling gold in the hazy June air.

I squint at the vehicle until it's out of sight, and then I take a moment to let the sun sizzle my skin like a little steak cutlet. My eyes wander across to the fields ahead, separated by wooden fencing and metal twine, and I mentally itinerate my tasks for today, tomorrow, and the coming weeks ahead.

Then the dust settles.

And I'm on my own.

*

About a minute after I put my foot on the pedal, already light-years away from the supermarket lot, I realise what I've forgotten.

Novelty cereals – the type that when you pour them into your bowl you feel like you're on an acid trip – are my favourite vice. Tame enough that my parents always indulged my infatuation, but with just enough E-numbers to really spice up my mornings.

Irritated by my lack of focus, I get a bit heavy-heeled as I pull away from the town square, fingers twiddling with the radio dial.

I'm going to have to ration my last box of Teddy Grahams. One teddy a day for the rest of the week.

Once I'm safely returned to the ranch I park up in the garage, grab my bounty from the back, and then make my way up the porch steps, arms laden with sun cream and bags of candy. A thousand new freckles later, I fish out my key and let myself in.

Our family home is an open-plan two-story wood and stone cabin, snuggled up between the garage, the shop, and the livestock barn and stable. It overlooks the land that we use for the animals and crop cultivation, and behind it sits one section of pasture, inclining gradually before you reach the bushy green forest and dark mountains beyond. In the winter it's a sparkling gingerbread house, loaded with thick sugar-icing. In the summer it's a sun-trap, and as desiccated as a coconut.

I stock up the cupboards, wash my hands, and then strip down to my underwear, throwing my clothes straight into the machine. I've sweat so much that I need a hosing, so I pad up the stairs to the gallery corridor and I treat myself to a fully-submerging soak. I rest my phone within arm's reach, lazily scrolling through my music library as I recline in my pouf of bubbles. I marinate, roll over, and then give myself one luxurious minute to stretch the muscles in my back, sore from all of the manual shit that I had to do this morning.

It's only mid-afternoon by the time that I'm out and dried but I slip into a clean pair of summer pyjamas anyway. The shorts are white with a black and red check, and the tank is a dainty cropped number. They're as girly as emo clothes go and I think that they're cute as hell.

I'm about to tread downstairs for a meeting with my candy haul when a much better idea suddenly appears in my mind.

My eyes slide over to Kaleb's bedroom door.

I back-step, flick the handle, and the door lazily wanes open. Would you look at that. I give it some extra encouragement with my hip until I have the full visual of his two-years-untouched teenage bedroom, and my heart-eyes instantly zone in on the object of my desires.

Kaleb's Fender.

I pad into the room and then drop down onto the floor, curling my feet up under my butt as I rest the guitar in my lap. *Kitty's Fender.* I stroke it with my fingers, thinking about how much better it would look in my room, and then I start strumming out a couple of chords, singing along with it.

I purse my lips when I reach the end of the song, my thumb a little sore because I don't have a guitar pick. *Yet.* I glance around the room, sure that there'll be a stray one somewhere in here for me to smuggle.

I mean, is it even stealing? Kaleb left it here, so obviously it's currently of no use to him. Plus, I'm not *exactly* stealing. It's more a case of *borrowing*.

The thing is, dropping out of college was a total freaking blessing. My parents were right – I *didn't* need to do a management course if my intention was to work full-time on the ranch.

And I would need to do one even less so if my intentions were to be a *singer*.

It's not something that I'm particularly vocal about with my parents, and even less so with Kaleb. I don't want to let them down and I don't want a bollocking for being a copycat sibling, so for the most part I just do my duty.

But if no-one's going to be around…

My mind flicks back to a poster that I saw on the pin-board outside the bar in town a couple of weeks ago. Every year just outside of Phoenix Falls there's a small town talent contest called the Barn Bonanza, which takes place in front of the giant barn at the back of the colonial hotel that hosted my high school prom, a night that was eventful to say the least.

The event is for people with huge musical talent – I'm talking the kind where you can sing, yodel, and ukulele at the same time. It's kind of an excuse for a big community get-together, but the winner gets a sponsorship with a nearby recording company, studio time, and the potential opportunity to get signed by Christmas.

Long story short, my parents are out of town, I have an abandoned guitar in my arms, and – oh yeah – *I can sing.* I couldn't believe my luck when Papa said that he would be leaving me solo these next few weeks instead of staying at the ranch with me. If everything stays according to schedule then there is no way that I am *not* competing in the Barn Bonanza this year.

I've already got in with the doorman from the bar in town so that I can have practice time on their stage, getting used to the equipment and maybe even a live audience. I'm a little nervous but I want to push myself, so I stay seated on Kaleb's floor for another half-hour, twanging out an acoustic version of the song that my parents were listening to before they left the ranch.

When I finish up my little jamming session I return the Fender to its previous place, although I'm thinking that it's about to have a three-week rendezvous in my room, and then I head back to the staircase, ready to hike up my blood-sugar with E-numbers.

That's when I hear it.

The gravel crunch. The soft serenade of window-muted metal music. A bellow of laughter followed by loud door slams.

My heart lodges in my throat and my body stills.

Then I sprint the remainder of the steps and run to the kitchen window, blood pounding as I peep outside.

When I see the car that has just pulled up below the porch my brain goes blank as if I've just experienced a trauma. Which is accurate. I feel colour instantly rise to my cheeks, and my neck heats up despite the shower I just had.

Suddenly I'm eighteen again, it's the end of May, and the boy from all of my forbidden teenage fantasies is holding my hand as we escape my senior prom. His guitar is slung over one broad shoulder and every few paces he glances my way to make sure that I'm not out of breath. He knows that I won't be, track star and all, and my cheeks turn pink with secret pride.

We're heading towards his Wrangler. He's going to take me to his SUV, the car most coveted by everyone in my high school, and he's going to kiss me.

Suddenly one of the doors from the hotel creaks open and he quickly pulls me to the side of the barn, hiding me with his body in case it's my brother. His chest is flush against mine as he peers around to check, and he entwines our free hands whilst we wait.

"Coast is clear," he whispers, the tips of his cheekbones sheathed in moonlight.

There's a soft fuzzy glow in the air and it only intensifies as he bows slightly forward, the curves of his lips millimetres away from my own. Heat flushes up my chest, sizzling every nerve ending, and then Madden flexes his fingers, reminding me that he still has a hold on me.

I definitely don't need reminding.

I turn around so that my back is to the ledge, facing the refrigerator and counting to ten. Then I turn back to the window to see if I've been hallucinating. Sadly not the case.

Madden Montgomery's Wrangler glints in the sunlight, its two occupants joking as they make their way up to the porch.

I stumble backwards, trying to work out what to do. Little electrical bolts are shooting up and down my arms, which probably isn't a good sign. I scamper to the small mirror hanging on our living room wall and do a quick appraisal. Flushed cheeks, crazy eyes. I swipe my hands over the top of my hair, trying to smother the flyaways, but I'm pretty sure that I just created more static. I try to calm my breathing as I listen to the thud of their boots mounting the steps outside, the soundtrack to my impending heart attack.

Thud, thud, shuffle, silence.

And then they knock.

"Kit!" Kaleb's voice bellows through the wooden pane of the door. "Open up! We're gonna fry out here."

I contemplate letting them.

"Kit!" *Thump, thump, thump.* No respect for his knuckles.

I walk to the door like I'm wading mud – hesitant, reluctant, and in major fear of *falling.* When I reach the interior side, I rest my hand on the lock, my head swimming with all sorts of questions.

Why is Kaleb here? Why is Kaleb here *now?* And why the hell is he not *alone?*

"Kitty."

I instantly still, because this voice is deep and low and *not* my brother's.

Madden.

"Open up."

My fingers hover over the handle as I mull over what's happening right now. Is Kaleb visiting? Is there a break in their tour? Or is he here indefinitely, to watch over things whilst our parents are gone?

My brain revs into full throttle.

Papa sent Kaleb because he didn't think that you could take care of the heavy lifting. Mama doesn't trust that you can protect the ranch. Kaleb brought Madden because he doesn't know what happened between you two.

I narrow my eyes at the door before glancing down to the little table beside the frame, hosting a dish for our keys and various other more questionable items. I pick up one of the pieces and then swing open the door.

Kaleb Hanson Lu and Madden Montgomery are the kinds of guys who you'd bet on in a bar fight. Big, broad, and dressed in all black, if they hadn't gotten into rock music then they would've gotten into a hell of a lot of trouble.

I try my best to avoid looking at Madden. For all intents and purposes, growing up I treated him with the dismissive nonchalance that you give to an unwanted sibling, but he's kind of hard to ignore when he takes up so much *room*. The whole backdrop behind Kaleb is entirely blocked by Madden's rigid frame, his hands fisted in the pockets of his jeans and his eyes trailing all over me.

Kaleb snaps me out of it.

"About time," he beams, and then he shoves his shoulder into my belly, swinging me over his shoulder as he barges inside.

I squeal like a little piglet and punch at his back with my free hand, my tummy churning like a dairy mixer.

"What the hell!" I'm kicking and screaming. Literally. My brother, unfazed, opens up the fridge and pulls out a soda.

"Miss me?" he asks, one arm extending so that he can pass the glass bottle to my other source of anxiety. I tilt my head to the side so that I can get a look at his face and Madden's eyes lock in with my own, his expression unreadable. His black spiky hair is in chaotic disarray, and his swollen muscles strain against the confines of his clothes. I try to transmit his tight black shirt a little message: *rip*.

Madden's gaze languidly trails up my back, stopping when it reaches my ass, arched high over Kaleb's shoulder. He gives his lip-ring a rough tug and then walks heavily into the living area.

I knee Kaleb in the chest until he finally puts me down.

"What're you doing here?" I ask, a crimson glow of rage shimmering all around me.

He pulls a bottle-opener from the drawer and pops the cap on his beer. "Nice to see you too."

His gaze flicks to my right hand as he takes a quick pull on his drink. He cocks an eyebrow.

"You gonna put the gun down or…?"

I look down at the pistol, weighing its sturdy handle in my fist.

"Can't be too cautious," I say before laying it gently on the counter. "Besides, I wasn't expecting visitors."

I give him a sceptical once over. His grin cranks up a watt.

"Seriously, why are you here?" I think for a moment. "If you came to see mom and dad, they literally just left."

He positions his beer bottle on the worktop as carefully as I lowered the pistol, then asks, "Didn't they tell you?"

My heartbeat kicks up a notch. He takes my silence as a cue to continue.

"We have three weeks until tour resumes and it coincides with mom's comp. When we put two and two together we thought it'd be good for you to have some extra hands to help out at the ranch whilst they're away."

So that's why Papa opted to go. He'd already found

me a replacement bodyguard.

"That's sweet," I say, trying to sound sincere. "But not necessary," I conclude, my foot tapping agitatedly.

I give him a pointed look. It reads: *scram.*

He pulls me into his arms and looks down at me, a surprisingly paternal look on his face.

"Kit, I'm not about to let my kid sister run a ranch in the back-end of a place like this on her own. Especially when I'm available to oversee things right now. You're a hard cookie, I know, but sometimes it's better to leave things to the big boys, okay?"

No, not okay! My eyes dart to the living room where Madden is making himself at home, one thick bicep resting on my fluffy love-heart cushion.

"Boys, plural?" I ask, not averting my eyes.

Kaleb follows my gaze and quirks up a smile. "Oh yeah, Madden's here too."

I slide my eyes up to my brother. *No shit.*

"You don't mind him staying though, right?"

My brain stutters.

"Staying?" I repeat, blood pounding in my ears.

Kaleb releases me in favour of his beer. He glances at Madden, then takes a swig.

"Before we started touring Madden was doing construction work with Jason Coleson, so he's gonna help patch up the barn whilst we have nothing better to do."

Jesus Christ, he's being serious.

"Do mom and dad know-"

Kaleb throws me a look, the kind that instantly makes a little sister shut up. "Do they know that I brought an extra dude, a guy who no one will fuck with, to help keep you safe on the ranch?" His eyes sharpen. "Madden's hung out with us since forever and he's my closest friend. Y'all might not be best buddies but I know that he sees you like a sister."

I certainly hope that he does not.

"He's my best friend, Kit. You know they'd be cool with it," he concludes sternly, completely evading my question.

Kaleb takes a deep inhale, watching me carefully from twelve inches above. I scowl back at him to prove that I'm not a pushover.

We have a ten second sibling standoff to see who will back down first.

I think about the guitar that's in Kaleb's bedroom and the beginnings of a plan formulates in my mind.

"Fine," I acquiesce. "Whatever. I'm…" I have to physically force the words out of my oesophagus. "I'm happy that you're here."

Kaleb instantly relaxes, smiles, and then bats a finger across the button of my nose.

"There's my sister."

CHAPTER 2

Kitty

"So Kaleb showed up, huh?"

Spoken with the confidence of a man not within shooting distance. I grip the cell phone that my dad's voice is trickling in through tighter in my right hand, fantasising about it being his neck. He has royally fucked up my summer plans.

I flash my eyes over to my two unwanted bodyguards. Kaleb splayed across the couch, checking the TV guide. Madden lifting the unopened soda to his lips, his eyes boring into my own. When our gazes meet he suddenly pushes the top of the bottle beneath a sharp white canine, bites off the lid, and then spits it into his free hand.

Good God. I turn my back to him and speed-walk to the back of the kitchen.

"Nothing a pistol can't fix." My voice is shaking.

Papa breathes a laugh down the line. "Keep him in check will you? Your mom and I count on you, you know."

Huh? I don't even bother hiding my confusion, irritation, rage.

"What kind of logic is that?" I hiss. "You made him come back here to look after *me*." I hook my fingers in air-quotes around the phrase "look after" because it's Kaleb that we're talking about here.

"Pumpkin." Stern. "You know that isn't why he's there. We trust you completely, and we know that you're not a kid anymore."

"Doesn't seem like it," I mutter, exactly like a kid would.

The authority in his voice takes a turn, going from Corporal Officer to Sergeant Major. He isn't joking around anymore. "You know what I'm talking about, Kit."

A deafening silence follows.

Phoenix Falls is as small and towny as a small town can get, so here at the ranch, being located even farther from civilian life, everything is more quiet, more suspicious, more *wild.*

"He's there to look after you in case of any incidents, that's all. You have my word." There's a gruff finality to his tone.

Incidents like wild animals? Rival ranch hands? Or is he talking about incidents of a different variety?

I peek over my shoulder, a soft waterfall of silky black hair slipping from around my collarbone and gliding down my back, and there he is, staring right back at me. He takes me in with an unhurried perusal, Kaleb across from him completely oblivious, and he grinds his knuckles against the dark stubble on his jaw. The rough scratchy sound causes a little shiver to ripple in my belly and Madden senses it like an animal would. When our eyes meet again there's a heated gleam beneath the surface.

Definitely incidents of a different variety.

"He's gonna be doing the work though, right?" I try not to sound like I'm begging.

"He's been told to take on as much as he can handle, and I trust that he'll honour that." Hmm, no comment. "No guy in their right mind would let his little sister take the brunt of a manual labour job, so I expect he'll be doing most of the hours."

Every cloud. Sometimes I don't mind small town sexism.

Sadly, I think that my thoughts transcend down the wire because he then adds, "And you will be doing your share of the work too, Kit."

I narrow my eyes. "But he'll be doing more."

He gives me a parental chuckle. "Don't work him too hard, Pumpkin."

I am going to work him like a husky.

"I'll call you once your mom's finished her first comp, okay? Tell Kaleb that we said hello."

It's only once I'm outside after the line goes dead that I realise the one thing I forgot to mention.

My second unwanted bodyguard.

*

There's an unfamiliar bag sat on the landing outside of Kaleb's room. I toe it cautiously with the tip of my flip-flop and then sweep my eyes over to the spaced-out beams in the gallery corridor's balcony panelling, contemplating punting the bag through with one quick boot.

"Do it."

A deep masculine voice hits me from behind and I practically jolt out of my shorts as I whip around to face him.

He's leaning against my bedroom door and his eyes are a taunting twinkling all-pupil black. My gaze flickers between his growing smirk to the room that he's resting against, and I take a shuddering inhalation as I try to stamp down on my hormones. For one moment he looks confused but then the realisation dawns as he puts two and two together. He's been to the cabin many times before and he knows which room he's leaning against. His grin widens.

"Neighbours, huh?" he asks, taking a small step forward. Slowly, like a serial killer. "This oughtta be cosy."

I downplay his confidence. "Surely Kaleb isn't having you room with him. There are plenty of other places that you could crash."

He gives his lip-ring a flick. "Such as?"

"The barn?" I suggest lightly.

We both glance at it through the window behind me. A piece of timber panelling slides slowly to the ground, then a small dust cloud poufs up around it.

When I face him again he seems to be even closer than before.

"I can think of a better location," he murmurs, voice husky. He gently nudges his temple against the pane of my bedroom door.

I bristle like a porcupine.

"Don't talk like that." I step around him until we've completely swapped places, this time with the breadth of a prairie between us.

He looks glumly down at his carry-on, then gives it a shove in the direction of my room.

"No," I command more firmly.

He holds my gaze for one long lingering moment and then his eyes trail down my body like maple syrup – slow, saccharine, and stuck in places that they shouldn't be.

"I haven't forgotten, you know." His voice is low and rough as he moves infinitesimally closer. Even with his temple resting on a tilt against Kaleb's door he's still standing over a foot taller than me, and the intoxicating heat radiating from the wide planes of his chest is almost lulling me comatose. "I was there that night, remember?"

I peep in the direction of the gallery banister to ensure that Kaleb is still outside finishing up with the cattle, and then whisper back, "And nothing really happened that night, *remember*?"

He blows out a hard exhalation. "This is how you're gonna play it?" he asks, his expression displeased.

When I don't respond, he shifts so that his acre-wide shoulders are bridging the gap from one side of Kaleb's doorframe to the other, his head dropping backwards with a dull *thud* against the panel. I watch the heavy roll of his Adam's apple as he swallows.

"I'm not bunking with your brother," he says, dry amusement undercoating his deep voice. "That bag's just full of band shi-"

He stops himself short and quickly glances in my direction. For a moment I'm confused, but before I can comment he grunts and rephrases. "The bag's full of band stuff. I'm sleeping in your guest room."

I still haven't quite come to terms with the fact that we're going to be sleeping under the same roof for the next few weeks, and I have to shift my body weight to try and disperse the throbbing sensation in my tummy.

He notices.

"It's cosy down there," he continues gruffly, his gaze slow-dripping down my torso until he reaches my shorts. "You can come anytime."

White hot rage explodes in my brain.

I can *come* anytime?! I am *not* having a summer filled with innuendos to edge and torment my already insatiable post-teenage lust – I simply refuse. Determined to show him how no-nonsense I intend to be, I propel myself forward and shove my palms into his chest.

Jesus Christ, is he made of marble? Madden doesn't move a millimetre. He suppresses a grunt, then shoots me a warning look.

"Don't give me that look," I snap. "You think we're about to rekindle a teenage blip from two years ago whilst you're staying in *my* cabin with my *brother*? Not happening. So if you're here to pester me about what could've been-"

"Let me fill you in," he bites out, shoving himself off of Kaleb's door and backing me up into my own.

With my ass pressed hard against the wood and nowhere further to go, I fold my arms resolutely and jut my chin in defiance.

"I'm here so that you don't get sliced, diced, or murdered whilst your parents are away. If you don't want to sneak around then-" He pauses for a second, rolling his bottom lip into his mouth. I cock a brow at him and his eye twitches. "Then that's fine," he chokes out, his chest heaving unsteadily. "But don't for one second think that I'm letting you out of my sight."

I'm so bemused that I'm almost laughing. "Are you kidding me? As if I don't contend with this shit enough already when it comes to my parents and Kaleb, now you want to roleplay as a surrogate brother too?"

His mouth lifts slightly at the corner. "Trust me, I don't want to be your brother."

He glances quickly over his shoulder to check for Kaleb again and then faces me, moving his body so close that our thighs are now only one twitch away.

"I'm just here to help keep you safe whilst your parents are out of town. And you're gonna let me."

His eyes burn into my own, the startling silver colour hypnotising me when so starkly contrasted against his sun-kissed skin. There's a subtle cherry-red glow spreading up his cheekbones and after a moment he looks away from me, his Adam's apple rolling.

"Unless there's something *else* you want me to fill you in with," he murmurs gruffly, "I'm gonna need you to keep those hands to yourself, okay?"

My eyes stretch wide, then drop to his jeans. Which, although he hasn't moved any closer to me, are now brushed up against the bottom of my tank.

My lips pop open and then I quickly snap them shut. He isn't... he can't be...

He's no longer the only person with a strawberry flush.

He's ready now? He could... he could do that now? My eyes flutter quickly away from the hard swell beneath his belt, my brain spinning in overdrive as I realise that my snappy little fight literally just made him hard. The thought of him being so virile makes my body grow heavy, my brain light-headed.

He still likes me. He still *really* likes me.

As he steps backwards, an endearing kind of guilt radiating from his thickly-built body, I allow my mind to process the fact that *I* still like *him*, and for the first time in our lives we're two semi-adults no longer under parental supervision. Okay, Kaleb's here, but if he wasn't it's pretty obvious where this little stay-over would most likely lead.

To the room right behind me.

But Kaleb is *here*, my brain argues back. And the main issue with that is that, given my summer plan, I'm actually going to need to stay in his good books. I've never purposefully pissed him off – I think that my general little-sister presence sometimes did that, but I always tread carefully when it came to Kaleb and his fuse – but I know that a sure-fire way to make an enemy out of him would be to encroach on his territory. A.k.a. shacking up with his best buddy.

I mentally sigh, my eyes unable to stop their wandering over the peaks and valleys of Madden's cotton-covered muscles, whilst I consider my two options.

One: indulge in the fantasy that Madden is quite clearly offering up to me, and then endure a lifelong domestic when Kaleb catches on.

Two: snuggle my way into Kaleb's good books so that he'll let me use his old Fender for the upcoming Barn Bonanza, therefore forbidding myself from alone-time with Madden during my rare month of filial freedom.

This time, I sigh out loud, recapturing Madden's attention.

I nod. *Yes, I'll keep my hands to myself. Yes, I promise not to taunt you.*

He takes it all in – the flushed cheeks, the unwilling nodding – and rolls his neck, his jaw muscles bunching.

"Well, that's good then," he concludes, his voice as reluctant as my expression. "You're a… you're gonna be good."

Unable to stand the feeling pulsing in the air any longer, he steps fully away from me and starts making his way to the bathroom. He pauses when he's just outside of it, giving himself a few long seconds of silent contemplation, and then finally he strolls right through, leaving the door wide open behind him.

A fuse explodes in my brain. Not a chance. There's no way that I can stay up here knowing that Madden is going to be fully naked and drenched in water *with the damn door wide open.*

I practically throw myself down the stairs, using my track-star history to propel myself like a missile. My head feels heavy with heat, my blood pressure still higher than it should be.

All things considered, I think that went pretty well. We seem to have reached some sort of truce, although ironically we were both unenthusiastic about it.

It's been two years since we last saw each other and we're both still interested in our unknown romantic potential – that much is obvious. But we're also aware of the giant obstacle that Kaleb will be, even though Madden doesn't know how sincerely I need to stay friendly with my brother right now.

On the other hand, Madden is obviously not willing to fight fair.

I glance up at the gallery corridor when I reach the bottom of the stairs. The bathroom door remains wide open, opaque steam pouring through it and the loud slap of the shower-spray infiltrating the air.

Lordy. My stomach flutters as I turn away from my temptation, my mind trying to convince myself that I can't smell his ridiculously delicious body wash from all the way down here.

I speed-walk to the kitchen and stow myself onto the far counter, tucking myself into the nook that will keep the gallery corridor out of my eye-line as I wait for Kaleb to finish up outside for the night.

Buckle up Bronco, my brain says as I steel myself. *You have a favour to ask.*

*

When Kaleb lets himself in his face looks tired, because today is probably his first day of manual labour in the past two years. Whereas I can see that Madden spends his free time ripping concrete boulders and flipping tires, Kaleb is leaner in his build. He's strong and he's fit, but I can tell that he hasn't been as active as he had to be when he was living and working here on the ranch.

I begin with an olive branch.

I did a little bit of witchy herbal research and then dug out the most placating tea that we had in our cupboard. Said a little prayer over it, and now it's in my hand, outstretched towards Kaleb like an enchanted apple.

His eyes sparkle when he sees the sweet nectar I'm offering and he takes it without hesitation, glugging it down whilst he smiles his thanks at me.

You're welcome.

"So," I say, drumming my fingers on the kitchen counter behind me. When Kaleb lowers the cup I can see that half of its contents has already gone. "How did you find your first shift?" I ask lightly, watching as the tea leaves work their magic. He's mellowing by the second. Excellent.

He lifts a shoulder and then drops it in a half-shrug. "Tough but enlightening," he admits, taking another sip. "But I think that this is a good thing, my being here. I wanna get my fitness back up." He thinks for a moment and then he adds, "Madden's a fucking beast. You should see him when he's hauling the equipment out there."

Don't tempt me.

"Uh, so, anyway," I say, re-steering our conversation. "I'm actually really glad that you're here too. I know I was weird this afternoon but I'm genuinely *really* pleased that you're here."

Am I over-egging it? Yes. But Kaleb's ego is so large that he gobbles it right up.

"Aw, Kit," he says, pulling me against his side for a half-hug, his other arm preoccupied with finishing his drink. Sip, sip. I hide my smile.

Time to bite the bullet.

"So I was wondering, since you're here and all, if you could possibly-maybe-potentially help me with something?" I'm opting for the *damsel in distress* route, hoping that his Y chromosomes won't be able to resist aiding the helpless little woman in front of him.

His gaze drops down to mine, his brow lifted in surprise. "You need help?" he asks.

Another win for feminism.

"Yeah," I say, nodding. "Do you think that you could do me a favour?"

He blinks down at me, trying to read my mind with our sibling synergy. I block him out, my smile steadfast.

My gaze flickers into his cup. "There's still a bit of tea left in there," I say encouragingly.

He sips it, his eyes never leaving mine.

"It's your old guitar," I admit, taking my opportunity whilst his mouth is preoccupied. "I remembered that you had it in your room and, the thing is, there's this little singing competition that I saw advertised – it's a tiny thing – and I thought that maybe I could enter it? And use your old guitar?" Emphasis on "old", completely avoiding the word "Fender". "I won't have to annoy you by practicing here – I got in touch with Dyl at the bar and he said that I could use their stage space if I need to."

Is it bad that I have to trivialise an event that's a huge deal to me? Yes. But am I going to use everything in my power to out-manipulate my self-centred brother?

Hell yeah.

Herbal concoction finished, he places the cup beside the sink and searches my eyes, still frowning.

"A music competition?" he asks, his brow furrowed.

I make an iffy gesture with my hand, downplaying it.

When I don't give him any further information he

raises his free hand behind his head, scratching at his hair like I've just stressed out his scalp. "Well…" he says, his face so displeased that he's almost wincing.

I know that he doesn't want to share the limelight with me, especially not when we're both interested in the exact same field, but I'm hoping that my belittling of the endeavour will give him the nudge to act charitably. After all, *I* am the sibling who stayed with our parents to work on the ranch, and there's no way that he'd expect anything *real* to come from my entering a talent contest.

I give him a dimply smile. He folds like a stack of cards.

"Okay, fine," he sighs, smiling back at me. "But you'll owe me," he warns.

I scrunch up my nose.

"Owe you how?" I ask, not wanting to do more than my share of chores on the ranch.

"Like, we're not actually gonna stay here like hostages for the next three weeks," he replies. "I wanna go out like a normal person, have some fun whilst I'm back in town."

Great. I chew on my bottom lip, suddenly anxious. "You mean, leave the ranch unguarded?" I ask.

He pinches my cheek and I squirm because it hurts. I punch him in the stomach when he finally lets me go.

"Just for a couple hours at a time. Unless you'd rather I bring the party here," he says tauntingly.

I roll my eyes. He can't behave himself for three freaking weeks?

Begrudgingly I give him a nod. "Okay, fine," I say, grateful at least for the fact that we're somewhat compromising right now.

He grins. "Awesome. So Madden and I are going out tonight, and you're coming with us."

I look down at my pyjamas, avoiding Kaleb's eyes, because all that I heard there was *going out* and *Madden*, and I'm thinking about how that's a situation that I definitely shouldn't be putting myself into.

Instead I give him another smile and say, "Sounds great!" even though I know that this is a terrible idea.

CHAPTER 3

Madden

This was a terrible idea. One minute my best friend's little sister is blushing up against her bedroom door, and the next minute we're dragging her out to a bar on a Friday night. What the hell was I thinking?

Clearly I wasn't thinking anything at all because now she's riding shotgun in my SUV. I avert my eyes back to the road, trying to erase the image of her bare legs curled up in the passenger seat from my mind so that I don't take the wrong exit *again*.

There's also the fact that I defiled their family bathroom this evening, beating one out as I pictured Kitty in those fuck-me pyjamas that she was wearing at five o'clock in the afternoon. I risk a quick glance her way as I slow down in front of a red light and she's attentively twiddling with the raw hem of her denim shorts. I steal a glance at her black cowgirl boots and have to physically restrain myself from taking her back to the ranch right this fucking second.

Besides, this serves me right. I shouldn't have been goading her the way that I have been, even if I've been more than a little infatuated by her since we were kids. I should respect the fact that Kaleb is her brother, not to mention my friend, and I should respect the fact that her loyalty to him is stronger than any interest she has in me.

And yet.

When I pull into the lot in the centre of the town square I lift my foot off the pedal, slowly easing the car into a free space with neurosurgeon-level caution. Slugs are crawling through the mud faster than us. I feel Kitty's eyes flicker to the side of my skull because this is the first time that she's ever been inside a vehicle with me and she probably wasn't expecting me to drive so cautiously. I'm pretty sure that she knows my history so I avoid her eyes as I slowly bring the car into park, an embarrassed warmth spreading up my cheekbones.

My mom was hit by a car when I was younger, and her passing away was something that neither my dad nor I ever got over. Our small family home, a cutesy Phoenix Falls bungalow, was full of her – her pictures, her colour choices, all of her memories – and my dad never did anything to change that, something that I was both grateful for and resentful about. I was happy that I could still feel her with us, but I was also so unbelievably depressed that she would never physically be coming back. Hence the snap decision to up-sticks when the band got a touring contract.

Hell, *I'm* the guy who sorted out the tour.

The crux of it is I'm touchy when it comes to driving.

And I should text my dad.

I cut off the engine and bring myself back to the here and now, my body vibrating as I take in my present predicament, namely the attitude problem I've got curled up on my right, and the older brother who's seated right behind me.

"You sure you're good being the DD tonight?" Kaleb asks, unbuckling himself and opening one of the back doors.

Even after years on the road together this guy still hasn't clicked onto the fact that my obsession with driving isn't an act of charity. It's an act of control.

I give him a nod and he cracks me his easygoing cowboy smile.

"Lifesaver," he beams.

Ain't that the truth. I don't comment as he dismounts and then starts making his way to the bar ahead of us.

And then it's just the two of us.

Kitty's practically twitching beside me, because neither of us knows how to handle this situation. Do I ignore my feelings because of Kaleb's presence? Act on them until she kicks me out? All I can smell is her sugar-frosting body wash and it's fogging all of the rationality right out of my brain.

To hell with her brother. Take her home right now and show her what she's doing to you.

I swallow hard, jaw clenched tight, and I look nervously down at my jeans. There are some situations that even black denim can't hide. I clench and unclench my fists on the wheel as the weight in my boxers grows harder and thicker.

I should not be left alone with this girl.

I shut off the engine and release my seatbelt, reaching into the back to find what I'm looking for. As soon as I feel the construction hoodie that I keep back there I shove it in her lap and then I haul ass out of the SUV.

She eyes me with cool indifference when I open the passenger door for her.

"You forgot something," she says and then she slaps the jumper against my chest.

I pull her out of the seat and then lock up the car behind her. "Don't want you getting cold," I mutter, pushing the jumper back into her arms. If she thinks that I'm going to let her stroll into a dive bar wearing a tank top that has the phrase "*ROUGH RIDER*" emblazoned across it in twinkling silver rhinestones, she has another thing coming.

"In eighty degree heat?" she asks.

"It's not that hot out," I argue obstinately.

A cicada chirps nearby.

"I'm twenty years old, Madden. This isn't my first rodeo."

A cold sick feeling trickles down my sternum. This *better* be her first rodeo. She's not twenty-one yet and I have every intention of shadowing her like a bodyguard tonight.

"Fine." I'm practically growling. I chuck the hoodie onto the roof of my car, and then I start dragging her by her wrist through the lot up to the bar.

She slaps at my hand. I grip her tighter.

When we reach the door the bouncer gives Kitty one glance and then turns to me with an offended look on his face. I've been here a million times before and in most of those instances I was underage, so I'm hoping that he'll give me a free pass and no hassle.

"Seriously?" the guy at the door says, stubbing his cigarette against the brickwork. "You tryna get put away or something?"

I simply stand there, giving him enough time to take stock of the fact that I'm two hundred and thirty pounds and itching for a fight. He gives Kitty another once-over and turns to me again.

"Twenty minutes tops," he says, and then he steps aside, begrudgingly letting us walk through.

"Thanks Dyl," Kitty calls back to him, sashaying in front of me as soon as we're inside.

It takes me a moment to process what just happened.

Hold on – she's on first name terms with the *bouncer?*

I spin her around. She bats her lashes.

"You're on first name terms with the *bouncer*?" I growl.

I think that I'm going into cardiac arrest. Why the hell has Kitty been frequenting a dive bar with so much regularity that she knows the guy on the door?

When she doesn't respond I dip my head closer to her so that she can really get a good look at the level of insanity in my eyes. "Care to explain?"

From here I can really smell her soap or her perfume or, fuck, maybe it's just her natural scent, but in contrast to the room that we just walked into she smells like a freaking cherry bakewell.

She chews on her lip for a few moments, her brow pinched in worry, and then she scrunches up her nose. "No," she says simply, and then she turns her back to me, ending the conversation.

It's crowded, rowdy, and smoked up like a sauna in here. The walls are lined with dim crimson string-lights, making it almost impossible to make out who's who, and the people are packed in elbow to earlobe. I look over the heads of the local clientele and try to scope out which booth the guys will be in. As soon as I catch a glimpse of Kaleb I hook a finger in the waistband of Kitty's shorts and start hauling her through the throng like a piece of luggage.

"Did you wake up on the wrong side of the cave this morning or something?" Kitty growls, digging her nails into my forearm in an attempt to unleash herself.

Now I'm really hard.

"What is your *problem* Madden? Seriously, let me *go.*"

"You really gonna let your brother see you in a top like that?" Yeah, I'm a broken record still twitching about her tank.

"You think my brother is going to read what's written across my chest?"

Maybe I don't give a shit about what your brother has to say. Maybe I'm more concerned with every other guy in here and how the second they read what's written across your tits they're going to be picturing something that I only want you doing with me.

I change tactics. "Who're you wearing that for anyway?"

"Wouldn't you like to know," she mutters back.

More than the air I breathe. I have to pierce my teeth into my lower lip to stop myself from asking the other question that's burning a hole in my frontal lobe: *is it true.*

I'm drawing blood by the time we reach Kaleb.

He's sat at a booth with two guys that we went to high school with. There's Tyler, who like me is French decent, and he played guitar with the band until we started touring. Then on the other side there's Chase, the human embodiment of a golden retriever.

I can see that there are already a couple of bottles half-drained on the top but Kaleb taps his card on the table, implying that he's about to head up and order a round.

"I got it," I say, my hand still securing the bounty leashed around my fingers. Kitty tries to jerk her hips away from me but I keep her tightly in place. "Whaddaya want, I'll pay."

"Seriously?" Kaleb gives me a grateful grin, then wags his finger between himself and Tyler. "Just the reg, we're not fussed."

I jerk my chin at Chase. "You want something?"

I try not to notice the way that his eyes are roaming up and down Kaleb's sister.

He shakes his head, reluctantly taking his eyes off of Kitty so that he can give me a half-smile. "I'm all set."

Kaleb slides out of the booth and we work our way up to the counter, Kitty still safely tucked at my side and her brother walking up ahead. I look down at the top of her hair, smoothly centre-parted and luxuriously glossy, and I move my hands so that I'm holding both sides of her hips, moving her in front of me so that I can shield her from the crowd with my arms. She shivers when she feels the press of my fingers against her body, and a wash of protective pride rips through my chest.

When we get to the front I shift so that she's

sandwiched between us. She throws me a nervous look over her shoulder and transmits a thought to me.

It reads: *This is going to be impossible.*

I nod at her. *I know.*

Growing up we were never enemies. We were a long string of secret glances and teenage tension whilst Kaleb paraded around between us, totally ignorant to the fire we were kindling. To his face we both acted indifferent, but when we finally tested the waters our little flicker ignited like a bomb.

Thank God tour dragged me away from her otherwise Kaleb would be an uncle by now and Kitty would be a widow.

"Chase is DDing their ride tonight, so it's only Tyler and I drinkin'," Kaleb shouts to us, pulling me out of my thoughts.

I glance over my shoulder at Tyler. RIP man. I would rather crawl through broken glass than shotgun with Chase.

I pull a twenty out of my pocket and push it towards him on the counter. Then I notice a fishbowl of lollipops so I throw one of those down too.

Kaleb quirks his brow. I jerk a thumb at the source of my public hard-on.

He laughs. "Cute." Then pinches Kitty's chin.

"So I'm not allowed a drink?" she asks, her eyes sparkling up at Kaleb.

Forget not being twenty-one, she looks about sixteen.

"You're underage," Kaleb says, as hushed as he can manage, although it's so loud in here that anything beneath a yell is inaudible. "We're lucky that they let you in here in the first place. If Dyl didn't know you…"

He trails off, to my absolute fucking dismay. Where the hell was he going with that sentence?

Ignoring the grenade that Kaleb just set off in my brain, Kitty whips around to face me, her expression stubborn. I frown, trying to understand the look that she's giving me.

Then it clicks.

Does she think that I can *overrule* Kaleb?

Holy shit, does my opinion hold more weight to her than her brother's?

Distracted by my realisation I forget to actually respond and apparently tonight Kitty isn't in a patient mood. With a disgusted huff she pulls away from me, snatching her body out of my grasp and immediately storming back to the booth. I go to chase after her but Kaleb claps a hand on my shoulder, bringing me back to the present.

Don't act like a psycho boyfriend in front of her brother, don't act like a psycho boyfriend in front of her brother.

"It's cool," he says, as if that'll in any way satiate my need to guard-dog her. "She'll be fine with the guys."

I don't fucking doubt it. I look back in their direction but too many patrons are obscuring my view of the booth. Steam pumping out of my ears I turn back to Kaleb, where he's finishing up paying for our order. I pick up the lolly and pocket it at the front of my jeans, but as I move to turn around I feel a hand gripping my shoulder.

In a second I'm grinning and chucking my forearm around his shoulders.

"What's good, man?" I ask, giving him a rough scrub before we pull apart.

Jason Coleson – thirty-something year old tough guy, my former employer, and CEO of Coleson Construction – gives me a lazy grin, stark white against his deep tan, and his eyes crinkle at the corners. I've known him forever because he's Tate's uncle, the guy who was my best friend at the start of high school. Tate transferred midway through but I still see him whenever we're nearby.

"Was about to ask you the same thing." He sweeps his eyes between Kaleb and me, a smile lifting the corners of his mouth. "You kids even old enough to be in here?"

"Are we here on the pensioners' night again?" I ask. "Shit, I hate it when that happens."

I grin as he attempts to throw me into a headlock but he gives in after a couple of seconds. I spot his older brother Mitch standing behind him, an impassive expression on his face as he watches our debacle.

"Hey Mr Coleson," I say, a little more formal this time because – knowing what God-fearing Tate Coleson is capable of – I don't doubt that his dad could fuck me up.

"Madden," he says curtly, voice so deep I feel it in my bones. Jesus Christ. Someone give this guy a beer.

"Want a drink?" I offer.

"I'm the DD," he says, his face unreadable.

Maybe we have a little more in common than I originally thought.

"You back in town for good?" Jace asks, jerking his chin at the barman when he catches him looking our way. He turns to me before the guy reaches us to ask for their order. "Always space for you on the team if you're looking for a bag."

I wait for him to order and then I shake my head. "Just passing through for a couple weeks. Staying with Kaleb up at the ranch."

Jace looks over to Kaleb again, nodding in understanding. "I know the place. I helped Hardy build that cabin," he adds.

Kaleb, the guy who turned away from manual labour to pursue a career as an adored rock-n-roller, is evidently out of his depth, probably unsure of what to say in fear of getting decked. I can't blame him. Jace and Mitch don't exactly radiate sunshine and bunnies. He gives Jace a little nod, tongue-tied for once in his life.

"Well I'm not gonna keep you," Jace says finally, turning to me again and pulling me in for another rough embrace. "But if you decide life on the road ain't all that hot…" He gives me a look, man to man. "You've got my number, kid."

I nod at him, grateful, and I make a note to keep that in mind.

I look over to Mitch who's just pulled a wad of notes from the pocket of his jeans. He senses my eyes like a jaguar and gives me a *can I help you?* look.

"Is Tate in town right now?" I ask.

Surprisingly, Mitch seems to lighten up a bit at the mention of his son. He shakes his head as he hands some cash to his brother. "He's just finishing up one of his comps out of town but he'll be back next weekend." Then, even more surprisingly, he moves his gaze to Kaleb and adds, "Think he's taking his girl up to your ranch soon, actually."

His girl being River, the bespectacled little tyrant that he's completely infatuated with, and who also happens to be Kitty's best friend.

I flash my eyes over to Kaleb. "Kitty's having River stay over?" I ask.

For some reason Kaleb's cheeks start flushing red and he mumbles something unintelligible.

Huh?

"River *and* Tate," Mitch reiterates, eyes briefly meeting my own. Our knowledge of what Tate is like hums like a secret between us. "He'll be there if she is," he finishes.

I give them a parting nod each before leaving them to it.

That I *definitely* do know.

Unfortunately, when we get back to our table and Jace's calming influence has vaporised completely, all thoughts of not acting like a psycho boyfriend fly out of my head.

There's been a rearrangement to the seating plan and I don't like it one bit. Two bulky guys I don't recognise are now positioned in the back corners of the booth, and Chase has rotated to Kaleb's former seat.

Which just so happens to be right across from Kitty.

Who, I should mention, is now drinking Tyler's beer.

I turn to gauge Kaleb's reaction but he's vanished to the other side of the bar, leaning against one of the other tables and chatting up his on-again-off-again high school sweetheart Chastity.

Fine. I *will* take on the role of surrogate brother.

Normal Madden on sabbatical, I wait for Kitty to place the bottle on the table and then I hoist her off the seat and begin carting her to the exit.

"What the hell? Madden!"

Mad by name, mad by nature. I zip-lock her against my abs with my forearm, her feet dangling high above the floor, and I use my free hand to shoot a quick text across to Kaleb. Should be something along the lines of, "*Sorry man – your sister's got me all hot and bothered so I won't be able to tolerate keeping her in this bar for longer than five minutes. Please hitch a ride with Chase and I'll keep you in my prayers.*"

Pocketing the phone I glance down over Kitty's body. She's thumping at my hand gripped tightly around her ribcage whilst inspecting the thick tendons in my wrist. My muscles flex on instinct.

"I'll bite you," she threatens.

"I thought you were a vegetarian."

She huffs then mumbles, "I won't let that stop me."

I bite back a groan. *I hope to hell you won't.*

I know that it's ironic that a girl beholden to work her parents' ranch is a vegetarian, but I don't comment. It's cute that she's a country girl but I can't help but feel like she's stifling herself to satisfy her parents.

Outside I slide my eyes over to "Dyl", who is watching us with far too much interest. He's postering up the notice board outside with more flyers for the Barn Bonanza, a local music competition that takes place in July.

Not liking his eyes on us, I hold Kitty a little tighter.

Once we reach the SUV I drop her to the floor and fish out my keys.

"Madden, we need to talk."

I unlock the car whilst simultaneously yanking my

hoodie from the roof. I stretch it open over my arms and then hook it over Kitty's head. She stubbornly retains it around her throat like a neck brace.

"Get in the car."

"It was just a sip," she replies, using her moody little sister voice on me.

If I'm being honest I'd kind of forgotten as to why I just hauled her out of the bar. Sadly now I'm having fleshed out flashbacks of her pouring the head of Tyler's bottle between her lips.

The last thing to touch her *mouth was something that was in* his *mouth.*

Renewed with bloodlust I rip the car door open, jerking my chin at the passenger seat.

"Get in," I repeat, moving a little closer than I should.

She shoves at my chest. "Don't tell me what to do."

I pull at my belt buckle. Is she trying to excite me or something?

Trying to retain my cool I take a step back, unclench my jaw, and grit out, "Please."

"We need to talk about this," she begins again but, not having the capacity for rational thought right now, I shake my head and open the door wider.

"At home. Get in."

She cocks an eyebrow at me but to my surprise she doesn't continue her fight, finally sliding inside.

It's only when I've punched on the engine and we're carefully cruising back to the ranch that I realise I just referred to her place as *home.*

CHAPTER 4

Madden

By the time that we're parked up outside the garage the interior of the Wrangler is hotter than hell. Kitty has taken the journey to simmer in her rage, so she should be reaching her boiling point any minute now. I, albeit unjustly, have been doing the exact same thing.

I don't un-strap myself from the seatbelt. God knows I can't be let loose right now.

Sensing the extent of my insanity Kitty kicks off her cowgirl boots, props her feet up on the dash, and begins drilling her nails on the window ledge. Even in the darkness of the cab I can see that they're sparkling red.

I keep my eyes on the cabin up ahead so that I don't have to watch her reaction. Probably a cocktail of disappointment, irritation, and justified feminine rage.

I can't help but notice that she's relented though, snuggling her little body inside of my construction hoodie, so maybe all isn't lost quite yet.

"I'm sorry," I rasp. My voice comes out low and hoarse. Hopefully she'll take it as a sign of remorse rather than what it actually is: my fucking sex voice. "That was… that was out of order."

"Mm."

Definitely disappointed. I swallow hard.

"When Kaleb told me about you dropping out of college, and that you were gonna be here on your own for a while I-"

"Kaleb told you that?" She spins around in the seat so that she can face me directly, winging her bare legs down from the front of the car and curling them up underneath her shorts. The toes of her pop-socks stick out from beneath her butt.

Now it's my turn to hold my tongue.

"Mm," I say, choking the truth back down my throat. Yeah, Kaleb told me. I'm the numbers guy, the person who organises everything that our band does. Any guesses as to why there was a sudden availability in our schedule coinciding so perfectly with *Home Alone: Kitty Edition*?

I redirect the conversation as far away from the truth as possible. "I'm just here to help Kaleb ensure that you don't get…" I wave a hand vaguely in the direction of the pastures. "Eaten."

"Eaten?" she laughs. God, her laugh is pretty.

"Coyotes, bears – don't act like you don't know what's out here. You're the one who's lived on this ranch for your whole life, you know how high risk this is."

"Eaten," she muses again, this time whispering it like a magic spell.

My mind goes straight down to the gutter, thinking about all of the other ways that she could get eaten.

"I didn't expect anyone to be watching over me whilst my mom and dad are away," she says, eyes glazed over as she looks at the ranch in front of us. "And I don't need protecting."

She arches her neck, tilting her head back against the seat.

"It's kind that Kaleb came by, but I think that you being here is going to cause problems."

A knife twists in my chest as I take in how sincere she sounds.

"For me *and* for you," she amends. "I don't want you to lose Kaleb over, like, a summer fling. If he catches us… having a moment or something-"

That grabs my attention. I lock my eyes in with hers and her lips part as she nervously tries to backtrack.

Too fucking late.

"So it's on the cards?" I ask. Give a dog a bone and all. "Me and you, this summer. If we're careful-"

"That's like the opposite of what I just said. Kaleb – your best friend, my *brother* – will cut you off like *this*" – she snaps her fingers to emphasise her point – "if he thinks that something's going on between us." She runs a hand through her hair and it spills like silk through her fingers. "Years of friendship, gone. Bye bye band."

Bye bye balls is more like it.

"It's worth it to me – you're worth it to me." I unstrap my seatbelt and twist my abdomen so that I can face her, hooking my bicep around the back of my headrest.

Her eyes drop to my chest and her lashes flutter

light-headedly.

Ah Jesus, this is not a good time for her to start waning on me – if I catch a whiff that she's even slightly tempted right now I'm about to become the worst best friend of all time.

"Eyes up here, princess," I tease, trying not to enjoy her perusal so damn much.

She looks shyly up at me, her brow pinched with embarrassment. Then she looks down at her lacquered nails, pretending to study them.

"This isn't supposed to happen," she whispers, her voice nervous. "You're my brother's best friend. I'm supposed to be, like, your arch nemesis."

I take a deep inhale as my eyes trail down her little body.

And what will you be arching exactly? my brain interjects. *Your back?*

I steel my jaw, forcing my mouth to stay shut.

"And you're only going to be here for a couple of weeks, right?" she asks, now twiddling with the lace trim on her socks.

"Three weeks." I blurt it out too fast, my voice way too deep for a conversation outside of the bedroom.

She nods, still avoiding my eyes. "So it couldn't be a real thing anyway, because you'll be back on tour soon."

I scan my eyes all over her, trying to accurately determine what it is that she's feeling. Does she sound… *disappointed* right now? Is she disappointed that I'll be leaving again?

I can't let myself believe that.

But I'll take whatever I can get with her.

"It can be anything that you want it to be," I say,

shifting a little closer to her and trying to ignore how edible she smells. "I'll do anything you want me to," I promise, gently tucking two fingers underneath her chin.

She looks up at me, those unbelievable eyes of hers twinkling with uncertainty and need and hope. "But Kaleb can't know," she whispers. Then she twists her lips to the side and adds, "And we'll have to be really freaking sneaky."

I bite back my smile. *This is going to be the best summer of my life.*

"Of course," I say, ducking down a little further towards her perfect parted lips. "Anything you want."

Her hands move down to my abs but then she surprises me because instead of pulling me closer she gives me a hard shove. I look down to where her nails are digging into the cotton of my shirt and my muscles flex with arousal.

When I glance up at her confused, she says, "Not here. Cameras."

What? As if that explains anything.

"Cameras?" I ask, looking out of the window behind her to see if I can get a glimpse at what she's talking about.

"Because of the land, and the animals," she explains, but I'm only half hearing her because her fingers are still exploring the muscles of my lower abdomen. I'm losing my breath and she's not even touching my bare skin.

It's been a while since I've had a woman but fuck if this isn't the horniest that I've ever felt in my whole damned life.

"Okay," I say thickly, swallowing like I'm parched. I

can't even remember what she just said.

When I hear the musical chime of her laughter my attention is drawn back inside the car. She's giggling, probably because she can tell that she's got a six-four ranch-hand buckling at her mercy, and I can't help but smile back at her.

I look down at her hands again, sliding dangerously close to my belt.

"You teasing me?" I ask, mouth lifted up at the corners.

She grins back at me. "Yeah," she whispers, cheeks flushed with mischief.

"Maybe I should return the fav-"

Before I can finish my sentence we hear the whiz of a car flash by.

She instantly pulls away from me, scrambling to the far edge of her seat in fear that it's Kaleb. Not gonna lie, that stings.

I look out at the back of the car, scoping it to see if it's Chase bringing Kaleb back, but I know in reality that it's way too early for that.

But the damage is already done. Kitty's so spooked she's sitting on her hands.

"Rules," she says suddenly. She sounds a little out of breath after her tentative exploration and my shaft grows heavier, aching in my boxers. "We need to make some ground rules for whilst you're here."

I nod. Anything to keep her talking. Anything to keep her in this car with me.

"If we're gonna… if there's the potential that we might…" Her sentences hang in the air as she chews on her bottom lip, trying to find the right words. Then she flashes me a pained look. "No girls."

I blink at her. *Huh?*

"Like, no *other* girls," she says, as if that's clarifying anything for me.

"Other girls?" I repeat, feeling clueless.

Then it clicks.

"Kitty," I sigh. I want to scoop my arms around her back, pull her into my lap, and show her how serious I am right now, but I also don't want to scare her with too much contact too soon. Instead I opt for clutching the sides of the seat around her, keeping her safely inside the confines of my arms, and she bites at her lip as my body heat envelops her. I try not to notice how fast her chest is heaving, her small curves trying to send my rationality into shut-down. "I'm not interested in any other girls. Look at me. I don't want anyone else."

She mutters something that sounds an awful lot like *"for now"* and her little lip juts out miserably.

"Kitty." Her eyes flash up to mine and they hit me like a bolt of lightning. "Only you, okay? It's always only you."

She considers my words for a couple of seconds and then I see a baby dimple appear in her cheek, her lips lifting at the corners. "'Kay," she mutters, the smile in her voice letting me know that she's sated.

I'm psyching myself to lean down and kiss her when a thought pops into my head. A thought that makes my triceps twitch.

"And will you do the same for me?" I ask, my shoulders swelling with envy at the thought of her seeing other guys. Yeah, I'm still thinking about Tyler's bottle in her mouth, and I have every intention of obliterating every last trace of him.

Her smile widens. Devil woman. "No girls?" she asks coyly. "I can't make any promises."

I groan, leaning further forward. I swear that this car has shrunk by fifty inches. "No guys *or* girls," I reply, stipulating the fine print because I am one jealous motherfucker, and I'm not giving Little Miss Bisexual a get-out clause.

"Fine," she sighs, rolling her eyes, but I can tell that she's joking from the way that she's nibbling back a smile again. "No guys, no girls… and we have to be really careful. Like, *nothing* over the friendship line if Kaleb's in the vicinity. No touching, no… no kissing." She glances up at me as if she's nervous to voice her thoughts, not knowing that me hearing her talk about us kissing is music to my ears.

Then she shatters the illusion real quick.

"So maybe we should start off as friends, to see if there's anything to build on anyway."

My heart misses a beat. Then another.

I'm almost a cadaver by the time I choke out the word, "Friends?"

I officially have a least favourite word.

She nods eagerly and another dagger works its way into my flesh. "If we keep it as friends to start with then maybe it won't be so weird for Kaleb if we seem a little closer, or if we decide to… if maybe it isn't just for…" She trails off, not allowing me to hear where she was going.

I submit anyway. "Yeah, okay, of course. Whatever you want. Just friends." *For now.*

"I know you aren't staying for long but I think that we should take it slow, especially because it's a secret and all."

She's twiddling with her socks again so I wrap my hands around her fingers, stilling them from their agitated work. I dip my head down to hers so that our foreheads can gently touch. She giggles a bit when my fringe tickles over her.

"Two friends with a secret," I whisper, so very aware of how close we are to kissing right now. So very tempted to suggest the option of *friends who make out. A lot.*

"A secret," she whispers back, her eyes shutting serenely. The curled tips of her lashes brush against the apples of her cheeks.

I rub my thumbs up the backs of her wrists and a happy shudder ripples through her.

Yeah. This is definitely *not* going to be just another summer fling.

CHAPTER 5

Kitty

Today's set to be another scorcher.

It's 5.30am, the sky is clear blue, and there's a rippling haze shimmying across the pastures as I hitch my dungaree straps up my shoulders, easing my way quietly through the back door so as not to wake the cabin's new residents.

First I tend to the cows, feeding them in their barn before I release them for the day and begin the beautiful task of mucking out the manure. I also set free my newly acquired baby goat, an adoptee I simply couldn't say no to when I saw that he was in need of a home. He lets out an enthusiastic bleat and then gambols head-first into a bag of feed.

Grain everywhere, I steer him safely into his make-shift pen and then I get back to mucking.

With shit up to my ankles, now seems like the perfect time to address the equally shitty word that's running a loop around my brain.

Friends.

Friends? Seriously? Who suggests to the guy that they've been crushing on their whole life that they should be *friends* during their one summer of potential romantic opportunity?

Worse still, he didn't exactly fight me on the issue, making me realise that no matter how pent up *I* may be feeling, the situation is definitely not that deep to Madden Montgomery. And why should it be? Madden's hot as hell, built like a tank, and a freaking *rockstar* for crying out loud. There must be people throwing themselves at him every night when he's on tour.

Every. Night.

After I lay down some fresh bedding I take my muck-vat out back to the composting heap, killing off about five million brain cells as the smell burns its way through my skull. I pump a gallon of soap onto my hands and start hosing them, all the while watching over the cattle as they lounge in the shady spot created by the shadow of the barn. I make eye contact with my favourite dairy cow hoping that she can offer me a pearl of wisdom.

She slow-blinks her lashes like a Furby, then flaps an ear and looks away.

Thanks Daisy.

Therapy session concluded, I mentally tick off my internal checklist. Morning chores done, next up I intend to go for my morning run through the forest before the weather gets too crazy. I've been solid about maintaining my track star fitness since high school and, plus, now that I have company in the house I can't exactly practice for the Barn Bonanza at home the way that I originally intended to.

Madden is *never* learning that I can sing. If he thinks that he influenced the biggest passion in my life then that would probably be the most embarrassing thing to ever happen to me. So a warble in the mountains it is.

The only other thing that I need to keep a sharp eye on now is the weather, because rain on a ranch in the summertime is a homesteader's kiss of death. Personally I love summer rain – it's atmospheric, refreshing, and crazy sexy – but the hay on the other hand?

Goodbye hundreds of dollars of cattle feed, hello five fields of mulch.

Turning off the tap I wipe my wet hands across the thighs of my dungarees and it's when I'm beginning to disrobe that I see him.

Madden's not a big fan of pyjamas and I am more than okay with that arrangement. He's wearing a pair of loose joggers that are clinging onto his hips for dear life and he's stretching thickly-muscled arms high up over his head as he walks farther away from me over to the kitchen, giving me nothing but the view of his bare tan back. He drops his arms to his sides and I watch as he flexes his hands. They're workingman's hands, enlarged from summer after summer of working with a construction company.

I like them. A lot. And not in a friendly way.

I hide back inside the freshly scooped barn to change from my coveralls back into my shorts, returning them to their peg, and then after a frenzied attempt to smooth the frizz at the top of my hair I begin to make my way back to the cabin.

As soon as I open the back door I can hear that

Kaleb's up too. I try not to be too bitter about that as the kitchen comes into view.

When I step over the entryway to the room there's some good news and some bad news.

The good news is that not only is Madden not a big fan of pyjamas, he also doesn't seem to be a big fan of *underwear.* He's leaning against the sink as he downs a glass of water, his free hand skimming the waistband of his pants like it's contemplating a journey down under. Join the club. When he catches me looking the faint trace of a smile line appears in the hollow of his cheek, and he runs his free palm up from his muscled abdomen to his swollen pecks. Who am I to deprive him of such mutually beneficial attention? I let my eyes wander to where he's giving me the show, nibbling at my lip as I fantasise about how warm and solid he would feel pressed up against me.

The loud rustle of a cereal carton brings me back to the bad news.

"Morning," Kaleb says groggily, twisting his body halfway so that he can pull me into a possessive side-squeeze. Thankfully Kaleb is a fan of both pyjamas and underwear. Sadly he is also a fan of *my fucking cereal.*

The last of my Teddy Grahams fall mercilessly to their doom, meeting their sorry end inside Kaleb's breakfast bowl.

Kaleb crunches up the cardboard carton and then throws it across the floor so that he can chuck it in the recycling chute later. Feels like a fitting metaphor for my dreams and desires. I look at the last of the teddies and then flash my eyes up to Madden, my cheeks warming in embarrassment at my own childishness.

His empty water glass is now on the counter and his head is cocked to the side in interest as he tries to work out what's going on inside my mind.

When he peers across to Kaleb's bowl his eye twitches.

I take a quick glance in the cupboard and note how all that's left in there is a sack of oats and a box of bran. It's my own damn fault for forgetting to buy cereal at the store yesterday. I deserve to starve.

I move from Kaleb's grasp as he takes the milk out of the fridge and then drowns the remaining teddies in it. I walk to the back of the room and flick on the kettle, hoping that I can tranquilise myself with herbal tea.

"Is that cereal hers, man?"

My head whips over my shoulder, eyes wide as I take in Madden's stance. Six four when barefoot, and his fists folded beneath his biceps.

Wow. His biceps.

Kaleb takes a spoonful and nods absentmindedly, crunching his way through their tiny bear bones. Madden cracks his neck and then meets my eyes. I have no idea what message he's trying to transmit to me but it is definitely not getting through. I don't have a chance to mouth anything over to him though as he rolls his shoulders, claps Kaleb on the back, and then trudges his way up to the bathroom.

Positioned behind Kaleb I allow myself to watch Madden as he walks off, appraising how *heavy* his gait is. It just looks so… encumbered.

Kaleb pulls me back to the present.

"I'm heading out for an hour, so Mad's gonna watch over everything whilst I'm gone."

My brain short circuits as I try to understand what Kaleb just said.

Did he just say what I think he just said? Madden's going to "watch over" everything?

Uh, what?

"Huh?" I ask, eyebrow cocked.

He waves a hand between us as if he's brushing away his previous sentence. I should hope so. "Let me rephrase – Mad's gonna watch over *you* whilst I'm gone."

Somehow that sentence managed to get worse the second time around.

"Kaleb." I say his name like a peace offering. "I don't need anyone to watch over me. I appreciate how fragile you seem to think that I am, but mom and dad don't babysit me when they're here."

"But mom and dad aren't here," he counters.

"O-*kaaaay*," I begin. "But it's 6am and the sun's beating down like it's nobody's business. You think a coyote's gonna stop by right now?"

"It's not just coyotes," he says simply.

Does this dude have an answer for everything?

"Then what?" I ask. "The daily psycho with a machine gun?"

"Yeah." *Slam.* His bowl rattles in the sink. "Not every small towner's a nice guy, Kit. And having this much land? You know that we've got enemies. Now stop being so stubborn and do as I say."

My irises turn red.

"Do as you *say*?" I'm laughing now, and not in a good way. "Who the hell do you think you are? You're not Papa, Kaleb."

I'm about to start comparing him to various

twentieth century dictators when Madden reappears, hair dripping wet from his quick shower and a towel slung around his neck. Water droplets glitter as they trickle over his swollen shoulders, dazzling me as they catch in the sunlight streaming in through the kitchen window.

He must have left his jeans in the bathroom last night because he's slipping the tongue of his belt into the holder as he calmly asks, "Everything alright?"

I almost sigh in relief. *Now it is.*

Kaleb cracks his jaw and then gives Madden a conspiratorial look, as if I'm some kind of criminal. "Keep an eye on her whilst I'm gone?" he asks, shaking his head like I've just got on his last nerve.

Stay in Kaleb's good books, I tell myself. *Think about the Fender.*

But then to my absolute horror Madden replies, "Sure."

My eyes flash to him, his deep authoritative voice settling low in my belly, and I part my lips, desperate to protest. He avoids my gaze, a displeasured look on his face, and then he turns around and walks back to the guest room.

Kaleb storms past me, heading upstairs so that he can freshen up before he goes on his mysterious "I'll be gone for one hour" adventure. When I hear his door slam shut I understand that this conversation is over.

I grab a banana from the fruit bowl and begin aggressively peeling it.

"*Narcissistic, misogynistic Neanderthals.*"

I'm muttering to myself like a crazy person. Which is accurate. I take a violent bite of my banana and begin stomping up the stairs myself.

Think about the guitar, all that matters is the guitar.

But still.

Fuck Kaleb, and fuck Madden. Okay, "fuck Madden" in a slightly different way, but fuck him too nonetheless. They both think that I'm *that* incapable? That I really *am* a damsel in distress?

Whatever. As soon as Kaleb's gone for the morning I'm going to do whatever the hell I want.

And no-one is going to stop me.

CHAPTER 6

Kitty

As soon as I hear Kaleb drive off in the Chevy I slip into my sports bra and a tank, and I stride out of the back door of the cabin. I catch sight of Madden measuring some loose planks by the barn, using that handy blue collar brain of his as he thinks about how to fix up the broken bits whilst he's here. How metaphorical.

When he notices me he does a double take, his eyes lingering momentarily on the text emblazoned across my chest.

"You look…" He lifts himself up from his crouch by the wood and he takes a few heavy steps towards me.

On the inside I'm laughing. *You're gonna treat me like a child when we're with my brother and then act like I'm a big girl once he's gone? Right.*

"You look… really, really good," he finishes, stopping to stand about two feet away from me.

I give him a quick smile. "Thanks." Then I breeze straight past him and start sprinting up the incline, heading for the protected canopy of the forest up ahead.

"Hey! Kitty, wait!"

His call is somewhere far behind me, along with all of the shits that I give. I'm immediately exhilarated, feeling the midsummer air against my skin, the stinging expansion of my lungs, the insane pounding of the man racing behind me.

I glance at him over my shoulder. So much for my Maria moment in the mountains.

"Quit chasing me," I shout to him. "Kaleb won't be gone for long and there are some private things that I need to do right now."

His cheeks are flushed red with exertion and he gives me a bewildered look from under his fringe. "What the hell kinda 'private things' you plan on doing in the forest?"

"Never you mind, stalker." I up my pace and try to ignore the fact that he's right behind me.

Why should I have to scupper my daily routine just because two dudes want to keep me under lock and key?

"Kitty," he huffs out, closer than before. I'm impressed that a man so built can keep up with a body as lithe as my own. I add an extra flair to my strides so that I can kick back some dust on him. "I can run *with* you, all you have to do is ask. I'm here to look after you, not to be a shackle."

Yap, yap, yap. I rev into full throttle.

"I don't want a bodyguard, nor do I need one." He's irked me so much that I'm talking like a Brontë.

"You've been relieved of duty, Officer. Scram."

Somehow he manages to match his pace to mine, running right beside me with a focused look on his face. The morning sunlight dappling through the leaves overhead make his eyes look striking and quartz-like.

"I thought you'd want to make the most of Kaleb being gone," he heaves out, brow furrowed in concentration. "Not run away from me the first moment you got."

"Well, we all make mistakes." I flash him a look and, so affronted, he stumbles.

Okay, now I feel a little bad. I slow down and back-step towards him.

"I'm kidding, Madden. That was mean, I'm sorry."

He bends over at the middle, hands on his knees as he catches his breath.

"How the hell are you talking when you just sprinted that fast?" he chokes out, tugging a hand through his hair and then standing upright again.

Even stood below me on the forest incline he's somehow still towering over me. I chew at my lip. Why does he have to be so darn good-looking?

"I have some secret things that I need to do out here and they don't involve you. We'll have other opportunities to hang out. And, no offence, but couples jogging could really give me the ick."

His eyes whip to mine, picking up on the one part of that sentence that I immediately wish I could undo.

"Couples, huh?" he teases.

I blanch, mortified. "It's just an expression."

"An expression that people use when they're referring to a *couple*," he grins.

I shake my head. "I didn't mean it like that, you know what I meant."

I'm spiralling like a neurotic prey animal, which seems about right.

My head's about to pop like a grain of corn when Madden grips a heavy hand over my shoulder, immediately grounding me. He looks deep into my eyes and says, "Hey, I'm just messing with you. It's okay, I didn't mean it."

I don't know if I like that anymore than if he *did* mean it.

"Hey," he says again, palms sliding up the sides of my neck. His eyes black out as he feels my six-billion-beats-a-minute pulse. "I'm sorry, I shouldn't be teasing you. I'll keep my mouth shut, okay?"

He cocks a small smile at me and then leans forward towards my ear, the scent of his heady pine body wash instantly infiltrating my bloodstream. The common sense in my brain vaporises into a cotton candy cloud of neon pink hearts and hot steaming lust.

"You tell me when you want me to talk." He dips his head to the crook of my neck and takes a heart-stopping inhale. "I know my place," he whispers.

Alarmed, aroused, and completely off my head, I stagger into his embrace and totally lose my balance. My foot slips on a sprouted seedling and, instead of clinging to the man-mountain in front of me, I throw my hands backwards and land on my ass.

My coccyx is screaming, my legs are akimbo, and my hands are instantly scratched up as they scrape across a decade's worth of twigs and branches.

"Oh my God, Kitty-" Madden drops to his knees and tries to regroup my limbs. I'm like a newborn deer only with less bodily control. "Kitty, I'm sorry, here-"

He attempts to wrap my arms around his neck when I suddenly feel a sharp sting in my left palm.

"*Ouch*," I whisper, bringing my hand under my chin so that I can inspect it at a closer range. I squint down at it, my vision still a little blurred, until I make out a tiny sharp splinter embedded in the soft flesh of my hand.

Madden sits back on his haunches, denim-clad thighs splaying obscenely between my knees, and then he wraps his fists around my wrist, bringing my palm gently towards him so that he too can examine it.

"Splinter," he mutters.

"Duh," I mutter back.

He gives me a sharp look from beneath his dark spiky fringe and then gently circles his middle finger around the affected area. He bites and sucks at his lip ring as he contemplates my palm.

"We need to get it out," he murmurs.

Of our systems, I don't add.

"I don't think my fingers can-" He stops talking so that he can concentrate as he tries to extract the chipping from my flesh. He really does have the world's largest hands, so unlike the artistic musician stereotype. His nails are neat and trimmed short, making them unable to grip at the splinter, and his fingers… well, they're the kind that were made to grip logs and bare knuckle fight so, to put it plainly, there's no way that he's squeezing a millimetre of wood out of me.

"You can't do it, it's okay-" I start, but he cuts me off with a look.

"I can do it," he says, a double-meaning that I'm

not getting burning behind his molten irises.

He pauses for a moment as if I'll come to some conclusion on my own but, seeing that that's not about to happen, he fills me in.

"I can do it," he repeats, a little hesitant this time. "Just not with my fingers."

Not with his fingers? I give him a cautious once over, trying to work out what the hell that means.

Am I crazy? Is he going to fuck it out of me or something?

"I can… suck it out," he finishes quietly, eyes on the scuffed flesh of my hand. "I can get it out using my mouth-"

"No, absolutely not," I stammer. "That definitely won't be necessary, but thank you-"

"Kitty," he breathes. His voice is so low it reverberates through me. "Kaleb isn't going to know. Unless you've got cameras up here in the trees too-"

I'm breathing harder now that I'm stationary than when I was sprinting fifty miles per hour.

It's been less than twenty-four hours since I suggested that we keep this ship afloat under the guise of friendship and now he's about to suck something out of my body? Did I accidentally reverse-manifest this?

"Madden, please." I try to ignore the butterflies fluttering in my belly. "I can try to get it out myself, I'm sure it isn't a big deal."

He hooks his left arm around my lower back, pulling us slightly closer together. "I used to work in construction, Kitty. Injuries like these can become infected."

"What are the chances that it'll *actually* become

infected?" I argue.

"None," he argues back. "If you let me suck it out of you."

We've reached an impasse. He stares down at me like I'm his life's mission and I scowl up at him like he's a pain in my ass. Unfortunately the pains that I *do* currently have in my ass are not Madden related.

After a tense ten seconds of mutual glowering I finally roll my eyes, submitting, and he lets out a relieved sigh.

"Fine, you can-"

I stop talking the second that his mouth meets my skin. It's warm and wet and more gentle than I was expecting. He grazes his teeth gently around the point of soreness and then slowly, painstakingly, he begins to suck.

My face scrunches up as he begins working the foreign-body out of me because it hurts in a way that's both good and bad. Combining that with the smooth rub of his lip-ring against my skin, my thighs are twitching with heat and daggers.

Sensing my discomfort he slows down on the suction and gives me a much needed distraction. The hand that's not gripping my wrist gently caresses its way up my back, Madden's warmth seeping into my skin like a heat pad, and he briefly glances up at me through his long black lashes, gauging my pain from the pinch in my brow. He works his fingers under the hem of my tank and slides them upwards until he reaches the back of my sports bra, tracing his fingers back and forth. After a moment he bows his head again, his fringe shielding his eyes in fluffy disarray, but I can still hear the low noises coming from the back of his throat as he miraculously teases the splinter to the surface.

Before I'm ready for him to pull away I feel the sting of the wood being released and then Madden's sitting upright, one fist still suspending my hand in the air.

He turns his head away from me and spits the splinter out of his mouth, then wipes his lips across the large swell of his shoulder. The stubble on his jaw scrapes roughly against his shirt. I fantasise about him doing that up my belly.

When he looks back down at me I'm suddenly aware of how compromising my position is, so I bunch up my knees and tuck them to my chest, hopefully looking a little less exposed.

Madden gets to his feet and then tugs me up by my elbows, breaking the silence.

"Done," he grunts, breathing deep and heavy.

"Thank you," I reply quickly. Then, too aware of how close we're standing, I add on the word, "Friend."

At least my mouth seems to have some self-control. If this was up to my other body parts, this conversation would definitely be over.

"'Friend'," he repeats, a quietly amused look on his face. "Is that our safe word?"

His hands slip from their grip on my elbows and slowly work their way around my back. When he reaches my shoulder blades he splays out his palms, and my head grows woozy when I realise that his two hand-spans? Yeah, they're bigger than my *entire back.*

Trying to bring us back down to Earth I ask casually, "How'd you learn how to do that?"

"The splinter thing?"

"Yeah." A thought enters my mind and I give him a dimply smile. "You been kissing splinters out of all the guys at Coleson's construction company?"

He smiles back at me. "How'd you think I got the job?"

A laugh bubbles out of me and I scrunch up my nose, trying to ignore the little exploration that his hands are currently enjoying around the narrow frame of my shoulders and up the curves of my neck.

"Another fascinating tank," he mutters dryly as his fingers tangle in my hair.

I look down, appraising the word *RAWHIDE* printed in bold across my chest.

"I'm a cowgirl, every cowgirl likes the Blues Brothers," I say defensively.

I'm lying of course. I wore this tank purely to befuddle that pretty boy brain of his.

He swallows but omits further commentary, avoiding my eyes *and* my chest. Turning his face slightly away from me he reaches into the front pocket of his jeans and then pulls out the baby pink lollipop that I'd forgotten he'd picked up last night. He unwraps it, pockets the clear plastic covering, and then holds it in front of my lips like I'm a kid who's just had a successful trip to the doctor's office.

My lips quirk into a little smile.

"Why're you trying to give that to me now?" I ask, my head shaking in amusement.

His expression is no longer blushing and boyish.

"'Cause I wanna kiss you."

His eyes burn into mine and the peaks of my chest begin to ache.

"But I know you wanna go slow," he continues.

"So if you put this in your mouth then I can't… I won't be able to…"

I pinch the stick of the lolly, unable to avoid brushing his thick fingers with the soft pads of my own, and when he lets it go I tuck it into my mouth, throwing it into my right cheek pouch like a hamster.

"Thanks," I say, weirdly enjoying how good it feels to be cared for.

With the sun shining right behind him a golden halo circles his spiked ebony hair, contrasting so starkly to his face shrouded in shadows.

He nips the stick that's jutting out of my mouth and I stop swirling it as he begins to tug. Understanding what he's doing, I marginally part my lips so that he can slide it out of me.

Beneath my tank, my nipples pinch and push against the fabric. What the hell? It's barely eight in the morning and he's already turning me on. On his *second day* of being here.

I don't think that I'm going to be able to survive a whole summer of this.

Madden twizzles the stick between us, its glossy head sparkling when it catches a break in the canopy overhead, and then he holds it up higher – not returning it, but *retrieving* it.

He shoves it into his mouth and compresses me against his chest. My eyes grow wide as I try not to go all Bambi-limbed again.

After sucking on it for a few seconds he slips the lolly out of his mouth with the hand that's not rubbing circles in the small of my back and he gestures with it to the forest running uphill behind me.

"Kaleb will maul me if I let you run out here on

your own," he states.

"Maybe I'll maul you if you don't," I reply.

He looks down into my eyes and there's a twinkle sparkling in his icy depths. "Maybe I want you to," he teases, and then crushes me against him tighter.

Feeling brave, I scratch a nail roughly up his abs and he throws his head back in pseudo-pleasure. "Oh yeah," he groans, his mouth tilted up in a grin. We're joking together and it feels good, but it definitely doesn't feel like *friendly* joking. My eyes travel down the thick column of his neck, entranced.

He dips his head forward again so that he can look down into my eyes and he tosses the lolly back into his mouth.

"I'm sorry about this morning, in the kitchen with Kaleb." He squints his eyes as if cringing at the memory and adds, "We were jackasses. I didn't want to fight him on it because I didn't want to draw any attention to… *us*… but…" He twists the lolly around with his tongue as he contemplates the rest of his sentence. "I should have. I should have been on your side there."

I pull the lolly out of his mouth.

"You don't need any more of this," I whisper, twirling the stick like a magic wand. "You're already too sweet."

Twin creases appear in his cheeks and his face breaks into the most stunning grin that I've ever seen. Laugh lines crease around the edges of his eyes, and then he dips down so that he can rub his forehead into my shoulder.

"Princess, you're the sweet one," he mumbles, his soft hair tickling me as he brushes it side to side.

I'm really not. Or, if I am, I don't want to be. The more that I allow myself to like Madden the worse this is going to be for me when he leaves. I really have got to try and keep him at arm's length – at a nice *friendly* length.

But before I can push myself out of his arms we suddenly hear a rustle at my rear, somewhere farther up the incline and deeper into the forest.

I whip around, startled, and Madden's arms lock me against his chest like a seat-belt. He quickly turns us so that he's now the one closer to the sound, and his eyes are hard as he scans through the trees.

"The hell was that," he mumbles, his chest rising and falling in large steady pumps.

I shake my head to signal that I'm not sure, but really I'm lying. I saw the flash of fur, and I'm betting that Madden did too.

We've been talking in hushed tones and we aren't in the sunniest spot, so I don't doubt the fact that some animals would risk a prowl if they suspected the area was safe. Okay, it wasn't a bear but it was big enough for me to know that Madden wants it nowhere near me.

Madden swallows and looks down at me, adrenaline rippling through his arms and making him clutch me tighter.

"Please, for the love of God," he says, his voice dangerously low. Predatorily low. It's a good thing that whatever was out here just shot back to wherever it came from because Madden is no longer in a friendly mood. "Whilst I'm here – whilst your parents are away – don't do your running up here. Please Kitty, for me. It's not safe. And I'm not opposed to the idea of hauling you over my shoulder to stop you."

Is that supposed to discourage me? I want to make a joke out of it but I can see from the hard set of his brow that he's being totally serious.

"I don't want you in harm's way. I don't want to lose-" He groans and shakes his head, discarding his sentence. I'm not sure what nerve we've hit but I decide that the best tactic is distraction.

I take the lollipop from his hand and give the head a little suck. He watches me, agonised, and when I hand it back to him it goes straight into his mouth.

Yeah, we're going to make a pair of really great *friends.*

"Fine," I say, agreeing to his terms. "I won't run up here whilst you're in town."

I push my body out of his arms and then reacclimatise my footing to the downward track. After a quick glance over my shoulder I can tell that he's already feeling a little better, his expression much calmer and more relieved.

"You can tail me," I say as I begin my descent, more cautious than before after my incident with the wood chipping.

"I would love to tail you-"

I shoot him a glare and he responds with a look that is definitely not sorry.

Friends for now, I think to myself, trying to ignore the fluttering in my belly.

And then we run.

CHAPTER 7

Madden

It turns out that Kaleb's important morning off the ranch was a pick-up mission.

And the thing that he was picking up?

"Dude," I say, gripping my fingers through my hair as he undoes the tailback trailer, un-strapping the hot tub from its clipped-in bonds. "Tell me that isn't what I think it is."

I'm stressed the fuck out. I spent the entire morning with my eyes locked on Kitty's magic little ass and I need to jerk one out before I die a death by hard-on.

"Pre-fourth of July celebrations, man," he replies, grinning at me like I'm not about to combust.

Hang on. He wants to orchestrate pre-fourth of July celebrations at his parents' ranch with his *little sister* around?

"You're gonna have a hot tub party here? With Kitty around?" I ask, eyebrows raised in disbelief.

I'm not insecure about where Kitty and I stand – I'm well aware that we're on the precipice of an active volcano, on the cusp of enjoying an exhilarating freefall before I meet my bone-crushing doom with her brother – but that doesn't mean that I want other guys around her, talking to her and shit.

"Yeah," he replies as he unfastens the last clip, then he leans backwards, scoping the best way to manoeuvre the tub.

"How much does this thing weigh?" I ask, folding my arms across my chest. Whilst he scratches at his forehead I risk a glance over to the fields, trying to catch a glimpse of Kitty.

"Not sure. You'll be able to lift it," he replies.

It looks as heavy as a small tractor but I'm not going to turn down an opportunity to impress Kaleb's sister if she just so happens to be walking by.

Right after I sort out the problem in my jeans.

"Think you can give me ten?" I ask, my voice hoarse as I try to hide my growing need.

"Yeah, whatever – I'm gonna shower off before we do this anyway. It's hot as balls out here."

My jaw twitches. *He* needs to use the shower? Get in the fucking queue, man.

"Sure," I say, my teeth clenched tight.

What the hell am I going to do?

I look around, scoping for somewhere that I can go and do my business. No way am I jacking off in the cabin if it's only Kaleb and me in there.

The forest maybe?

I turn around looking for my out when suddenly a flash of obsidian catches my eye – Kitty's long black hair glimmering in the early morning sunlight as she hauls a stainless steel can of milk from their cooling den, working her way towards us so that it can be taken to be pasteurised.

I reactivate like I've just been hit with a defibrillator.

"Here, let me."

I stride over to her, dismissing that amused eye roll that she just did as more of a show for her brother rather than mocking my desire to baby her, and I grip my fingers under the slots, replacing hers as she hands it over to me.

"Just put it in the-"

She stops short when she looks at the hot tub on the tail of the truck.

"Uh…" She raises an eyebrow and then looks up at Kaleb with squinting eyes. "Is that a hot tub?" she asks.

He smirks as he chugs back a mouthful from his water bottle and then he replies with a grin, "Yeah. You're not gonna tell mom on me are you?"

Her eyebrow climbs even higher. "Surely you'd be more afraid of dad."

He nods in agreement as he finishes the bottle. Then he throws it through the rolled down window onto the passenger seat and moves around to the back of the truck, squatting at the attachment key that's joining the carrier tray to the Chevy. He unwinds the mechanism, freeing the vehicle from the plate carrying the hot tub and then gestures to the open-top bed, jerking his thumb at it whilst tipping his chin in the direction of the milk that I'm now carrying. How the hell did she carry this? Surely this is way too heavy for her.

"Pop it in there. Kitty'll cover the bed once they're all in."

Kaleb, apparently done with his participation, begins heading towards the cabin, so I allow myself to slide my eyes up and down his sister as I heave the milk into the back of the truck. That tank she's wearing should be illegal.

"You taking this to town?" I ask, voice getting lower as my brain cells turn to ash. There is not one clean thought left in my head.

"Yup," she replies absentmindedly, tapping away on her phone. "The other cans are back there if you wanna get them for me," she adds on, eyes still glued to her screen.

I lean against the truck momentarily, watching her in studious silence as she continues ignoring me. As if I didn't have my hands running all over her an hour ago. As if she doesn't know how stiff she got me this morning.

Aware that she's gonna continue ignoring me I head to where the other cans are waiting and one by one I haul them into the truck for her, quickly so that they don't curdle before she's made it to town.

When I'm done I cover the bed, give the Chevy a slap on the rear, and then turn around to look down at her.

She's still texting.

Who the fuck is she texting?

"Who are you-"

I'm about to ask her even though I have no right to do so when she suddenly looks up. She pockets her phone and, after a sweeping glance at the cabin to check that Kaleb's safely inside, she lifts herself onto the toes of her cowgirl boots and plants a tiny peck on the side of my cheek.

My heart thunders in my chest like I'm a teenager again.

"Thanks," she says quickly, and then without a second glance she hops into the driver's seat, straps herself in, and peels off the gravel faster than I'd like her to be driving.

In seconds I'm alone, standing in the dust-caked driveway, with nothing but the swing of the barn door for company.

Wait a second.

The barn.

I take a look over my shoulder towards the currently vacant barn, freshly cleaned out and totally empty.

Huh. Would you look at that.

I grind the heel of my boot into the dirt, contemplating if this is really fucking wrong or not.

I know that it is. But I also know that I don't care.

I turn around and start making my way over to it, my brain burning with the new visual of Kitty holding that giant can of milk in her sexy little top.

When I get inside I push the door so that it's fully closed and then I lock the latch, hoping to God that Kaleb doesn't try to get in here for the next ten minutes.

It feels hotter in here than it did out there, the warmth of the cloying June morning clinging to the wooden panels and radiating upwards from the freshly lain straw. Too horny to not jack off but not horny enough to beat one out in a cow stall, I move to the booth at the back of the room that's stocked up with ropes and various other pieces of ranch maintenance equipment. I rest my left palm flat on the plank in front of me whilst my other hand slips my belt buckle loose, unzipping my fly and then tugging down my jeans.

I stifle a groan of relief as my shaft is freed from the denim, giving me the room to expand and thicken fully. I tuck my hand into my boxers and rub my thumb over the head.

It's too much. I bow forward, grinding my head against the wall as I take my hand back out of my underwear, wiping the pre-cum on the side of my jeans.

I'm not sure I can even do this. A couple of tugs and it's gonna be over.

Breathing heavy, I tilt my head to the side, subconsciously acknowledging what else is in the booth. I blink slowly as if I'm seeing it for the first time when a hook adorned with a couple items of clothing comes into view.

A roughed up pair of denim dungarees.

A dusty red and black check flannel.

And a black cotton tank top.

Incapable of finesse, I yank the whole lot off the hook and then drop everything except for the tank. It's so over-washed that it's gone translucent and there are holes around the neckline and a gash up the back. Presumably it's been hanging here to die for the past year at least, no longer usable and long unworn.

Swallowing hard I lift the top to my face and I gently press my nose into it, sniffing at the soft cotton.

I'm not sure if I'm in Heaven or in Hell because this little tank smells sweeter than sugar. It's falling to pieces and she still fucking wears it.

She shouldn't be wearing it. She shouldn't.

Keeping my forehead against the wall in front of me I lower the top to my crotch, and I lightly press it against myself. I squeeze my eyes shut as my temples tighten, the need for release weighing heavy in my sac.

I slip the fabric into my boxers and wrap it around myself, cursing because this shit's softer than silk. I clench my teeth together as I tighten my grip, desperate to unload this aching weight.

Biting my teeth into my lip-ring I fist one rough tug, pumping my whole length into the softness of Kitty's tank, and it's the best feeling that I've ever felt in my life. I want to thrust into it in pure ecstasy, allowing the fact that she's been wearing this, the knowledge that her scent is rubbing all over me to squeeze me to the brink, but at the same time I know that I can't.

Would she forgive me? Yeah, she's so sweet that I bet she would. But would I forgive myself for defiling something that she's probably been wearing forever? Hell no.

I slip her tank out of my boxers, cursing because even *that* feels good, and I swap it from my right hand to my left, scrunching it against the wall as I shove my fist back down my underwear.

I picture her with me, in front of me, wearing that *RAWHIDE* top that needs to be incinerated. She's wearing a pair of her cute denim cut-offs and her used holey tank is dangling from her fingers. She knows what I need and she holds it between us, giving me permission to take it.

I push my forehead against hers, silently asking her

to do this for me, to help me get there, and she understands. Of course she does. She knows me better than anyone else.

Still holding her top, it's her hand that slips down my boxers, enrobing me in softness and warmth, and then she begins to grasp and grip and pump me senseless.

"Cum," she whispers, looking up at me through her lashes, her lips parted and perfect for kissing.

I want my tongue in her mouth. She's wearing that tiny top and her sweet little shorts but she shouldn't be wearing anything at all.

I shake my head when she gives me an encouraging nod. We've only been here for fifteen seconds and I want to last as long as I can. I need to show her what I can do for her.

"It's okay, I want you to," she continues, lips lightly kissing against the stubble on my neck. Fuck she feels so good. "Before anyone catches us, Madden. No-one's allowed to see."

I'm desperate to last but I know that I can't, not with the smell and the feel of her all around me. With both of her hands gripped around my shaft she tosses me faster, making me groan and buck. Then she stands up on her tip-toes so she can kiss her way up my jaw. Goosebumps ignite up my back and my shoulders, and I lean into her harder, wanting her to know how little control I have left. It's fucking obvious but she needs to know. She has to know how desperately I want her.

"Kitty," I whisper, dipping my head low so that I can finally catch her lips. She's right there, she's ready to be kissed, but somehow she's still just out of reach.

My body swells and tenses until I can no longer see

a thing.

CHAPTER 8

Kitty

I scroll through the photos that Mama sent to our family group chat – her winning her first competition of their trip, a Quarter Horse medallion draped around her neck as she grins a big white smile at my dad behind the camera. I scan my eyes over her everyday cowgirl outfit – a pair of mid-wash blue denim jeans, hoisted around her small waist with a thick leather belt, wherein a huge tiger's eye gemstone is positioned in the centre of the bronzed buckle, and a tight navy shirt buttoned up to her chin. Her cocoa brown cowboy hat is the cherry on the cake.

It takes every ounce of my good-natured sibling loyalty to not tattle on Kaleb's hot tub agenda, which he has been storing for the past week underneath one of the wooden vehicle shelters my dad built a few summers ago, preventing it from getting fucked up in the sunlight. Instead, I flick off from the page of photos, open up my contacts list, and click the call button at the top of the screen.

"Hey Pumpkin." My dad's maple syrup drawl comes in through the speaker after a couple of seconds. "You see the pics?"

I nod even though he can't see me and I set the call to speakerphone so that I can collate my garb for the shower and wash the day's worth of cowpat, dirt, gravel dust and hay off of me before I become too tired to care.

"She looks amazing," I say, pulling a fresh pair of pjs from my dresser. "And first prize too."

"She's a superstar," he agrees. Then adds, "Just like our baby girl."

A warm feeling spreads through my chest and I scrunch my nose to hide my smile. "*Papa*," I groan, feigning embarrassment.

"And you look just like her too these days," he continues. Then he asks, "Kaleb being good?"

I hear a bottle top popping somewhere in the background.

"Define good," I say dryly. I can get away with masking the truth with sarcasm because Papa doesn't really understand half of the stuff that I say anyway.

"Is he doing his fair share around the ranch?" he questions, then takes a swig of whatever he's drinking.

I plop my underwear on top of my pjs and then scoop up the clothes pile, grabbing my cell as I leave my bedroom. "Yeah, he actually is." *Alongside having impromptu jamming sessions every night and organising some hush-hush secret pool party.*

"Hay need cutting yet? I checked the weather and it's still looking dandy, fingers-crossed."

"I'm gonna get Kaleb to do it next week," I tell

him, kicking up a leg so that I can shut my door with my foot.

"Next week," he muses quietly.

I hear him scratch at his scalp, deep in thought.

I understand why when he asks me, "You got any plans for the fourth?"

"I don't, but Kaleb probably does. And River's coming up just after," I admit.

My dad knows that River is my best friend from high school and he's met her on a couple of occasions. I can sense him nodding, placated, through the phone.

"You know what Kaleb has planned? Nothing at the ranch I hope."

I hip-bump the bathroom door open and dump my clothes on the counter. Then I cross my fingers behind my back. "I'm not sure what he has planned yet. Maybe it's better if you ask him."

"Can you put him on the phone?"

"I'm about to shower," I say. Code for: *I do not want to be any way involved with you potentially finding out what Kaleb has planned.*

"Okay Pumpkin, I'll leave you to it. I'll text Kaleb and ask him to give me a ring."

RIP Kaleb.

"Love you, Papa. Tell mom congratulations."

"Love you too, Pumpkin."

There's a click and then the line disconnects.

I back-kick the door shut and then flip the lock, stripping out of my dirty clothes and throwing them into the wicker laundry basket.

It's been about a week since Madden and Kaleb pulled up and it's been weirdly good having them around. Ever since the splinter incident I've been on my best behaviour because I don't want Kaleb to know how I feel about his best friend, and with the barn restoration that Madden's taken upon himself he's so shattered that he's been passing out on the sofa most evenings. Undoubtedly, him being unconscious does make avoiding our feelings a hell of a lot easier.

Plus, I've also managed to stay out of their hair under my milkmaid disguise – carting the dairy load to the factory and then stopping by the bar so that I can get in some practice time, courtesy of the key that Dyl smuggled for me.

Horrendous employee, very handy buddy.

I twist on the shower head and hold my hand beneath the spray, checking the temperature of the water. It's warm but I like being cooked alive, so I browse the shower gels in the wall cubby as I wait for my incinerator to heat up.

As I lean forwards, knocking my knees against the side of the tub, a dark blue bottle that I never paid attention to before catches my eyes.

Stepping into the bath and under the jet streams I reach up into the holder and lift out the bottle, running my eyes over the text on the label.

Midnight Pine. Relatable. I click open the top and give the body a little squeeze, lowering my nose to the opening so that I can breathe in the scent. *His* scent. A small mound of gel leaks up out of the plastic and I close my eyes as I take it in.

It's heady and strong like freshly rubbed pine leaves, and dark too, like campfire smoke. That day when we were toying with each other in the forest and he held me close to him after extracting my splinter, the warm scent radiating from his skin was *this* scent.

And the combination of *this* scent mixed with his skin…

Opening my eyes, I make a quick glance towards the door, checking that it's locked, and then I squeeze out one glossy dollop, alight with anticipation.

I'm sure that he won't miss one spurt of body wash.

I cup my hands under the water, now hot enough to boil vegetables, and then I rub my palms together, creating a thick, foamy lather. I arch my spine so that the spray can cascade down to my naval and then I lift my hands to my clavicle and start gently massaging. I grip and rotate my fingers down my arms, loosening my muscles from the day's physical exertion.

I should indulge like this every day – God knows I need it what with all of the hauling I do – but for some reason I'm still so shy about my body, even when I'm basically home alone.

Why am I so tentative about touching myself? What repercussions am I afraid of with regards to my own body?

I shake my head at my own neurosis. Going down that neuropathway is way too deep for a shower. I should've stuck some music on before I'd got my hands all wet.

I stroke my hands up my throat, giving it a little squeeze before I slide them down over my chest. I peer down at myself, delicately rubbing the lather around my small curves and thinking about the fact that I'm now coated in Madden's thick, warm-

A hard rap on the door shocks me out of my thoughts. I jolt like a deer in headlights.

What the *hell* am I doing? *Bad* Kitty. He isn't even

in the room and I'm still allowing him to fog up my brain.

"Occupied!" I shout out, my hands now moving double-time over my belly and ass and down my legs.

I don't know who I want it to be out there the least. Kaleb, who will follow me around all evening until I lock myself in my room in order to ensure that I'm not going for a midnight jog with the coyotes? Or Madden, who will realise in the space of three seconds that I've pumped his soap all over myself like a tiny little perv?

Spooked out of my mind I quickly rinse off, rain-checking my self-massage for another evening, and then I scramble out of the bath, huddling under my towel to keep the heat in.

The knock on the pane sounds again so I bang back at them with my right fist, chucking the towel on the floor and then slipping into my underwear.

"Who the hell is it?" I bark out.

I pull on my shorts and a clean pyjama top and then, disgruntled, I whip open the window, praying for a fast air-circulation turnaround as I head back over to the door.

"Who-" I pull the door open and my jaw drops to the floor.

Wow.

Caked up in mud, sweat, and drying brown paint Madden rubs a flannel towel around the back of his neck whilst his other hand grips the edge of the door frame. His oiled-up bronze skin, glistening with exertion, radiates the warmth of a man who's spent the entire day in a sun-trap, baking in the summer heat as he toils hour after hour. The belt that he wears is partially loosened, allowing his jeans to slip and expose the deep V which slices up from his groin to his lower abdominals. Which, I should mention, are completely exposed due to the fact that he's *shirtless.*

"Oh," I say, involuntarily obviously.

With his head ducked down so that he can continue wiping the sweat from around his shoulders he glances up at me through his lashes. His eyes are tired from his labour but still sparkling with our secret.

I'm eye-level with his chest so I let my gaze sweep across the width of it for another luxurious moment. I think that I'm regressing because right now the only thoughts that my brain can cook up are words like *Muscles* and *Meat* and *Huge.*

He taps his thumb against the wooden frame to recapture my attention. I flush like a criminal as I meet his eyes again.

"I gotta shower," he says, his voice all deep and hoarse. "Sorry for rushing you, but I'm seizing the fu-" He stops himself mid-sentence, swallows and re-completes it. "I'm seizing up," he finishes.

I nod, entranced, but I can't seem to move. Probably because I don't want to. If we could just stand here like this for the rest of the night, I would wholeheartedly be okay with that.

Aware that I've become nonresponsive, he lets out a chuckle, an amused twinkle in his eye.

"Come on princess, in or out," he smiles, the tips of his cheekbones ruddy with pleasure. "Or," he continues, dipping closer so that he can lower his voice to a conspiratorial murmur. "We could do a bit of both if you'd prefer."

My eyes pop wide and my legs turn to jelly.

"Ha-ha," I say, trying to keep my voice casual but

really I'm all a-wobble. I turn briefly back to the bathroom under the guise of slinging my towel into the laundry bin, but the fact of the matter is that I'm trying to get my hormones under control. I briefly squeeze my eyes shut, trying to flush out the impression that his pecs have burned into my retinas.

Christ. I bend forward to pick up my towel when I feel a change in the airflow behind me. Or maybe it's a change in the pheromones. I glance at Madden over my shoulder as I stand and I instantly note the change in his demeanour. His body has become still and his pupils have blacked the hell out.

Suddenly I realise why.

"It's not what it looks like," I lie quickly.

More like, it's not what it *smells* like.

Which, again, would also be a lie.

"Did you…?" He breaches the threshold of the bathroom, eyes trained on the product cubby in the shower. I risk a glimpse in the same direction. The suddy bubbles of Midnight Pine shimmer as they slide down the bottle.

Damn it.

"You used my shower gel?" It's a statement disguised as a question.

"Nope." I'm a serial liar tonight.

His eyes slide back to me, half-mast with arousal. "Kitty," he drawls deeply. "I'm obviously not mad at you for doing it."

He takes another step closer, closing the gap, and I stay completely still. Watching me carefully he gradually lowers his face to my collarbone, exposed in my summer pyjama tank, and then he gently presses his lips against my skin.

I'm warm and clean from my speedy evening shower and he's hot and dirty from barn renovating all day. The contrasting combination is like a shot of heroin and I shudder dramatically as his lip-ring digs into me.

He takes a deep inhale and a low sound rumbles in his chest. I can feel his hands hovering at my waist, desperate to get his palms all over me.

"Where's Kaleb?" I whisper, the fear over my brother catching us mixing in with the pool of pleasure whirling in my belly.

"Still outside," he murmurs against my skin, his soft black fringe tickling my jaw. Then, "Jesus, this smells so good on you, Kitty."

He lifts himself up again until he's towering a good foot over me. I step back so that my ass is pushed up against the sink. He follows me immediately, hands gripping into the porcelain on either side of my hips.

"Why'd you use it?" he asks, voice so low it's fossilising.

Stupidly, I tell him the truth. "I wanted you on me," I whisper, too scared to speak the words at a normal volume.

He closes his eyes momentarily, Adam's apple undulating as he swallows hard.

"I want that too," he replies, hands sliding closer to my pyjama shorts. "Maybe if Kaleb stays over at someone else's one of these nights-" he begins, but he's suddenly interrupted by the hoots of loud voices coming from outside.

Voices?

"What…?"

I look into Madden's eyes and I can see the present

moment dawning on him again. We're back in the real world now, away from the heady make-believe land where it's just the two of us. After one last sweeping look down my throat, clavicle, and to the ribbon on my shorts, he takes a lumbering step back, giving me the room to move around him.

"What's going on out there?" I ask, brow furrowed.

"Uh, he's…" Madden waves his arm behind him, gesturing vaguely in the vicinity of Outside. At least I'm not the only one who can barely string a sentence together right now.

Not knowing what he's attempting to say I brush past him, leaving him alone to un-seize in the shower, and I walk down the landing, eyes on the windows facing the front of the cabin as I descend the stairs.

There are loads of cars outside, blinding headlights illuminating our living room as they idle in front of the wooden fence.

Have I forgotten something?

When I reach the bottom step I watch as Kaleb appears from the cow barn to greet the visitors, high fiving the guys and jerking his chin up at a whole host of girls.

Now I remember.

It's almost the fourth and Kaleb's having his hot tub party.

CHAPTER 9

Madden

Damn it, Kaleb.

Of all the nights he had to throw his pre-fourth of July party on *this* one, the one where I've got Kitty letting me suck her skin in a steamed up bathroom whilst telling me how much she wants me *on* her.

That makes two of us, princess.

I shut the door, not bothering to lock it because if Kitty wants to come back in here then I'm not gonna be the one to stop her, and I shove my jeans down my thighs, my belt snapping fully open as the denim breaches my quads. I kick my pants off my legs and turn on the shower faucet, the water already steaming due to its previous occupant.

I quickly hose myself down because I'm coated in dirt from the ranch, but a big part of me is revelling in this feeling. It's been two years since I was working at Jason's company and I can't deny that I've missed it; the hard wear on my body as I spend each day hauling and hammering, exerting myself past what my muscles originally thought they were capable of. Even though it's only been a week since Kaleb and I came to watch over Kitty on the ranch, I can already feel my body reacclimatising to the non-stop labour, the pleasure that comes with being physically overworked.

Don't get me wrong, I'm grateful that our band has been a success in so many small towns across the country, but working myself to full capacity from dawn until dusk is what really gets my engine going.

I squirt out a pump of shower gel, fucking loving the fact that Kitty is now covered in this too, and I quickly scrub it up and down my arms, over my torso, and everywhere else. God knows how Kitty will feel about Kaleb bringing half of Phoenix Falls to her parents' ranch but I don't want her alone out there if I can help it.

Best case scenario would be if she sees Kaleb's party, doesn't give a shit, goes to her bedroom where I can find her on her own, and I sneak in an hour of her company, undisturbed and still a secret from her brother.

Worst case scenario? My breathing gets heavy just thinking about it.

If I leave this bathroom and find her wearing a stringy bikini as she gets chatted up in the kitchen by some small town brute you can bet your ass that I'm going to be playing the over-protective *I'm here to look after you* card. Or maybe I'll put those teenage years of illegal bare knuckle sparring to use again and let out some steam by busting a few jaws.

Either way I obviously need therapy.

I rinse off the suds and rub a clean towel over my

hair and body, squinting as a soap droplet runs into my eye. The temptation to use the towel Kitty threw into their laundry bin is so overwhelming that I almost do it. Mentally chastising myself I toss my towel on top of hers and then shuck my legs back into my jeans, albeit not wearing boxers this time because I'm not gonna wear a dirty pair, but I'm also definitely not going to waste another second going down to the guest room for a new freaking 'fit. I zip my fly up and wince as the metal scours my shaft.

I hope that isn't the only action I'm getting tonight.

I slip my belt back through the buckle and then open the door, ready to head downstairs to whatever's awaiting me.

Please don't be wearing a bikini in front of all the guys, I think to myself, my mind spinning with a jealousy I'm not justified to have.

I try thinking rationally.

It's harder than it sounds.

Even if Kitty *was* stripped down to a bikini in front of the guys, it wouldn't really matter. Girls wear bikinis all the time, and it isn't even a sexual thing – it's a comfort thing, so that they can get in and out of a hot tub without destroying their underwear.

The cords in my neck tighten as I think about all of the things Kitty could get up to in a hot tub.

With someone else, my brain adds sardonically.

I grab a fistful of my hair and give it a rough tug, willing myself out of this unhinged possessive mindset.

It's the twenty-first century, I remind myself. *No acting like a caveman.*

When I reach the bottom of the staircase I check the kitchen at my left to see if Kitty is mercifully inside ignoring everyone. I sigh when I see that it's completely empty.

I turn right, where she also isn't curled up on their living room sofa watching a movie, but I add that to my mental *Things To Do Whilst I'm Staying At Kitty's Place* checklist as I trudge to the backdoor, leading to the barn and Kaleb's hot tub via the rear route. I force my feet into my boots and then I pull the handle.

I can smell the party as soon as I step outside.

Sometimes Kaleb makes me homicidal. Doing this around his sister? I roll my shoulders to try and shake off my irritation, only then realising that I still don't have a shirt on. Fuck me sideways. It's not an issue seeing as most of the people here won't be wearing too many items of clothing either, but I don't want it to look like a threat around Kaleb's guys. The problem with being big and cut is that, once another guy spots you, all that he sees is a challenge. A fight. And when you add a pool full of chicks into the mix, it's just not a good combination.

Kicking at the grit as I traipse around to the front of the barn, my jaw instantly clenches as the hot tub comes into view. It's packed.

In a macho attempt to prettify the dirt-space between the cabin and the outbuildings Kaleb has strung up some patio lights, illuminating the pool in a sultry summer's night glow. At least they'll help me scope out Kitty.

"Hey man," Kaleb calls to me from a log that he's set up around the edge of the tub. It's like a wooded fairyland meets Wild West orgy.

I jerk my chin at him, meeting him at his stump.

"Your sister here?" I ask quietly, keeping my voice

low so that the guys around us won't hear. Then, remembering that I'm not supposed to act so interested, I add, "She wasn't inside is all."

"Oh, yeah," he nods, then swigs at his bottle. A wash of disdain trickles through me.

He points straight ahead, directly across the water. "She's over there."

I'm already on my way when he adds on, "You think I shouldn't have?"

I stop and look at him, understanding the vagueness of his sentence when we're surrounded by guys puffing joints and girls looking for a hook up. He's asking me if I think he shouldn't have hosted a party and, subsequently, if he shouldn't have let Kitty come out here and join him. Yeah: if he shouldn't have *let* her. Is it archaic? Yes. But I guess that not all of those protective caveman genes have fully left our systems despite the millions of years of evolution after all.

I grimace at him to express my view on the matter, hating the feel of eyes on me from the hot tub.

I trudge around the wooden porch chairs as I make my way to the other side, wishing that it was just Kitty and me out here, with no-one to distract her and no-one to stop us.

A tight feeling grips at my chest when my eyes finally land on her.

She's not in a bikini thank God but she is still wearing her cute pyjamas and, honestly, that's almost worse. There's nothing a guy likes more than when a girl wears a sweet little outfit that he was never meant to see.

The fact that she's not dressing up for anyone

unlike every other person out here? That's like heroin to a guy.

She's not interested in me? Then she must be fucking priceless.

Unfortunately Tyler must agree with me as he's resting his arms on the outer side of the hot tub, flexing his biceps like he's putting on a mating display. Kitty's sat on a deck chair in front of him, her knees bent up as she peels the label off a bottle that I'm two seconds away from ripping out of her hands.

Probably sensing the serial killer energy that I'm emitting Tyler glances my way and quickly recomposes. He stands up slowly, water dripping down his abs, and then he climbs out of the water and sets himself on the ledge.

Tyler's a big guy, but knowing that I weigh at least thirty pounds more than him calms my mind like a mug of Valium.

"Hey," he says, his tone the equivalent of *fuck off*.

"Hey," I say back, my expression giving *you first*.

"Been a while," he continues, eyes slipping down to Kitty and then back to me.

I can't look at her right now or I'll lose my train of thought so I keep my gaze steadily on Tyler.

"Not really," I reply. "It's only been a week."

I give him a smile that reads *could've been longer*.

He nods as he takes in my mood, but there's a mutual understanding beneath both of our hostilities. Since the day that I met Tyler we've always been too alike – the same heritage, the same interests, and the exact same *type* – but it's never been an issue with us. Until now. Because this is the one *interest* that I'm never letting him take from me.

"It was good catching up." He smiles down at Kitty and I see her cheeks flush red.

My fists are itching to meet Tyler's face.

"See you around," he adds, a little extra salt for my growing wound.

He meets my eyes as he moves to go, the silence between us speaking volumes. I jerk my chin at him, a sort of conciliating apology about the fact that, right now, we can no longer be friends. This is too important to me. She's too important to me.

He nods in agreement and brushes past me.

Fucking finally. I look down at Kitty's deckchair and, seeing as she's all crunched up at the back of it, I straddle the front half, forcing her to look at me.

"Hey," I say, leaning slightly towards her and trying to meet her eyes.

She avoids them completely but she's smiling which is a good sign. She scrunches up her nose and then shakes her head, turning her face to the right so that she can continue ignoring me.

But she *is* smiling.

"Sorry. Again," I say, even though I'm not sorry at all. I want to steal her all night. I want to steal her every night. "I'm a brute, I know."

She laughs and her eyes flash my way, sparkling like crazy when they meet my own.

"You're not sorry," she says, lifting up her right foot and prodding her toes roughly in my chest. It's not a gentle shove, and I fucking love that.

I'm also loving the fact that she's not caring that Kaleb could potentially see us messing around right now. Unless that's because we look like two friends. Which I hate.

I take her ankle in my left fist, stroking her bone with the pad of my thumb.

"I'm not sorry," I concur, my voice lowering again.

Her smile falters a bit as the air between us grows heady, and she pulls her foot away, stashing it against her butt.

"You like Tyler?" I ask. I'll admit, I'm not a subtle guy.

Her brow furrows and her lips pinch into a pout.

"No," she mumbles, sullen like a teenager.

"It's okay if you do." A barefaced lie.

She rolls her eyes at me. "It's loud out here and I wouldn't be able to sleep in there if I tried to right now, so I may as well be out here. And I *did* want to catch up with him – we discussed some things at the bar that night and I wanted to hear his opinions again."

I distract myself by cracking my neck because I hate every single part of that sentence.

"Is that his drink again?" I ask, far too invested.

"Would you have a problem with that?" she retorts, cocking up an eyebrow. "You're only here for a few weeks, remember? So maybe you should stop pretending to stake a claim."

Now it's my turn to raise my eyebrows.

"Pretending?" I ask. If only she knew.

"Yeah." She throws the bottle into the dirt and it lands with a thud, its contents glugging out with one quick gurgle. "You'll be back on the road in no time, so this really isn't a good idea."

Her sudden mood swing takes me by surprise. I rake a hand through my hair as I try to re-rail the conversation.

"I can prove it to you Kitty," I say as quietly as I can, keeping my voice beneath the bellows happening all around us. A splash sounds to my rear and a cannonball's worth of hot tub water sprays up my back. I don't bother turning to see which idiot just dive-bombed the hot tub. "I promise, this isn't pretend. If you'll let it be something more, I promise I'll-"

She holds up her hand and I instantly stop speaking.

It looks like she's counting to ten. As someone with a history of pent-up rage I understand.

I wait her out.

After a shaky breath she gives me a small smile and another nose scrunch that I want to tattoo on my brain.

"I'm not asking you for anything," she whispers, swinging both her legs beneath her ass so that she can lean forward slightly. I try not to notice the way her tits plump up for me when she squeezes her arms together, but that's kind of hard to do when she's not wearing a *bra.* My eyes flash back up to hers as my abdominals contract and tighten.

She's not wearing a bra.

"Now *I'm* the sorry one," she says with a nervous laugh. "I shouldn't have gotten all huffy like that or… or flipped on you. I know what you're offering here."

No you don't. You have no idea how fast I'd give up everything to stay here with you.

Her spirits seem to have resettled because she gives me a naughty smile and says, "Hey, we're pretty good at communicating though, aren't we?"

Are we? I have no relationship experience so, other

than lying through my teeth when I'm being a jealous piece of shit, I have no reason to play games with her. Why wouldn't I tell her the truth? I want her to know how truly, deeply I want this. Us. Her.

I nod anyway, because we seem to be back on track and I don't want it to go off-road again.

"Yeah," I say, my eyes dropping down to her hand which is laid flat on the wood of the chair between us.

I give her ring finger a gentle rub, wishing that I could kiss her right now but begrudgingly willing to wait for a better moment – for the *perfect* moment. My mind runs through everything that's happened since Kaleb and I got here a week ago – my raging desire to rekindle things with Kitty, the happy accident of bumping into Jace, my need to "stake my claim" whenever I see Tyler – and my brain gives me a little nudge towards a thought, currently just out of reach.

I glance over my shoulder to check that Kaleb's not watching and then I swoop my hand under Kitty's palm, interlocking her fingers with my own.

I give her a squeeze and her cheeks dimple sweetly.

"We're more than pretty good."

CHAPTER 10

Madden

The next morning Kitty has a surprise for Kaleb of her own.

"River's coming up earlier than expected," she says, re-washing her hands in the sink. She's just come inside from dealing with the animals and there's straw-dust floating all around her. My eyes trail down her exposed legs as I lean against the counter, scratching at my jaw as I take in her scuffed pink knees. God, she's tiny.

I shift my body weight as certain muscles begin to wake up. If Kaleb wasn't here right now…

Kaleb almost drops the bottle of milk in his hand, snapping me right out of my fantasy.

"What?!" Crimson heat climbs up his neck.

Kitty raises an eyebrow at his outburst. "I said River's coming up earlier-"

Kaleb puts the milk on the counter and tilts his head towards his sister, his eyes almost as wide as hers.

"I heard what you said," he says, a desperate twinge rattling in his voice.

I step between them because he's acting unhinged. I breathe out a confused laugh and then clap him on the shoulder, trying to slap some common sense into him.

"You alright?" I ask, eyeing him sceptically.

I hear a quiet laugh coming from Kitty behind me. Luckily for her, Kaleb doesn't.

"Yeah," he says, shaking his head solemnly. I'm no psychologist but that seems a little juxtaposed. "It's just, uh…"

I raise my eyebrows at him. "Yeah?" I ask, confused as hell.

Now that I think about it, he was even being shifty when Mitch mentioned River coming up at the bar last week. Why would Kaleb be weird about that?

"I can tell him if you want." Kitty's quiet voice sounds out at my back.

Kaleb lifts his head and twists so that he can look at her around my torso.

"It's stupid," he says.

I can almost hear Kitty rolling her eyes.

"Go upstairs Kaleb, you have a big task today anyway. I'll… fill Madden in whilst you're getting ready."

Kaleb's big task is their summer hay cutting agenda. It's vital for them to do it before any chance July showers hit Phoenix Falls.

Kaleb doesn't argue with her. I release my hold on his shoulder and watch him cautiously as he mounts the stairs.

I turn to Kitty for the explanation, although a big

part of me stops caring about getting one the second that I lay my eyes on her again. A very big part of me. Instead I'm thinking that this conversation can get picked up at another time and that maybe right now we should have that kiss.

Kitty, on the other hand, is all business.

"Kaleb's got a crush," she says simply, reaching up to open the cupboard above the stove and assessing all of the new cereals I bought for her.

It's like Walmart in there now. Multicoloured Fruit Loops, Teddy Grahams, those chocolate-chip circles that look like little cookies – I went to the store yesterday afternoon to pick up bottles for Kaleb's get-together, and whilst I was there I decided to buy all of those vegetarian-friendly pretty cereals that Kitty's been obsessed with since she was a teenager.

She taps a finger against her chin, contemplating her bounty like a little duchess.

"I really oughta thank Kaleb for getting these," she mumbles.

Heat prickles up my cheekbones but I choose not to correct her.

"Who does Kaleb have a crush on?" I ask in an attempt to re-steer the conversation. I'm immediately distracted when she jumps up to grab the box of her choice, her little curves bouncing with the movement.

My boxers are suddenly too tight for me, and I grunt as I subtly try to rearrange myself. Her tank tops are gonna be the death of me.

"River, of course," she replies, her tone saying *duh*.

I literally have no idea what we were just talking about.

"River?" I ask, my voice a little breathless. Then I

register what she just said and I'm suddenly more alert. "Wait, River, as in-"

"As in Tate's fiancé, River," she says, her eyes sliding to mine.

We share a look. Mine says *oh shit* and hers says *I know*.

"Kaleb obviously can't stay here tonight," I realise. "'Cause if he goes sniffing around River, Tate would…"

A bit of context. Tate Coleson is the greatest guy I know – humble, God fearing, and totally in love with his fiancé – but, because of all of that, he isn't the type to let things slide when it comes to the things that he cares about. He's traditional and no-nonsense and boy would that dude look good in orange.

"Yeah," she agrees, a petal pink flush settling on her cheeks. "I guess Kaleb can't stay here tonight."

Which means…

I raise my eyebrows.

Oh.

And with Kaleb not being here tonight, does she mean that maybe…?

Suddenly the look that we're sharing is blazing with heat.

Fuck yeah, I think to myself.

Thank God for Tate Coleson.

*

Kaleb's been in the world's foulest mood and if he wasn't on hay cutting duty today I bet every note in my pocket that he'd be strumming out sad songs in his childhood bedroom right now. It's a good job that he's preoccupied on the fields because it's only a little after eleven when Tate and River finally pull up.

Kitty's just come back from a milk-related mission in town and is currently dusting out the barn that I've almost finished renovating, so I head inside the cabin to open up the front door.

I lean against the doorframe as I watch Tate park up the car, easing into a shady spot beside the detached garage to the right of the cabin. He's driving that piece of scrap that his dad calls a truck, probably because he's got his bike strapped down in the back and, unlike Tate's monstrous black Ford, a few new scratches will blend in just fine in the bed of Mitch's vehicle. The windows are partially rolled down and I can hear that Tyler Childers "Feathered Indians" song that he loves so much playing on the stereo.

I roll my eyes. Tate is six-four, tan as hell, and pushing two-hundred and forty pounds, and yet he's still the sweetest guy that I've ever had the chance to meet.

When he cuts off the music I watch as he turns to face the vision in pink to his right, and a soft chime of laughter drifts into the warm hazy air. He leans towards her, probably giving her a peck, and I grind my boot in the gravel as I wait for them to wrap it up.

He opens the driver's door and steps into the dirt, a cloud of sandy particles kicking up around his heel. When he spots me he gives me a flash of white teeth and a quick jerk of his chin.

"How's it going, man?" he calls out.

He rounds the front of the "truck", pulls open the passenger side door, and then I hear the thud of his tiny fiancé hopping down from the step, followed by the door being closed and their shoes scraping up the dusty driveway.

Tate gives me an easy smile when they come into view, walking with the confidence of a man who gets it twice every morning and three times a night. River beside him is lucky to be walking at all.

Tate wraps one heavily pumped arm around River's shoulders and manoeuvres her so that she's walking directly in front of him, his forearms binding her petite clavicle so that he can clutch her tightly against his abs.

"All's good," I reply, giving him a quick smile of my own. "Saw your dad not too long ago and he mentioned that you were stopping by."

He gives me a smile. "Hope we're not intruding too bad."

River snorts and I flash her a look, trying to work out what I'm missing. Little demon. I know that Tate gets the good side of her but I don't doubt that she can still be hellish when she wants to be.

When they step inside Tate moves his hands so that they're wrapped around River's collarbones, and he gives her a little squeeze.

"You got a bathroom around here?" he asks me, scoping out the interior of the cabin. It's all open plan down here, with the exception of the guest room at the back that I've been staying in, so he looks up to the gallery landing, guessing that the bathroom will be up there.

I nod and jerk my thumb over to the stairwell. "It's just up there. There aren't too many rooms and the door'll probably be open. Keep the seat down," I add on and, after another little squeeze, he unleashes himself from his fiancé and starts climbing the stairs.

River gives me one disgruntled look, turns her back on me, and then heads into the kitchen.

"Sup emo," I say, following her like the brother that she never wanted.

"Suck a fuck Madden," she says dryly, her expression bored.

I can't help but smile. Even though she's all cutesy dresses and pastel colours now I still remember what's underneath that candyfloss exterior. I recall her high school days, before she took that gap year working for Tate's dad and then started her degree at college.

I know how dark and cut-throat she really is.

"Don't hold back," I tease, folding my arms over my chest as she opens the fridge. "You're quite a contradiction you know. No one would expect such a bunny rabbit to be a hardcore metal baby."

She pulls out a juice box, inspects the label, then puts it down again. "I like hearing men scream."

I laugh. "I bet you do." God knows what she and Tate have been getting up to this summer.

She rolls her eyes. "Leave me alone, Madden. Go write Kit a poem or something."

I raise an eyebrow. Then I narrow my eyes.

Annoyingly this seems to lift her spirits. She picks up the juice box again, punctures it with the straw, and then takes a long antagonising suck, eyes scorching into my own.

"Yeah," she says. "You thought that I wouldn't know? I mean, speaking of contradictions, surely you could say the same thing about Kit."

I clench my jaw as my blood pounds through my veins.

"All-black everything on the outside, yet so soft and

silky on the inside?" she suggests, a taunting glow shimmering all around her. "But maybe," she continues, suddenly dropping her voice to a whisper. "I guess you wouldn't know how soft and silky she is on the inside."

I stop breathing completely. A red cloud of envy sheathes over my brain.

"What did you just say?" I ask, my irises aflame.

What the hell does she know? That I'm obsessed with Kitty? That I haven't got to her… soft bits yet?

How does she know?

Her responding smile is enough for me to want to smash my head through a wall. She takes another long draw on her juice box until the carton turns concave. She tosses it into the waste-paper basket on the floor and gives me an unbothered shrug.

"I've been through my share of shit and misunderstandings, so I know now to trust my gut. I can just tell. You're all…" She waves her hand vaguely in front of my abdomen and makes a kind of disgusted wincing face. "Pent up."

I can't help but laugh. I mean, she's not wrong. I turn around and close the fridge door so that I can press my forehead into it and cool off.

"So," I grunt, then cough because I feel uncomfortable. "Kitty hasn't been... Kitty didn't say-"

It's her turn to laugh. "No Madden. *Kitty* didn't tell me about your nonexistent romance."

A shudder runs through me. Thank God.

I turn to face her because there's another question on my mind – namely, does Kitty talk about me at all – but River holds up a finger to silence me before I can begin.

"No more questions," she commands. When I open my mouth to speak she holds her finger up higher and gives me a withering stare. "No."

I bunch up my jaw muscles. *Fine.*

"Kitty's out back if you want to go see her," I say, seeing as our conversation is clearly over.

She brushes past me without a parting glance.

The last thing that I hear from her as she steps outside is a little shriek and, "Is that a *hot tub*?!"

CHAPTER 11

Kitty

River and I climb up onto the hay bale, one of the last that we had in storage from last year's harvest, and we wiggle backwards onto the flat top so that our feet dangle above the dirt. She's taken a shine to my baby goat because of the heart-shaped patch on its furry butt, so she's holding it under her arm like a nineteenth century farm girl.

She grinds her ass into the straw to try and find a more comfortable position.

"It's so scratchy," she says, tugging down the hem of her dress, trying to salvage the backs of her thighs.

"We should tuck our knees up," I suggest. God forbid another splinter.

River laughs and I turn to look at her because I'm not sure what I just missed. When she sees me staring she gestures to the field in front of us, where Kaleb is doing the most impressively neat and efficient hay cutting of his whole entire life.

"I don't want to flash your brother," she whispers, giggling, and her eyes dart over to the barn where Tate is. I think what she really doesn't want is for her fiancé to turn my brother into puree, which all things considered is very thoughtful of her.

I'm certain that River has no idea how hard Kaleb's been crushing on her since high school. In fact, I think that she simply sees him as an extension of me, therefore labelling him as some sort of sexless extraterrestrial.

I nod in understanding and dust the flyaway hay off the backs of my legs.

I'm wearing a pair of denim shorts so I'm not at risk of flashing Kaleb thank God. I hitch my knees up under my chin and River lies backwards on the bale, stroking the goat's knee tuft.

"How's college?" I ask, and my tummy hums nervously. Now that I'm a dropout I'm a little insecure about how she'll think of me.

She puts my mind at rest.

"It sucks ass," she replies, her face dead serious. "If you aren't training to be an astronaut or something then there's literally no reason to be there. Plus, whether I like it or not, we're living in the twenty-first century, and even I can admit that it has some perks. You know how brilliant it is to be self-employed? How quickly you can set something up for yourself online? When I was working with Mitch and he showed me his accounts I almost had an asthma attack. In, like, a good way. He's literally rolling in it, and the best part about it is that he loves what he does."

I contemplate that, feeling a little better. "I think we're both too small to be astronauts," I say.

She nods in agreement.

Then I ask, "So why don't you drop out? I'm not suggesting that you should, but if you wanted to…"

She twists her lips to the side, mulling. "My mom, partially. Even though she moved to a different teaching post at a school across the country I can still feel that… that need to impress her with this thing that she always wanted for me. And," she scrunches up her nose, laughing slightly. "Then there's Tate and Mitch of course."

A shocked laugh bubbles out of me and she gives me a wry smile.

"Mitch too?" I ask. "What's it to him?"

I knew that Mitch kind of took a surrogate father role in River's life but I wasn't sure how invested he really was.

"He's, uhh…" She twists her face up, half amused, half embarrassed, as she tries to force the words out of her mouth. "I mean, they're both… they're…" She swallows. "They're kind of paying some of my tuition."

My mouth drops to the floor. "What?!" I screech.

Even the goat bleats in amazement.

River squirms on the bale and her skin heats up under the midday sun.

"Don't hate me?" she says, still smiling nervously. "It's just that because Tate didn't want or need to go to college… and Mitch had been building up a kind of college fund for him…"

There's a shy, guilty look sparkling behind her eyes. It's not necessary. I'm thoroughly impressed.

She drops her voice to a whisper, as if she's guarding a secret. "I know it's unorthodox, Kit, and really unusual, but… they *like* supporting me. Tate and his dad are so strong, and kind, and they like looking after me. And that's so *nice* for me, considering that…"

Her sentence trails off and she reclines her arms above her head. Her giant engagement ring casts blinding refractions across the straw.

She doesn't need to say anything else though because I know what she was going to say.

She's never had a father figure before. It's *good* that she's finally being spoiled.

"Are you gonna show me then?" she asks suddenly, an excited look on her face as she tilts her head my way.

Oh God. I know exactly what she's talking about.

I turn away from her, lifting my chin up, and I say nonchalantly, "I don't know what you're talking about."

She gives me a prod in the ribs and I squirm like a little bug.

"Ow!" I call out, but I laugh with her anyway.

"If you're going to be singing in front of the whole town then practicing with me is a good starting point," she says diplomatically.

Annoyingly she is correct.

I haven't sung in front of anyone except River really ever, and even that was years and years ago.

Huffed, I confiscate the goat from her. I pick it up under its belly and then hoist it into my lap, much to its absolute dismay. It thumps into my crotch and then lets out a painful warble.

River laughs. "You can't be worse than her."

I raise my eyebrows as if to say *you never know* and then add, "He's a boy, by the way."

Instantly she's squealing and I swear that Tate strides into my peripheral, checking that everything is actually okay.

Whippedamundo.

"*Eww*, why didn't you tell me?!" River sits upright, mortified, and shuffles to the farthest edge of the bale.

I start laughing but then, due to the look of horror on River's face, I set the goat down on the ground away from us, letting it curl up contentedly in the shady spot.

I take the little tube of candy scented hand sanitizer from my front pocket and pass it to River. She proceeds to squirt out half the bottle.

For a girl with a male fiancé she really does hate men – human or not, she does not discriminate.

Eager to distract her from whatever memory was just triggered I say, "Okay, I'll sing for you, but I have to be quiet. I don't want him to hear."

River looks up from her hands, which are now rubbing excess sanitizer into her legs. "You don't want who to hear?"

I swallow, then mouth *Madden*.

She narrows her eyes. "Why? 'Cause he's a loser?"

I laugh. "No, not because he's…" I slide my eyes over to her wherein she's looking pretty pleased with herself. "It's just… because he's in a band – even worse, he's in a band with my *brother* – I don't want him to think that *my* interest in music came from, you know, *his* interest in music."

I cringe at the thought of it alone, but River's demeanour softens completely.

"Kit," she says, her voice consoling. "I mean this in the nicest possible way but… that is totally fucking bonkers."

She twists onto her side, the straw making a scratchy sound as she props her chin into her palm, her elbow scraping across the hay.

"Madden doesn't *own* music. Just because he's interested in something doesn't mean that *you* can't be interested in it too. Besides," she concludes, her eyes tightening even further. "For all you know, *his* interest in music, his desire to be in a band, all of that may have stemmed from *you*."

I shake my head. "He doesn't know that I like music. He doesn't know that I can sing."

She turns her head to look out at Kaleb, the dull whir of the machine loud in the summer air. "That's not exactly what I meant," she murmurs, her look contemplative. "I was thinking more about why he may have wanted to join-"

She stops herself short and turns to look at me again.

"Never mind. Anyway," she continues, jerking her thumb over to the tractor-pull. "That thing's so loud even I'll be barely able to hear you. Which song are you gonna do?"

I scrunch up my nose, unable to hide my smile. I pull out my phone so that I can search up the song. "I'll be playing Kaleb's Fender whilst I'm singing so I wanted to do something… sweet. Something that won't make people's ears bleed," I admit, laughing nervously.

She peers over my shoulder to inspect my screen.

"You could never," she says. Then she reads the name of the song that I've typed in. "Oh," she hums, moving her hand next to mine so that she can scroll through the lyrics on the search engine. "Oh Kit, I love it."

"Really?" I ask, feeling a little apprehensive. "It's not exactly your taste."

She scoffs and then throws herself back down onto the hay bale, her curls splaying all around her.

"You know, Madden said something similar to me when I came in. It's weird to me to think that y'all assume that I'm so dark all of the time – I mean, maybe I was when I was seventeen but I've grown a lot since then. Now," she says, spreading her arms wide as if to embrace the beaming sun. "Now I just want the *light*."

She arches her body, luxuriating in the warmth, and then turns onto her side again so that I have her full attention.

"Okay," she whispers, tapping her finger against the song title on my screen and giving me an encouraging secretive smile. "Show me whatcha got."

CHAPTER 12

Kitty

After Kaleb finishes sheathing the hay pastures he takes his cue to dip.

"Why's he leaving? Doesn't he like me or something?" River asks as Kaleb re-emerges from the cabin, newly showered and dressed in clothes that aren't ninety-percent hay.

I flash my eyes over to her. "Er, not exactly."

"Then why isn't he helping Tate and Madden finalise the new panelling on the barn? We aren't sleeping in his room, so I didn't think that us hanging out this weekend would be a problem."

Yeah, they *aren't* sleeping in his room, they're going to be sleeping in the *guest* room.

Meaning that Madden is now on the market for a new location to crash.

My brain does a fizzy short-circuit when I think about where that situation could lead.

I shiver. We'll cross that bridge when we come to it.

"He wants to stay over with some of his other buddies whilst the band is having their downtime. They never get to stay in town so it's a treat for him." Half true, so that's good enough.

"Oh." Slightly perkier now. "So who's he staying with?"

I let out a nervous chuckle. "Um, some guys who were in the same year as him at high school. You might remember them – er, Chase and-" I lower my voice. "A guy called Tyler."

Her eyes flick to mine, shimmering with newly awoken interest. "And why is Tyler's name a secret?" she asks.

I whip around to ensure that Madden isn't in the vicinity and then I hiss, "It isn't."

She raises an eyebrow. "Convincing. It wouldn't have anything to do with M-"

"Yes, fine, yes it does," I say quickly and she quirks me a pleased little smile.

"Go on," she encourages. Shameless. For some reason we're also heading over to where Kaleb's hauling ass into the Chevy so hopefully he'll be able to act semi-normal around River today.

I whisper quickly, "Tyler used to be in the band but dropped out before they went on tour. They sort of fizzle when they're near each other. Maybe they both mutually hate each other or something."

"Or both mutually like *you*," she mutters, giving me a pointed look.

I blush and then look away, grateful for the impending distraction of watching Kaleb pee his pants.

He must have heard us coming because he sighs once we're right behind him.

"You gonna keep those rain clouds away from my hay whilst I'm gone?" he asks, his back to us as he stuffs some of his junk up in the backseat of the truck.

I roll my eyes. "*Your* hay?" I ask, amused. I turn to River and mumble, "The guy cuts the fields down once and suddenly it's 'my hay'."

A laugh tinkles out of her and apparently it shoots right up Kaleb's spine because he instantly jerks upwards and smashes his head against the roof of the car. He grunts, rubs a hand through his hair, and then hauls himself out of the truck, an expression of sheer panic on his face as he looks down at us. Well, more specifically, as he looks down at *her*. He takes one glance at her little gingham dress and his pupils dilate like he's on crack.

"Er, sorry," he says, for no reason whatsoever.

"What for?" River asks, smiling cutely. Totally oblivious to the sweat running down his cheekbone.

"Er, nothing, sorry."

I have to physically restrain myself from face-palming this idiot.

"Have a nice time with your friends," she says, her cheeks apple-ing.

Honestly Kaleb should count himself lucky because if he wasn't my brother there isn't a cat's chance in hell that River would be wishing him a polite adieu.

He swallows. "Thanks." Then he clumsily shoves himself into the driver's seat. He's giving off busting-for-the-bathroom vibes but interestingly River doesn't seem too spooked. She gives him a quick wave and then we turn for the barn.

"That was nice of you," I say, eyeing her curiously.

"I fucking love your truck," she mutters, and a

laugh bursts out of me.

Of course she wasn't saying goodbye to Kaleb. She was saying goodbye to the *truck*.

"That makes a lot more sense," I confess, and she gives me a guilty smile.

"Anyway," she says, chipper again. "Why not make the most of having all of these handymen around to do your work for you today, and give your high school best friend an evening of fun on the farm?"

"First of all," I say, holding up a halting hand. "This is a *ranch,* not a *farm*."

"Tom-ay-to, tom-ah-to. I saw your hot tub earlier and thought that maybe I could get Tate to drive me into town, buy a bikini, and then we can do a…" She wafts a hand through the air like she's summoning the rest of her sentence. "A girls' night. Sounds cute, right?" she asks, excitement making her cheeks flush raspberry pink.

Tate must hear us coming because he walks around from the side of the barn, paint splattered and glistening with sweat. River walks casually over to him, curls bouncing all glossy and plush, and she stands onto her tippy-toes so that she can give his jaw a peck.

He looks down at his palms, dirty from the work, then wipes them on his jeans before enveloping them around her shoulders.

"We're having a girls' night," she explains, before turning to give me an enthusiastic grin. "But I need a bikini," she adds.

I'm about to watch their exchange unfold when the barn door swings open, Madden attentively checking the hinges. With the music that's playing in there he probably didn't hear us, so he seems sincerely surprised to see us gathered outside.

He flicks his eyes to River and Tate and then, noting that they're currently enraptured, he steps towards me, gaze scanning just over my shoulder.

"Your brother gone?" he asks, his voice low and gruff.

I nod my head when his eyes meet mine.

He gives me a steady once-over and then breathes a deep inhale, a warm glow spreading up his cheeks.

He asks quietly, "You got plans tonight?"

My three second pause makes him tug at his lip-ring.

"Um, well-" I begin.

I'm cut off by a sharp, "Yes, she does."

Madden's eyes flash over my shoulder and River appears at my side.

"She has plans with me tonight," she says, pretending to inspect her nails.

Tate moves to stand beside Madden. Neither of them seem particularly happy with this arrangement.

Madden's jaw muscles bunch and roll.

"Right," he mumbles, his flush growing more severe. "Okay, that's fine. I'll just be..." He turns to face the interior of the barn which, admittedly, he has renovated incredibly over the past few days. It looks brand new with its fresh panels and a lick of paint.

He looks into my eyes again, his sharp silver irises like a stab to the gut. He really is devastatingly beautiful.

"I'll just be in here if you need me," he says at last, and with one parting look he goes back inside.

*

"I'm thinking about getting a belly button piercing," River says, fingers prodding keenly around her innie.

It's night-time and the sky has turned dark and velvety, tiny stars winking like crystals above the horizon.

I look at her belly, warped by the bubbling hot tub water.

"A belly button piercing," I repeat, a little sceptical. I look over to the barn wherein Madden and Tate have been hanging out all day. Tate's since gone inside to get a shower but I can still sense Madden's presence out here from the pulse of his Alpha pheromones.

"For Tate?" I ask, already knowing the answer.

She glances over to her left hand, safely out of the water and holding onto the ledge of the pool, and her rock sparkles back at us.

"Maybe," she says, a little smile on her lips. "I can't tell if he'd love it or hate it though. I think I should ask him about it tonight."

I nod absentmindedly and close my eyes. The warm evening air combined with the piping hot water is giving me the spa night that I didn't know I needed. Sometimes I really underestimate my body's need for soothing.

When I open my eyes again River says, "When Tate and I leave you can come with us if you want, so that you can practice Kaleb's guitar at our place, where Madden won't hear you."

I contemplate that and nod. The bun on my head wobbles dangerously.

"That's a good idea," I agree, re-knotting my hair.

"Although I'm sure he would love to know you can

play," she adds, her eyes watching me cautiously.

I scrunch my face up. "You know what the problem is? It's that I think that I know that. Seriously, I'm more worried about him *liking* it than anything else. If he finds out that I can play guitar, and sing, and that I want to potentially pursue a music career more seriously myself, I'm scared that he'll be so into it that Kaleb will realise there's something going on between us, freak out, ban me from using his guitar, and then totally scupper my chances of having my voice being heard in the first place."

It comes out in a fast anxious blurt and River's eyes are wide by the time that I'm done.

"Kit," she says. "If Kaleb's that insecure then that's his problem. He needs to get over it."

I shudder, shaking off all of my Kaleb and Madden related anxieties, and I reach into our fishbowl of candy, propped up on a chunk of chopped tree bark. We've essentially cooked up a candy salad.

River observes my perusal with a smile on her face and then asks, "What's with all the sweet stuff? Your cupboards look like they've been stocked by the Pied Piper."

I stuff a Red Vine between my back teeth and then rip it apart like a savage. Chewing, I say, "Other than the stuff that I bought when my parents first left, I actually have no clue. Since Kaleb got here he's been stocking up on all of my favourites."

I suck up the rest of the stick between my lips and then I get to unwrapping a strawberry Starburst.

"Kaleb you say," she murmurs, her gaze boring into me intently.

I shrug. "Yeah, I guess. Who else would be doing

the shopping?"

She stares at me for a few long beats and then shakes her head. "Yeah, you're right I'm sure. I just had a thought is all."

I'm trying to work out what her mysterious thought was when I see a figure exiting the front door of the cabin. I give River a little splash.

"Here comes your probation warden," I whisper, and she gives me a wily little smile.

She lazily tilts her head in the direction of my gaze and Tate's hulking frame, backlit from the sconces surrounding the cabin, grows larger and larger until he's bearing down at us from the edge of the tub. I sink down into the foaming bubbles until I'm nothing more than a pair of razor-sharp eyes slicing into the darkness. River recomposes her face so that she's in alluring vixen mode, a small smile threatening the corners of her lips.

She turns around, the strings of her pink bikini floating around her waist, and she asks teasingly, "Are we having too much fun, Officer?"

Tate's large tan fingers, emblazoned with River's name, drum lightly on the ledge of the hot tub. He jerks his chin towards the house, chest heaving as he watches her bob amidst the ripples.

"It's getting dark out, baby. We should get to bed."

I roll my eyes. Just act like I'm not here then.

River covers Tate's knuckles with her palms and then heaves herself so that she's exposed from the belly button-up, a siren about to lure her bounty. The water cascades down her bare back like a rapid and then sloshes noisily into the whirring pool.

Tate's eyes dip down to River's chest and, after a

momentary pause, he swallows hard.

"Five more minutes," River whispers. I can hear the smile in her voice.

Tate nods, hypnotised, and then leans down to kiss her chastely. I look away to give them their privacy and my eyes wander to the open door of the barn where Madden is aligning the replaced beams, lit by the glow of an oil lamp like a Victorian serial killer.

When Tate's shadow shifts across the shimmering ripples in the pool I turn my attention back to him, hoping that by having my stare burning deeply into his skull he'll get the hint and skedaddle. He's no longer kissing her but he is still standing here.

I hook a toe in River's bikini bottoms and give it a little tug. She throws me a smile over her shoulder and then sends her fiancé on his way, his gait heavier after the little preview that she just gave him.

"Jesus," I mumble when he's out of earshot, his large silhouette ascending the porch steps. "I don't think that I've ever seen a man that infatuated."

River makes a happy humming sound, her sparkly nails dancing with indecision over the candy bowl. She plucks up a lolly, unwraps it, and shoves it in her mouth. Then she scooches next to me so that we both muse over her giant diamond.

"It's because I'm a pain in the ass," she replies, twisting her hand so that the ring catches in the light. "He wants to service me, it's in his caveman DNA – much like-"

She glances over her left shoulder in the direction of Madden's hushed grunts. I can hear the soft thud of the wood as he dutifully stacks the panels. When River turns back to me her eyes twinkle behind her glasses.

"Fascinating how impassioned that guy is about fixing up a barn that isn't his. One might assume that he's…" She pauses for extra drama. "*Interested* in its owner."

She pulls the lollipop out of her mouth, it's bulbous head a pretty powder-puff pink, and then she holds it out in front of my lips.

It reminds me of the lollipop that Madden got for me at the bar that night – the lollipop that we shared in the woods. It sets a kindling alight in my stomach and I give River an eyebrow raise after glancing at the lolly. We share a long silent glance, riddled with things that we don't usually talk about. Words like *bisexual* and *exploration* come to my mind. *Tate Coleson* and *will murder me* follow quickly after.

We're only messing with each other so we both start laughing at our giddy girlishness, and warm flecks of hot tub spray tickle at our faces.

Suddenly a hand darts out from above us and snatches the stick away.

"Absolutely not."

The water splatters as we recoil in shock and I arch my neck backwards so that I can see our second warden. He's upside down and absolutely livid. I'm not sure if the steam in the air is radiating from the hot tub water or literally from Madden's chest.

He chucks the lolly onto the ground, his eyes never leaving my own, and River makes a noise of disgust, rolling her eyes as she lowers herself into a jet-stream.

I roll around and scowl at him.

He crouches down in front of me and then leashes a hand in my hair.

I'm so shocked that my body jolts and pinches, the

warm pool in my belly battling an onslaught of confused surprise and heating arousal.

"You want her spit in your mouth?" he asks, his voice deep and menacing. His eyes are so molten that I almost burn looking into them.

"Don't be such a Neanderthal," I bite back, attempting to detangle his hand from my hair.

He grunts and grips at me tighter. He looks so incensed, so jealous and enraged, that pleasure throbs between my thighs.

He looks over my shoulder and jerks his chin at River. "Think you could…?" His sentence trails off but it's obvious where it's headed.

Think you could leave us to it?

"Kit?" she asks, prodding her long toe in the back of my leg. I turn my head over my shoulder to look at her, Madden's grip slackening slightly so that I can twist, and she raises an eyebrow, asking for my confirmation.

I feel Madden's fingers begin to slide up and down the back of my neck and all common sense trickles out of my brain.

I nod my head and she heaves herself out, quickly bundling up in her towel and flip-flopping back up to the cabin without another glance.

When I turn back around to Madden his eyes are running across my clavicle, then up the centre of my throat. His grip re-tightens when he finally reaches my eyes.

"Sorry. For being a thug," he says hoarsely, his thumb rubbing circles into the side of my neck.

"No you're not," I whisper, pressing up against the very edge of the tub so that I can be as close to him as our barrier allows.

"No I'm not," he murmurs, his other hand dipping into the water and caressing against my lower back.

Waves of anticipation flood through my body and long-dormant need reignites down below.

"I wanna kiss you," he grunts, his lips millimetres from my own. "I need to kiss you."

I bob in the water, revelling devilishly in the push and pull of our new game. The *hate to want you, but can't help but need you* game.

His concentration wanes momentarily as he zeros in on my lips and I take the relaxing of his hand around my neck to pull away from him completely, moving backwards until I'm on the other side of the hot tub. He blinks as if startled and then looks at me questioningly.

I smile at him like a little imp and then, with the swish of my foot, I flick a spray of sparkling water droplets up the front of his shirt.

"Then come and get me."

CHAPTER 13

Madden

I scratch my hand at the back of my neck, biting at my lip-ring.

"You want me to get in the tub?" I ask, brow rising in amusement.

She settles herself onto the submerged bench on the side farthest from me, wiggling her ass until she's nice and comfortable.

The corner of my mouth quirks into a smirk. Temptress. But she continues feigning interest, propping her feet up onto the seated ledge and avoiding my eyes as she waits me out.

I can't help myself. I walk around the tub until I'm stood by her feet and I look through the ripples at her glittery toe nails.

Possessed by animal instinct I dip both of my hands into the water and I wrap my hands around her ankles, rubbing my thumbs into her until she uncrosses her legs for me.

Jesus, she's soft. I gently lift her ankles out of the water, her warm wet skin slippery in my palms.

Now that I've got a feel for how fucking light she is all I want to do is get her underneath me, and see how high her legs can go.

I place her feet back into the water and take one last glance at the cabin to her back. No chances that Tate and his fiancé are going to be unoccupied right now so it should be private out here for just the two of us. I say a quick prayer for Kaleb to not make any surprise appearances and then I reach my arm to the back of my neck and rip my shirt over my head.

Kitty's eyes slowly trail down my torso, and my chest heaves under her gaze. I toss my shirt onto the ground and then kick off my boots and socks as my hands make work of unsheathing my belt. When I'm down to nothing but my jeans I give her a few last seconds to change her mind, although my fingers are itching to tug down my zipper and get in there with her.

She looks up at me through her long, dark lashes, and the soft light from the cabin reflects against her eyes.

"You want me to get in?" I ask her again, my voice no longer light with amusement. It's low and gruff and it makes a shiver ripple through her chest.

"Yeah," she says quietly, eyes dropping down to where my fingers are paused. I flick the button open and her breathing hitches. Then I yank down my zipper because I'm done giving her a show. We can have a re-do some other time because right now – when I'm finally going to be able to kiss her for the first time in *two fucking years* – is *not* the time.

I kick off my jeans so that I'm wearing nothing but my underwear and I grip my fists into the ledge of the tub, quickly heaving myself over the border and instantly being met with hot steaming bubbles. It seeps straight through the cotton of my boxers and lashes at the muscle that's growing heavy behind them.

I wade the few steps from my side to the centre, the hot spray splattering up my abdomen as I shift my weight in the water. Kitty's eyes haven't left my body, roaming over each muscle like she's cataloguing them for a textbook. I'm taking that as a good sign. When I'm finally right in front of her she swings her legs down from the bench and lowers her body up to her chin.

I bend forward so that I can get my hands under her knees and then I lift them slowly until they're knocking at my ribcage. She chews nervously on her lip and takes a glance over her shoulder, thoughts of her guests and – much worse – her brother obviously nagging in her brain as well as my own.

When she turns back to me again, looking much more relaxed after realising that we are in fact totally alone, another thought resurfaces in my mind.

"The cameras," I say gruffly, wanting this conversation to be wrapped up before it's even begun. I have much better plans for the rest of our night. "The other week, you mentioned that you have cameras-"

She waves her hand as if that's old news and her toes scrape up the backs of my thighs. Holy fuck. I lean a little further towards her, wanting my cock pressed nice and hard against her pussy.

Her breathing shakes and my eyes drop down to

her tits. They're obscured in the water and I need to see them. I almost growl, the need to take them in my mouth overwhelming.

"I took them down from the barn just before you started working on it," she breathes out, her knees trembling underneath my fingers.

I exhale a sigh of relief. "Okay, that's good-"

Then I stop short.

Hang on. The *barn?*

"When you say the barn," I begin, my mind racing at a million miles per hour.

Shit, shit, shit.

"You mean the outside of the barn, right? To watch for, er, animals or something." *Probably should've kept those up then, all things considered.* "Or burglars and thieves, right?"

"Yeah." She says it like I'm stupid. Fucking accurate.

Then, dropping like a tonne of bricks in my stomach, she adds, "And the inside too, of course."

Of course. Of fucking course.

Of course I *jacked off* in the one section of this ranch that was wired up with *cameras.*

My hands are gripping her knees way too tightly and her eyebrows are raising as she senses the shift in my mood.

"But you took 'em down before I got here." I ask it like a statement to try and prevent the inevitable "no" that I'm about to get.

"No," she says. Obviously. "I took them down a few days ago so that you wouldn't have to paint around the wires."

I lower her legs into the water and tug my hands

through my hair, the water that was just dripping down her thighs now running down my face.

Fucking shitting motherfucking hell. I really am an idiot.

She shifts on her bench, raising her body up from the water so that it pools around her waist. Her beautiful tiny waist that I should've had my hands on five fucking minutes ago.

"Why does it matter? What's wrong?" She looks around us as if she's searching for an answer. Her eyes light up when she thinks that she's found one. "Is it a band thing, like you need an NDA, or I'm not allowed to have you on film or something?"

God, she's cute. No, I don't think that I'm so important that I require an NDA. I'm grateful that the band can tour and earn a fuck-tonne but I don't give a shit about someone taking my picture.

I care more about the fact that there is now a video of me beating one out for her *parents* to see and, better yet, I've got my fist clenched around their daughter's *used tank top* whilst I do it.

"Please tell me the footage doesn't live-stream to your dad's cell or something," I ask. Beg is probably a better word for it.

She gives me a nervous laugh. "No… why?"

I let out a relieved sigh. "Can we delete the footage?"

Now she looks really freaked out. In fact, worse than that, she looks angry.

"Delete the footage? What the hell did you do in there, Madden?"

I hold my hands up, trying to prevent the escalation of her rage. "Nothing bad, I promise, it's just… when

I first got here, and I was in there checking things out I…"

There is no way that I can tell her what I did in there.

"Please just trust me," I plead with her. "Can you delete the tapes from the past week for me?"

She stands up, the water sloshing down over her body and landing with a slap around her hips. I keep my eyes locked in with hers even though I'm dying to finally take a look at her breasts.

Don't look down whilst you're having a serious conversation with her, do NOT look down whilst you're having a serious conversation with her.

"I have to check those tapes to ensure that we don't have anyone staking out on our land, Madden. Protecting our ranch and keeping it safe is ninety-fucking-percent of this job."

I couldn't hate myself any more right now. All that I *want* is to keep her protected and safe. I've learned from what my dad and I went through and I refuse to repeat that catastrophe.

"Kitty, baby-"

She shoves me backwards and a grunt leaves my chest. At least she's fighting me. Fighting means feeling.

"Don't 'baby' me," she says, her tone lifting in defiance. "Either tell me what you did or-"

"Fine." We're not sinking this ship just because I'm a moron, but there's also no way that I can look her in her eyes and tell her what I did at the same time. "Watch the tape – it's the one from the day after I came." I almost choke on my own choice of words. "Came *here*," I rectify. "It's the one from the day after I came here, to this ranch, with your brother."

She's looking at me like I'm insane. She's right. I am.

"In the morning I went in there and…" I trail off because I've already fucked this up and I don't want to keep her out here any longer than she needs to be. "Please just watch the tape and then delete it. I don't want your parents to see it."

I don't want your parents to know what a dirty fucking dog their future son-in-law is.

"My parents?" She's truly astounded now. "What does this have to do with my parents?"

Oh God. "Nothing, definitely nothing to do with your parents, Kitty, honestly, please."

I shove my fist into my mouth. Anything to shut myself up.

"Please. And I'm sorry, okay? For… for everything."

I turn around and leave before I can make things any worse.

CHAPTER 14

Kitty

Obviously I'm going to have to check the tapes.

I had every intention of checking them as soon as I stomped out of the hot tub last night but I was so riled up that I worried for what I'd do if Madden actually *had* done something terrible. Maybe some mild strangulation. After he got back into his jeans he picked up the rest of his stuff and headed into the barn without a second glance.

I knew what he was doing. He was waiting for me to go back inside the cabin before he came inside too, ensuring that I didn't actually get murdered in the darkness – which, all things considered, is sweet and annoying. He came inside about five minutes after I did and he locked up everything outside too. And I mean *everything.* I know this because I was stalk-watching him from the shadows behind the banister, and I had to scamper like a ninja when he finally made his way through the back door.

Now I'm cross-legged on the counter and angrily crunching my way through a bowl of sacrificial teddies. River's sitting next to me in solidarity, leafing through her pocket Bible like it's the morning paper.

Irritatingly Madden is currently right in my line of sight given the fact that River and Tate were in "his" room yesterday, so instead of taking up Kaleb's offer of using his room, and seeing as he definitely wasn't staying in mine, Madden slept on the couch last night. Which serves him right. Asshole.

Tate descends the staircase, hair dripping from his shower, dressed in jeans and about to pull a plain shirt over his head. Madden uses it as his cue and enters the kitchen with him, probably thinking that I won't claw him like an animal if we have an audience.

Not true.

Madden glances over to Tate, eyes flicking down his back.

"You need to get that girl a pair of mittens," Madden mutters to him, probably thinking that we won't be able to hear them from here.

I automatically have to shift my body, crossing my legs a little tighter. His voice is frustratingly gruff in the mornings and I freaking hate how much my body enjoys it.

Tate looks over his shoulder, the majority of his large back still exposed, and he attempts to glance down at himself, wherein there'll undoubtedly be an array of small red kitten scratches marring the sides of his ribcage. Defeated he just breathes a laugh and gives Madden a man-to-man look. For some reason that makes me even madder.

River's body stills next to me and she flashes me an

apologetic look. We didn't discuss what definitely didn't happen between Madden and I last night but nothing needed to be said – no woman wakes up in this foul of a mood if she did anything worthwhile the night before.

I roll my eyes and shake my head, giving her my best *forget about it* look. Besides, she's the one who came up with the merciful plan to give me some guitar practicing time today, and I'm all the more thankful that I won't be anywhere near this sickeningly hot pain in my ass.

Madden's looking at me with a slightly wounded expression, so that makes me perk up a little. At least he's as put out by last night as I am.

Tate finishes pulling down his shirt and then comes up to the counter so that he can scoop up his fiancé, hitching her around his waist like a koala bear whilst she continues reading her book over his shoulder. When he goes over to the fridge to see if there's anything that he can put in his tank Madden begins to walk cautiously my way. A dangerous game for him at this present time.

I shove in another mouthful of teddies to prevent myself from hissing at him.

He hooks his thumbs in the belt loops of his jeans and then looks up at me from under his lashes. His head is tilted low for the full puppy-dog effect.

"So," he begins, voice all deep and quiet.

I continue my angry crunching. He rolls his lip-ring and then lets out a sigh.

"Did you watch the tape?"

"Nope."

"You gonna?"

"Yep."

He swallows hard. "When?"

"Don't know." A lie, but he doesn't need to know my little plan.

He bows his head lower and nods, eyes on the floor. "Okay. Well, if you wanna find me later I'll just be chopping up the old wood so that it can be added to the timber pile-"

"I'm going to need you to watch the livestock in the fields whilst I'm out this morning," I say, as curt as I can manage whilst still being polite enough to ask for a favour.

His head lifts up, eyes molten with curiosity. "Out?" he asks.

"Yeah, I'm going with River to their place at the lake for a bit."

This is also apparently news to Tate because he closes the refrigerator door and then starts talking in quick, hushed tones to his fiancé.

Madden opens his mouth as if to protest but then quickly snaps it shut again as he gauges my expression. At least he remembers his place.

"Okay, of course, anything. You just want me to keep an eye out or…?"

"Yeah." I put the cattle out this morning like I usually do. Even though a midday Wild West ambush is unlikely, I'd still rather Madden kept an eye on them so that I don't come back to a bloodied up massacre.

I scoop in my last spoonful of cereal and then slide off the counter. I'm so eager to not touch him that I practically dislocate my spine as I squeeze past his concrete-boulder frame.

I take my bowl to the sink and he tails me like a

tomcat.

"Okay, I'll do that, I'll just…"

I scrub at my bowl like I'm trying to turn it into a diamond.

He sighs behind me and I try not to enjoy the warmth radiating from his body, seeping into mine. I quickly rinse off my bowl and then give it an aggressive towel-dry before putting it on the rack. I just want to get the hell out of this room without any further delay.

"You ready?" I ask River, who's still sitting comfortably on the side of Tate.

She lifts her head and nods, and then disentangles herself from her fiancé, dropping down to the floor.

"Yeah, I'm ready. I just need to go upstairs to get *that thing*." She gives me a meaningful look that's about as subtle as a slap in the face. "Wanna help me?" she asks, eyes going crazy wide.

I almost laugh. She may as well have *LET'S GO AND GET KALEB'S GUITAR* written in ink across her forehead.

I roll my eyes. "Sure," I mutter, amused, as we traipse out of the room and begin mounting the stairs.

"Good going Detective," I mumble to her when we're finally on the landing.

She turns to look at me with an innocent expression on her face and whispers, "Well, if Madden thinks that we're up here for *me* then he won't be interested in sticking around to see what we're getting, so that means that we should be able to get the guitar out undetected and therefore maintain your, um, music-hating pretence."

I breathe a laugh as we head to my room. I go to

the corner where I've been resting Kaleb's old guitar, tucked safely in its case. "I don't pretend to hate music," I whisper back to her. "I just don't act like it's something that I'm particularly interested in."

River leans her back against my doorframe with a *yeah, yeah* look on her face and mumbles, "Some sense that makes."

We leave the room and I shut the door gently behind myself, jerking my chin at the gallery railing so that River can scope out from a bird's eye view if Madden's still down there. She peers over the banister and then shakes her head.

"Must've gone out back," she says. Then, as we quickly run down the stairs, she adds on a quiet, "Told you so."

I nod, impressed. She did.

We hightail it to the truck that Tate drove here in and then River hastily opens the back door so that I can stuff the guitar inside. I hop in after it, and River climbs in behind me.

Tate turns around from the driver's seat, giving River a questioning look. Having a plus one in the car probably isn't how he expected his morning to go but with River's blessing I know he'll be more than amenable.

River leans over the centre console to give him a little peck on the cheek, and the physical effect that she has on him is visceral. He instantly relaxes like he's just taken a sedative and then he turns back to the wheel without any further discussion.

He kicks the engine to life and soon after we're easing off the gravel and out onto the blacktop.

"Tate's got another motorbike comp next week,"

River explains to me, fingers rubbing cherishingly up and down the book in her lap. "But we're staying at the lake tonight and we'll travel up during the day tomorrow."

"I hope I'm not intruding." I say it for Tate's benefit seeing as the lake house is his property, but I'm pretty sure that he's tuned me out like a very selective radio dial.

River shakes her head. "We won't even be in this morning so you'll have the place to yourself."

"Where are you gonna be?" I ask her, hugging onto the guitar as Tate dodges a particularly grisly pothole.

"Church," she replies with a smile, flattening out the skirt of her dress.

I give her a little once-over, admiring the lightness that seems to be emanating from her these days.

"Are they new frames?" I ask after a beat, only just registering her glasses.

Being so used to seeing her wearing them for so many years I hardly notice that they're there, but I'm pretty certain that these ones are new. They're large and rounded with pink champagne frames, big enough that they reach the middle of her cheeks and so retro in style that they make her look like a baby pin-up from the fifties.

She makes a cute face, twiddling with her Bible double-time.

"Oh, these?" she asks, fidgeting on her seat. "Um, yeah, they're my new frames," she mumbles quietly, turning away from me as an embarrassed dimple puckers her cheek.

My heart pulls tight. "They're so cute," I say to her, and then I give her a little prod in the waist, making a giggle burst out of her.

"They're okay, I guess," she mutters, the apples of her cheeks glowing Honeycrisp pink.

"They look amazing, baby," Tate says from the front, watching her with a serious expression through the rear-view.

She wriggles her butt, eyes never leaving her lap. Tate's eyes flash to me and I almost have a heart attack. I'm pretty sure that this is the first time in almost a decade that Tate Coleson has ever looked at me.

"I've tried to tell her," he says in that deep drawl of his, glancing at the road again before returning his eyes to mine. "She just won't listen."

I nod and then turn back to River, giving her a squeeze around the shoulders.

She scrunches up her nose and then punches me in the arm.

"Ow!" I howl, but now we're both laughing, so I sigh contentedly and lean back in my seat, head finally free from thoughts of the past week.

*

River and Tate leave to go to church about forty minutes after we get to his place, leaving me in peace to practice my chords. It's been a while since I've touched this guitar so I do a little warm up and then I pull up the notes on my phone, testing out the strokes.

After I get the gist of it down I begin playing it from memory, adjusting a note here and there when I find one that I like better, and I strum leisurely whilst I look out at the lake, back reclined against one of the wooden deck chairs and my skin cool under the shadow from the porch roof. A light breeze trickles through the woods behind the water and the emerald canopy flutters like butterflies wings.

When I next check my phone an hour has passed and my curiosity has grown too large to be contained.

I strum out one last run-through on Kaleb's Fender and then I lay it to rest in its bag. Then I tuck my knees up to my chin and unlock my phone, only one agenda pulsing through my mind.

Those cameras that were up inside and outside of the barn? I wasn't lying when I told Madden that they don't live-stream to my dad's cell.

They livestream to *mine.*

I open up the app which has been pestering me with notifications in the absence of my using it, and I click on the file storing the last week's worth of footage, bar the days since I disconnected the cameras. I know that I should have checked through the old files sooner but, given the fact that no animals went missing, I hadn't felt the need to be excessive.

I click on the file storing the video from the day that Kaleb and Madden arrived and I speed through the footage, checking for anything amiss just in case.

Nothing unusual there, I click through to their second day.

It's the last video on the app because this was the evening that I took them down. It starts with me feeding the cows before letting them out for the morning and then cleaning up the barn.

I remember this morning way too clearly. It was the morning of my run, my splinter, and then our semi-realised truce. I tap through the hour wherein I went for my unsuccessful run but then pause it when I see Madden entering through the large door.

He walks to the booth wherein we store some of the appliances – rope, barn clothes, equipment – and then he bows his head forward as if he's taking a breather. The camera is on the wall right above him so I lean further into my phone as I try to work out what's going on.

I wait a few seconds, narrowing my eyes at the footage.

Then I gasp, my phone clattering through the gap between my thighs as soon as I realise what's about to happen.

Warmth burning up my cheeks, I pick up my cell and I hold it a few inches from my face, my lips parting more and more as I watch Madden reach into his jeans and begin to touch himself. When the sounds coming from his chest vibrate lowly through the speakers I quickly tap the volume until it's almost mute and then I sink further down into my deck chair, belly swirling with throbbing heat.

Just as I think I know what's about to happen Madden looks to his right and yanks my tank from the wall. He breathes it in deep, and then pushes it down his pants.

I stop breathing completely.

He only keeps it down there for a couple of seconds but it's long enough for me to see that he's been… *utilising* it. He slips it out, groaning, and then he fully unleashes himself, long, thick, and so painfully rigid that it makes me push my thighs together in trepidation.

I can't believe what I'm seeing. He's so big, so

ready, that my chest begins to heave.

After a few more seconds of watching him pump his length, his biceps bulging and his strong hips thrusting fast, I press hard on the top button of my phone, forcing it to power-down and disallowing myself to see anymore.

My head is literally pounding, and my cheeks are burning with a warmth that has nothing to do with the weather. My whole body feels like a livewire, frazzled with a stimulus that's now running riot in my system.

I press my hands against my belly, trying to calm the storm within.

That video, that *audio*, that footage of Madden… it's not what I expected.

I take another shaky breath.

It's a million times better.

I look down at the Fender, thinking about how it's going to have to stay stashed here for a bit and I'll collect it at another time because I have something that I need to do right now.

I need to get back to the ranch.

CHAPTER 15

Madden

How exactly do you apologise to someone for jacking off in their barn?

I glance down at the small goat that's ramming its head into my leg as if it's going to give me some advice, and then I get back to looking out over Kitty's cattle field, the guest room sheets that I just threw in the washer now swaying gently to my left, strung between the barn and the stable, and already dry in the mid-morning heat.

I grind my boot into the earth and give my lip-ring a twang. Presumably at some point during today's absence she's going to find a second to check out what I did. She had that *I'm not letting you off the hook* look on her face before she set out to leave so I know that she's intending to come back with a vengeance.

And for that reason I need to put up an equally strong apology gesture.

I slip my cell out of my pocket, first responding to a

message from my dad – Clinton "Call me Clint" Montgomery – wherein he's given me his next week's schedule. He works at the county police office and instances sometimes occur that mess with his formal hours. I scan through the list and then text him back, promising that I'll see him at some point during my final week here, but that I'm not yet sure which date will work best. For all I know, Kitty'll be kicking my ass to the dirt when she comes back so my current calendar is a little up in the air.

I breathe out a deep exhale when I send him the text, already imagining heading through the doorway of the old bungalow. Thoughts of my mom flash sharp in my mind and I wince at the memories. My emotions are more in check now than when I was a teenager, but sometimes I still get a little bit thrown, my feelings undulating from sadness to anger to guilt.

I breathe through it until I'm back to the present moment, the sun beating down on my skin, the air thick and still.

Then I get back to my phone and click on a name that I never usually dial.

For good reason.

"Yo, yo, yo!"

Lord help me.

"Chase?" I ask, one hand gripping through my fringe.

"What's up, man?" he asks. I can hear him smiling.

Incredibly on brand, Chase the golden retriever works at his parents' bakery, wherein he splits his time between icing cookies and getting high out of his mind.

"Need a quick custom order?" I ask.

I glance at the dirt-track that leads out from the ranch as if Kitty's about to come stomping up there before I've managed to put something together for her.

"Always," he says, and I hear a pen click snappily through the receiver.

"Do you do drop offs? 'Cause I'm tied up right now," I add.

"Yep."

"And you're not the driver?" A plea more than a question.

He breathes a laugh and says, "I can't drive right now, bro."

No shit.

"What're you after?" he asks.

"One of those giant cookies – like a good fifteen to twenty incher," I say. "Do you do those?"

"Yeah we do cookies the same size as my di-"

I slam my thumb down on the end call button. Then I let out a frustrated growl and redial.

"Yo, yo, yo!"

I grind my fist into my forehead.

"It's Madden. Again," I say. "And I'm looking for a baker who's not a pervert to get me an express delivery on a custom cookie."

He laughs on the other end of the line. "Hit me with the details."

I try to picture the perfect cookie for Kitty.

"Black icing for the text, and maybe a flowery border or something, but make that black too." I think for a moment. "Do you know that cereal that looks like…" I can't even believe what I'm saying right now. "You know that cereal that looks like… tiny bears?

They're called, uh, Teddy Grahams. If you've got any on hand, or if you could run to a shop nearby, d'you think that you could add some of those around the edges?"

He's silent for a good ten seconds. Then he says, "This phone call's gonna destroy your street cred."

I am well aware.

"What writing do you want on there?" he asks finally.

Now it's my turn to pause. "I'll text it to you."

I pull my phone away from my ear and shoot him a quick text of the apology that I want written.

He snorts as soon as he reads it.

"And you called me a pervert?" he asks. "I don't even want to ask."

"Please don't."

"How fast d'you need it?"

"Like twenty minutes tops. You got something pre-made?"

"Of course."

"Then we're all set." I go to end the call but then one last idea comes to mind. "Hey," I say, before he can hang up. "Do you do flowers by any chance?"

I hear his notepad open again. "There's a florist next door." Of course there is. That's quaint as hell Phoenix Falls for you. "I can run round and add something to your order if you need it."

"Black roses," I say immediately. "Whatever they have that's like… pretty but kind of emo. That's what I'm after." *In every area of my life.*

"Sounds good. Text me the address and we'll be there in twenty."

"Done and done."

I end the call and, impatient for Kitty to come back angry at me or not, I get to chopping the pile of no good tinder that I pulled from the newly finished up barn. The goat baby keeps me company.

After around fifteen minutes I feel my cell vibrate in my jeans.

I pull it out expecting it to be Chase. I almost drop it to the dirt when I see the name on the screen.

Kitty has ignored almost every text that I've ever sent her, so much so that I thought she'd blocked my number. When I see her name flash up in the message bubble my heart thunders aggressively in my chest.

I sit down on the stack of planks and read the text.

I'll be back in 10.

Holy shit. I have to ask.

Did you watch it? I'm so sorry.

There's a ten second pause, then a text bubble that pops up and quickly disappears. When it appears again she simply writes:

Yes.

Is that a good yes or a bad yes? I'm not sure so I send her another *sorry* and an *I'll make it up to you* and then I shove my phone in my pocket and haul ass to the back of the cabin, baby goat hot on my heels. I have to physically block it to stop it from squeezing through the door with me and then I lock it out for good measure. I can't have any distractions right now.

This is okay. I have a feeling in my gut telling me that she's not too mad so I'm going to run with that. Chase's delivery driver will be here in five, Kitty will be here in ten, and then I can re-apologise to her all over again.

What could go wrong?

I walk to the kitchen and try to think of what to make for her to drink. She's probably so mentally violated right now that I ought to make her something medicinal.

A hot toddy? A milkshake?

Chicks dig milkshakes right?

Not having a clue how to make a milkshake I settle for one of those fruit teas that turns the water a pretty colour, brewing it for a couple minutes and then pouring it over ice.

Then I hear it.

I swing the front door open without checking whose wheels are crunching up the gravel because my mind is so one-track right now that I don't even contemplate who else would be pulling up.

Big mistake.

"Hey man." Kaleb shuts the door of the Chevy and then trudges up the driveway, feet kicking at the dirt.

Shit.

"Hey." Voice more tense than a criminal during jury.

"Sorry for being gone so long – I ended up going to Chastity's."

Wish you'd fucking stayed there.

"It's all good," I lie. "You gonna bale up that hay out there?" Meaning: *please dear God go out back so that you don't set your eyes on what I'm getting delivered for your sister.*

"Yeah, just gonna shower first."

He mounts the last porch step, pulls his boots off, and then heads straight for the stairs.

Hopefully his shower will give me just enough time to destroy the evidence of my Not Safe For Kaleb cookie and the bouquet that Chase will have fingers-crossed failed to get for me.

No such luck.

A minute after Kaleb disappears into the bathroom a driver on a motocross bike skirts up the gravel, stabilising it and then dismounting. He pulls off his helmet and then whips his baggage carrier around to his front.

It's a sight to behold. He's wearing an all-black biker outfit, sans the jacket to accommodate for the heat, and he's got a bouquet of roses sticking out of his cookie pouch. Hardcore.

"You the cookie man?" he shouts out to me as I speed down the porch steps.

I hope to God that Kaleb didn't just hear that.

"Uh, yeah."

I pull my wallet out of my pocket and slap a wad of bills into his gloved up hand. He doesn't even count it. Instead he completes our swap, passing me a pizza style cookie box and a giant bouquet of baby pink roses. They couldn't be further from what I asked for, so that's great. One look at these and Kitty's never gonna talk to me again.

"Thanks man," I say as he remounts his bike. He slips his black headgear back over his blond surfer curls, flashing me a *you're welcome* smile before he peels back down his tire tracks.

And coming up in the opposite direction is Kitty in the back of Tate's Ford.

I can't tell if this is perfect timing or if I'm about to be the victim in a joint Hanson Lu homicide, but I stand my ground at the bottom of the porch, one hand holding a giant cookie and the other holding the flowers.

Tate pulls his car around so that Kitty can hop out of the back and he jerks his chin at me in a quick *hi-bye* whilst River scrambles over the centre console and into the shotgun seat. Then he eases back onto the road and all that's left is Kitty standing amidst the dust, black hair gently waving in the drag that the truck left behind.

"Kitty," I start but she shuts me up, running straight into my arms and throwing her hands around the back of my neck.

"I'm sorry for being such a freak," she says quickly, eyes huge and imploring as she stares up at me. Those long black lashes dazzle all of the common sense out of my brain.

She's not mad at me?

My abs clench at what that implies.

She liked the tape.

"You weren't being a freak, but we can't do this now," I whisper. "Your brother just got back and I need you to hide this stuff."

"What stuff?" she asks, pulling away slightly.

I raise my hands, gesturing to what I've got in them, and her little dimples make a reappearance.

"You got me apology roses?" she asks, cheeks glowing like morning sunshine.

"Yeah, and uh…" I shake my head. "This stupid

cookie."

"A cookie?" Her eyes are sparkling now. She withdraws herself from my torso and grabs the box from my hand, opening it up to read it.

She throws her head back and laughs the best laugh that I've ever heard.

"'*Sorry for my hard on'?*" she whispers, grinning. Then she pulls one of the Teddy Grahams off the border and starts crunching on it. "This is the best cookie ever."

I make a mental note to thank the fuck out of Chase some time.

"We need to hide it baby, if you don't want Kaleb to see."

She gives me a wry look. "And where do you think we should hide it?" she asks, eyebrow hitching deviously. "The *barn*?"

Thank God my hands are full, otherwise she'd be bent over my shoulder and we would *both* be on our way to the barn right now.

"Your room," I say gruffly. "Please, he'll be out any second."

She plucks off another teddy and stuffs it between my lips. Then she takes her flowers and her cookie and presses her tits up against my pecs. I swallow hard to try and disguise the grunt that's rumbling up my sternum.

"I'm sorry that I made you feel the need to be sorry," she whispers, pushing against me harder. Checking behind me for Kaleb, I turn back to her and run my hands down her back, stopping when I reach her ass and hauling her up against my abs. I walk us backwards into the cabin and then set her down on the bottom step of the stairwell, giving her a rough slap on her ass to encourage her to run to her room. She lets out a little gasp of surprise, pink lips parting and eyes going black.

"Go on baby," I murmur, one second away from losing my mind and finally kissing her.

She takes a few steadying breaths, brow pinched in indecision, and then she nods.

"Thanks," she whispers again, and then she turns on her heel and dashes to her bedroom.

CHAPTER 16

Madden

Happy 4th.

I reread Kitty's text about ten times before shooting her one back, with a smiley on the end for good measure. Then I turn my phone fully off because that's enough baby-softness for one day.

Plus, I've just woken up at two in the afternoon and I'm the only one who's not down at the lagoon yet for the annual Fourth of July celebration. I haven't been able to attend it for the past couple years due to touring with the band, but you can bet your ass that if Kitty's going, so am I. I try not to get too het up about the fact that Kaleb drove them down there instead of me, but at least she texted so that I know she's okay.

I take a deep breath as I look over to my right where the garage is, the shaded spot where they park their sparkling sapphire blue Chevy stomach-droppingly empty.

I start counting to ten.

She's okay. She texted, and you know that she's okay.

I didn't fall asleep until way too late last night because of all the maintenance we had to do around the ranch. We had to kick the working up a notch due to the sudden summer storm warning that the weather broadcaster claimed is threatening the area. After Kaleb baled up all of the fields of straw yesterday, he showed me around one of their monster machines and taught me how to wrap the hay for storage, so I spent the entire evening taping them in some sort of candy pink ranch cellophane. I cross my ankles as I take a sip of my coffee, leaning my shoulders against the door frame out back, and I glance over to the open stable doors, stuffed up with what looks like a hundred giant marshmallows.

When I reach the bottom of the mug I chuck the rest out onto the dirt and then turn my phone back on because I'm an addict in need of another Kitty hit. I blow out an agitated breath when I see that she hasn't opened up my last message and I scroll back up through our entire conversation history, disastrously one-sided.

On the plus side, it gives me hope that she'll be this dismissive with every other guy hounding her phone.

On the downside I know that the meaner she treats them the more they're gonna wanna chase her.

Damn it. To prevent myself from smashing my forehead through the wall I check my other messages, only opening up the ones from Jason Coleson. I skim over the messages, a little bummed that I'll have to decline his invite.

I would one thousand percent rather head over to Jace's house right now and attend the Coleson's

Fourth of July barbecue over a sordid beer soaked rager down at the lagoon, but my intentions would become pretty fucking obvious if I drove across town, stole Kitty away from her brother, and then took her to a family get-together that's more intimate than dinner with the Corleone's. If she wants us to be a secret then I'm not about to be the one who shows our hand.

Time to go find her.

The cattle are being kept in the barn today seeing as there's not going to be anyone here to watch them throughout the afternoon, so I lock up all the doors and head inside the cabin. I rinse out the coffee mug, take a quick shower, and then, grabbing my guitar, I finally head out.

I unlock the Jeep and shove my guitar case down on the floor at the back so that it doesn't get knocked around too much. Then I duck into the driver's seat and peel out of the ranch.

I haven't played the thing once since we got here. I've heard Kaleb strumming out a couple tunes here and there but he's the singer so his skills on the strings aren't of much consequence. It's not as if I'm gonna forget how to play because I've been playing it since forever, but I know that I really should be getting back into the rhythm of things before we leave for the road again.

A feeling of disgruntlement settles in my abs, making me grimace as I pull off the side road into the main square of Phoenix Falls. Jesus. The thought of being on the road again should not be making me feel so empty, and yet all I can think about is the one thing that I'm going to be so mad at myself for leaving behind the second that I'm all packed up and set to go.

No. I swallow hard, fists gripping into the steering wheel tighter than they should be. I need to relax. I can fix this. I can make it all work out.

But how the hell am I going to make it all work out?

It's another fifteen minutes before I reach the clearing at the start of the forest, a makeshift dirt track signalling the parking area that's a little deeper inside. I bump slowly over a series of stones and tree roots, teeth grinding together as I imagine Kaleb doing fifty down this thing, Kitty bouncing in the passenger seat.

I instantly decide that I'll be the one driving her home.

Fuck getting wasted at a Fourth of July rager, I'm going to make sure that she's getting into my car as soon as she's done here. I don't trust anyone else to take care of her the way that she deserves.

Once I reach the parking bay I ease into a gap between two other cars and dismount the SUV with only one agenda in my mind. *Find Kitty.*

I'm so fixated that it takes me all the way until I've reached the lagoon to realise that I've left my fucking guitar in the backseat of my car. I groan internally, wondering how to stop being so whipped in the hopes of recouping a couple brain cells. As I scan my eyes around the water, crystal blue and sparkling as the sun illuminates the surface through a big gap in the overhead canopy, I find the next best thing.

Kaleb, dressed in a pair of his scuffed up ranch jeans and a black shirt, is sat on a solid slab of stone overhanging the water, Chastity and a few of her friends with him. They're wearing trucker hats, jean shorts, and stringy bikini tops, and one of them is playing music at volume three million on her phone. I make my way over to Kaleb and signal him as soon as I catch his eye. I don't want to step one foot closer to the oestrogen circle that he's found himself at the centre of.

He gives me a quick grin, whispers something into Chastity's ear, and then gets up and meets me at the edge of the water.

"Wanna come up?" he asks, tilting his head back slightly in the direction of the women, probably assuming he can wingman me or something.

"Just got here," I say. Translation: *no.*

As if subconsciously reading my brain he suddenly says, "I think Kit was helping the guys build a campfire up there." He jerks his thumb somewhere through the trees to his left.

My brain glitches. Who the hell are *the guys?*

"What guys?" I ask, my forearms twitching.

"You know, the usual crowd."

That does not make me feel any better.

"I last spotted her with Tyler so, actually, that probably won't be of interest to you."

My eyes go blank, a red haze descending on my vision.

"Oh, and Chase said she could ride home with him in case you drink too much tonight."

A dull ache starts pulsing in my temples.

"You left her with Tyler," I say flatly, my voice the kind of calm that scares small children. "And you wanna let Chase drive her home."

Kaleb nods absentmindedly, attention momentarily pulled behind him as the girls start laughing at an explicit Lana Del Rey lyric.

I take his distraction as my cue to dip so I give him a quick slap on the shoulder and tell him, "I'll catch you in a bit."

I'm halfway around to the other side of the water before he even notices that I'm gone.

After about a minute of crunching my way through a shabby pathway of sun-scorched twigs and brittle, I hear it. The snapping sizzle of a midday campfire being prepared for the night's food, and the tentative twangs of someone brushing up on an acoustic guitar. I change my direction a little, heading more to the right, but then I stop dead in my tracks as a light melodic voice suddenly entwines with the air.

It's a girl and she's singing the first verse of Bring Me To Life by Evanescence. Quietly, I step a few feet closer, hoping to catch a glimpse of her from my position on the outer edges of their set-up, but there's a group of guys right below me obscuring any view of the people sat around the fire.

I can tell that she isn't the person who's playing the guitar because when she's about to reach the chorus a few chords get botched. She pauses, waiting for whoever's by her side to get back on track, and then she sings the most beautiful high note that I've ever heard in my life.

Who the hell…?

Amazed, I kick my way through the parched thicket until I'm shoulder to shoulder with the group of guys who have been watching her for the past minute. My breathing stops. A painful sensation lodges deep in my chest and my eyes grow wide as I realise what a fucking idiot I've been.

Of course it's her. Who else could it have possibly been?

Kitty's got her knees bent up as she perches on a log, the sun beaming straight down through the leaves and illuminating her in a holy golden spotlight. She's wearing a red tie-neck top and a pair of shorts that are covered in little rhinestones, making up the shape of the American flag.

From this angle, she's also unintentionally flashing her denim-clad pussy for the whole audience to see. My jaw ticks aggressively as I think about what's going through every guy's mind right now and I squeeze my nails into my palms, desperate to calm down.

That's no longer possible when I see the guy sat next to her.

Tyler stops playing as soon as he notices me standing there and an easy grin spreads out across his smug face.

The veins in my neck constrict the longer that I look at him.

Kitty let him know that she could sing… she told him that she could sing before she told *me* that she could sing. Why the *fuck* would she want Tyler to know before me? Why?

My brow creases and I turn my gaze to Kitty.

Her eyes are wide and her cheeks are changing from drained of all colour to sugar-frosting pink. She grips her fingers into her knees. Flashes a shocked look over to Tyler, then back to me.

The guys who were watching haven't seemed to notice anything weird about the sudden pause, instead taking the break to pop open a few new drinks and flick through some music on their phones.

I step past them until I'm right over her, my own eyes blacking out as I take her in from this angle. Fuck. Why did she have to be so pretty.

"You can sing?" I ask, my voice low and ringing with hurt. Because, yeah, I'm fucking hurt.

"I-" She's about to start saying something when Tyler suddenly murmurs something to her.

In fucking *French.*

My last grain of composure explodes like a grenade.

"You talk to him in *French*?" I'm so aghast that I can't actually bring myself to shut the fuck up. Do I sound like a jealous asshole? Yes. But do I give a fuck?

Tyler takes the wrong moment to start talking in English and he mumbles, "I'll be doing more than just *talking* to her in French-"

That's it. I step forward with every intention of unhooking his guitar strings and tying them nice and tight around his stupid neck when Kitty bolts upright and presses herself between us. We're all on our feet now and this is three seconds away from getting real ugly.

"Madden," she pleas.

I stare down at her, jaw hard, and I try to transmit her a thought.

I'm so angry at you.

Her eyebrows pinch in the middle and her eyes widen and sparkle. Guilty as sin.

"Yeah, Madden, back up."

The smile in Tyler's voice makes me want to chloroform him.

I slide my eyes over to his, gratified by the fact that I'm so much bigger than this piece of shit. So what if he's six-one? That's short to a guy my height.

I smile down at him, eyes so emotionless that I'm probably giving him the creeps.

"Madden," Kitty whispers, pressing her little paws palm-up against my abs.

I have to stifle my groan as her touch ignites a surge of heat down to my groin, my shaft quickly hardening and growing heavy in my jeans.

"Step aside," I grunt, biceps flexing hard with adrenaline.

I don't know what I'd rather do right now: hoist Kitty up around my waist and fuck her hard against a tree, or wrap my bare hands around Tyler's throat and throttle him until he's unconscious.

Maybe both.

Probably fearing for that nice shiny guitar in his hands Tyler suddenly takes a step backwards, chest heaving like he's ready to go but eyes flickering with self-doubt, and he mumbles something else in a rugged French accent that makes me want to break his jaw.

Kitty turns her head to him and gives him a curt little nod. I cock up an eyebrow 'cause what the hell's she nodding to him about, and then I watch with un-sated rage as Tyler brushes past the other guys and heads up towards the water.

Au revoir motherfucker.

"Madden, let me explain-"

I tangle my fingers into her hair, tilting her head back so that she can look up into my eyes and see how mad I am right now. How riled. How jealous.

"Madden-"

"Not here," I say gruffly, sorry to be cutting her off but eager to get her somewhere private so I can finally show her how she's been making me feel every damn day since high school. "I know a place."

She nods up at me, that same sorry expression still arching her eyebrows upwards. Feeling one brief flash of kindness, I unhook one of my hands from the back of her neck and smooth my thumb gently over the little crease in her brow. Her forehead relaxes and as I'm about to pull away she quickly reaches for my wrist, batting her lashes apologetically as she presses her lips softly into my palm.

My muscles tighten at the feel of her gentleness and a groan rumbles in my chest.

Don't worry princess, I think to myself as I pull my hand away and begin to walk her backwards, deeper into the forest. *We're about to get to that part.*

CHAPTER 17

Kitty

When we're fully out of sight from the others at the camp Madden grips his hands around the backs of my thighs and hauls me upwards. I'm straddling his middle as he descends parallel to the water and, with every step that he takes, the zipper of my shorts scrapes me up and down, my body slipping lower and lower until I'm wrapped around his hips.

I hum quietly as the metal grinds against me and Madden flashes me a look, burning with anger and lust.

"You'll let me explain, won't you?" I implore quietly, hands tentatively stroking their way from the bulging muscles at the tops of his shoulders to the strong sides of his tan neck. He hasn't shaved in a while and his dark stubble scratches at my palms.

He makes a low grunt and then starts moving us further to the left, trudging so closely to the rocks that water flecks begin splashing my bare thighs. He's not looking into my eyes anymore so I can't quite gauge how he's feeling.

Although the steel rod rocking hard against me is a slight clue.

"Madden," I whisper as he shoves another low-hanging branch out of our way, smoothing his other hand flat against my hair to prevent it from getting tangled in any stray twigs. The loud startled flap of birds taking flight sounds out somewhere to my left and Madden glances over in that direction, a stern look on his face.

I have to quash my brewing smile, a warm sparkly feeling spreading in my stomach, as I soak in the sensation of him carrying me through the woods like a caveman, hands running all over me and so overtly aroused that he's barely capable of speech. I know that it's stupid of us to be so far out here, away from everyone else, especially given the animal warnings we get reminded of during the summer mating season, but I'm currently so lost in my hormones that, right now, I don't care.

He suddenly drops me to my feet and starts ushering me backwards, using nothing but the jerk of his chin and his relentless pace to direct me. I stumble immediately and his hands quickly swoop forward, clutching his forearms securely around my lower back and dipping down so that he can press his forehead into my own.

My heart stutters and I close my eyes, keeping them shut until my ass hits off a sharp stone wall.

I pull away briefly and take a quick peep to the side, checking our surroundings. He's brought us to some sort of hidden cave, entirely entrapped in dark stone walls and with the trickle of the nearby water resounding around the room in an echo.

When I return my eyes to look at him, his own gaze has dropped to the band of my shorts, two of his fingers hooked around a belt loop and tugging at it roughly as if testing the resilience. He looks back up at me and a shiver runs down my spine.

"I don't wanna talk," he says quietly, his voice so deep that I can feel it in my belly.

I shake my head. "I can do the talking."

His cheek ticks up slightly, a wry look passing fleetingly over his features. "There are other things that I'd rather us *both* be doing right now."

"I thought you'd want an explanation," I say, and his face hardens again, the memory of what happened not ten minutes ago suddenly fresh in his mind.

He tips his chin in agreement and he unleashes his fingers from my shorts, moving them around my hips and then flattening them, warm and firm, against the dimples in my back.

"Make it quick," he whispers roughly, eyes entranced by my lips. Then he presses his body completely into my own, the rigid shaft beneath his jeans suddenly digging hard into my stomach, and as I bite back a small gasp he adds on one low final, "Please."

Now that he knows that I can sing I feel stupid for ever wanting to hide it from him in the first place. Whatever teenage logic I'd been clinging to at the start of my twenties has now entirely disappeared, and the words tumble from my lips like water off a lily-pad.

"I didn't mean to lie to you. I thought it'd be embarrassing if you knew that I can sing, if you knew how…" I cringe before I even say it. "How *alike* we are."

Shut up, shut up, shut up. I'm practically making myself gag with embarrassment.

I should've taken his advice and kept my mouth shut.

"What I mean to say is…" My brain goes completely blank as I try to find what it is that I apparently mean to say, and the way that Madden's eyes are burning into mine right now definitely isn't helping.

I swallow. "What I mean to say is that I like singing, a lot, and I also like you… a lot."

Kill me now.

"But, uh, those interests aren't entwined, if you know what I mean. Like, me liking singing has nothing to do with me liking you, and, uh, vice versa."

I pause to try and gauge how he's taking this revelation. Luckily his eyes are still darker than a serial killer's, so I obviously haven't turned him off too bad with my floundering.

"So with Tyler-"

Madden's eyes sizzle and his spine snaps straight. Lord above have mercy.

"Let me rephrase that. There's this show in town that you've probably never heard of – the Barn Bonanza? Do you know…? Anyway, it doesn't matter, the point is that it's this, like, talent show and if you enter and win it you can get a sponsorship so that you can make music with a local record company. Basically, they'll give you a test run to see if you're actually worth signing. It's an acoustic thing so I asked Kaleb when y'all got here if I could borrow his old

Fender but because I didn't want you finding out-"

I'm definitely saying all the wrong things because Madden's expressions have gone from irate to hurt to murderous in the space of the past fifteen seconds.

"Because I thought that you'd think it was, like, lame or something, I haven't been able to practice at the cabin. So Dyl's been letting me in to use the bar during the day and I thought that, this afternoon, because Tyler has a guitar too, I could do a little bit of practising before I go on stage and, you know, shoot my shot."

He stares at me blankly, a dark molten glare simmering behind his silver eyes.

I try to relieve the tension by bending my fingers into the shape of a pistol and giving him a little, "*Pew pew.*"

His eye twitches.

"Put the gun away," he says tersely.

Thank God. I try to smother my small dimply grin, relieved because we're back to playing now, and I tuck my finger-gun safely away into my invisible thigh holster. I give it a pat and then raise my hands to show him that I'm unarmed.

"Wanna frisk me?" I ask teasingly.

He lets out a gruff unabashed groan and slowly, cautiously, I begin trailing my fingertips up his abdomen. He lowers his forehead back to mine and a flame ignites in the centre of my belly.

"You done talking now?" he asks, one palm smoothing down over my ass and the other climbing North until it's fully leashed in the back of my hair.

I nod.

"My turn?" he enquires, hand rubbing harder

against my behind.

I hide my naughty smile and nod again, but he shocks me right off my newfound high horse. His fingers tug suddenly in my hair, surprising me backwards, and the hand resting on the back pocket of my shorts dips beneath the denim hem, slipping straight up the back of my underwear, cupping his labour-hardened palm roughly around my soft cheek.

"I'm gonna say this once and then I'm done," he says brusquely, his voice nothing more than a growl. "Never go to another man to fill your needs again, Kitty."

Then, with one last look, he hoists me up and kisses me.

I moan, soft and startled, right into his mouth and he crushes down on me harder, a low rumble in his chest. Hungry and impatient, he tilts my jaw and slants me open, sliding his tongue slowly into my mouth, and then caressing me with long intense strokes. The hand in my underwear is rubbing and squeezing and I'm so overwhelmed that I can't hold in my gasp, my mind too distracted to remember how to coordinate my fingers so that I can explore him in return. I tighten my thighs around his thick abdomen and, feeling my heat flush against him, Madden strengthens his grip, his tongue thrusting deep. I can't keep up with him and I make a tiny pleasured whine, my brain evaporating into nothing but twinkling dust.

Then he grips my wrist in his left hand and embeds it roughly against the solid shaft in his jeans.

I stop breathing.

Madden's length... Madden's length is longer than my hand span.

Perceiving my unfamiliarity with our newly broken touch barrier, or perhaps sixth sensing the fact that I'm about to blackout, he loosens his grip on my hair and slows his pace, his right palm running down the side of my neck and then giving me a light squeeze. Butterflies flutter in my belly as I nervously reach up to return his affection, fingers stroking up his jaw and then into his dark, thick hair.

He grunts and pulls away, pupils dialled out.

"Too much?" he asks hoarsely, eyes beseeching into mine.

I shake my head. My one single brain cell rattles around in there.

"Words, princess. I need you to use your words."

I try to find some.

"Uh…" *Great start, Einstein.* "No, it's… it's…" Oh dear. Another tragic onslaught of verbal diarrhoea cascades out of me. "It's just been a really long time since I've done anything – like, I mean *anything* – with anyone so I'm just not very good. I mean, I'm out of practice. I can learn," I add, voice hopeful, for good measure.

He watches me, truly curious, and then after a moment of slow consideration he flashes me his perfect white teeth, his cheekbones glowing warm and ruddy. I look longingly at his sharp vampire canines and then start chewing dreamily into my lower lip.

"'Out of practice'," he repeats on a deep exhale, eyes languorously trailing over my chest. His gaze shifts to my throat where his fingers are toying with the strings of my bikini, tied haphazardly beneath the neck of my top. He dips down, stubble scratching over my exposed collarbone, and he tugs at the string with a rough pull from his teeth.

I make a startled sound and he kisses gently at my neck.

"Fuck baby, you make me so happy," he whispers, his mouth hot against my skin. A pleasured ripple runs down my core and I realise that I'm hearing him curse for the first time ever. With the combination of the still summer air infiltrating the cavern from outside, and Madden teasing every inch of my body, I'm beginning to dangerously exceed the recommended bodily temperature.

"You've never sworn in front of me before," I whisper up at him, my palms exploring his pectorals and then giving them a little squeeze.

Solid as a rock.

Madden breathes out a laugh as he watches my perusal and then he nods at me when our gazes lock again. "'Cause I'm tryna be a gentleman with you, Kitty," he says, searching my face. His expression looks hesitant for a moment and then he adds, "I'm gonna be a gentleman with you, everywhere except the bedroom. That's the one place that I'm gonna drop the etiquette and let you see me for what I am."

I tighten my hold on him, nails biting into his biceps and calves crushing us groin to groin. He makes a quiet wordless sound as the warm denim of my shorts rubs him roughly through his jeans.

"And what are you exactly?" I ask, teasing him with a smile.

He smiles back and then moves his mouth to my throat.

"An *animal*," he replies, and then he sinks his teeth into my neck.

I howl in delight, laughing uncontrollably as he nips and tugs. His attack is surprisingly gentle at first but then it slowly becomes rougher and rougher, our smiles fading into parted lips, and my laugh diminishing into whimpers and whines. His licks turn into sucks and his kisses turn into bites.

One of his large hands slides to my chest and, after slowly acclimatising to massaging and squeezing, two digits begin rubbing circles around my sensitised nipple.

I moan in agony, arching my back off the wall, and my soft sounds entwine with the thrum of the running water.

"More," I plead needily, pulling him upwards with a tug from my fists buried in his hair.

He pulls a pained expression, wincing slightly as he strokes his large palms up my jaw. My nipples have pebbled through two layers of clothing and his arousal has grown so hard that he's bruising my skin. He knows what I want, and I know that he wants it too.

"I wanna fuck you," he whispers, brow taut and tendons flexing. "But it shouldn't be out here, like this. Not for our first time. It should be…"

He looks away from me for a moment, his eyes glazing as he pictures whatever's going on in his fantasy. When he turns back to me again he grips at my chin and presses a hard kiss against my lips. I try to move with him and it makes him pull away, groaning as he rests his forehead against my shoulder.

"In your bed," he says, voice tense. "Get you nice and comfortable and then I'll pump you real slow."

My thighs clench around him and his hips thrust instinctively, rocking me roughly against the stone wall.

His hand runs down over my thigh, knee, and calf, only pausing when he reaches the top of my boot.

"And these," he murmurs, pulling back so that he can look at what I'm wearing. He grips his fist around the sole of my cowgirl boot, hitching it upwards so that I'm opened wider against his body. I bite back a mewl. "I only want you wearing these."

I can picture it so completely. The height difference. The size difference. Madden – big, broad, and tan as hell – standing over me as I lay back into my duvet, body bare bar for my pair of cowgirl booties.

I try to shift the power dynamic, hoisting myself higher up his body and kicking my heels roughly against his ass like he's one of our quarter horses. His jaw flexes but he takes it like a man.

"You're gonna let me ride you?" I ask, rubbing my breasts up against his torso.

His eyes flutter closed momentarily, his cheeks flushing red. "Jesus Kitty, I…"

Pleased, I reach up and peck a series of small soft kisses against his neck, jaw, and cheeks. His hands move more gently than before, stroking me sweet and slow.

When I look up at him again he has a molten look in his eyes.

"Use my cock however you want," he says hoarsely, grinding himself against my thigh to relieve his aching bulge. "Whatever my girl wants," he grunts, "my girl gets."

CHAPTER 18

Madden

I need to be tranquilised.

It's a fucking miracle that we don't leave the cave looking like two victims of a zombie apocalypse given how close I was to ripping her tight red cami apart so that I could finally get my mouth on those sweet little tits.

When I finally set her down on the dry stone floor her legs give way like a newborn lamb, and I have to re-orientate her with my knee hitched between the apex of her thighs. She gives me a desperate look, another plea for me to take her right here in the middle of the forest, and I grind my teeth together, forcing my eyes away from her so that I don't end up doing exactly that.

She pulls my shirt away from my abs and runs her fingers up them. I shiver because her body's freaking freezing. I guess that that's a tiny-girl problem. Not enough inside of her, so she has poor circulation.

I can fix that.

Mind spiralling to somewhere that it definitely shouldn't be I plant my foot back on the ground and then give her one last kiss before I start walking us into the open sunlight. She grips her hands around my neck like a coconut crab, begging me to keep going even though we both know that I'm not gonna. I'm gonna do the gentlemanly thing.

And then, when the time is right, I'm gonna get real ungentlemanly.

I pull away from her and she whines like a spoiled princess. My cock jerks aggressively in my boxers. I love it when she's a brat.

"Start walking," I manage to huff out, chest heaving like I've been doing cardio all afternoon. Very nearly was the case.

"You're a tease," she puffs out angrily, brow furrowed down to her toes. I can't help but smile as she starts stomping up the incline, giving me the perfect view of her ass and a nice reminder that soon enough I'm gonna have those boots leaving imprints all the way up my back.

I readjust my shaft and then start following after her.

"Kitty," I call out to her, trying to catch up.

She starts speed-walking.

"Princess," I say instead. Her footing pauses momentarily but then she continues her military march.

I jog the small distance between us and then hook my forearms just underneath her ribcage, somehow still towering a foot above her even though she's ahead of me on the slope.

I press a hard kiss into her exposed shoulder, tasting her sweet skin, warm and salty from the sun. I can't taste any sun lotion though, which explains her intergalactic array of cinnamon freckles.

"I'm sorry," I murmur, rubbing my chin back and forth over her skin. She shivers a little and I tug smugly at my lip-ring. Yeah, she likes it when I rub her up with my stubble. Noted, princess. "You know I'm gonna make it up to you when the right moment comes."

I lean over her so that I can watch her face and she pouts disappointedly, sulking like a kid.

"What if the right moment never comes?" she asks.

Is she implying that she thinks I won't ever get her into bed? I will literally murder her brother if I have to.

I decide not to admit that, instead saying, "It will, baby. I promise."

She huffs loudly, then holds up her pinkie. I immediately envelop it with my own.

"Blood oath next," she says, and I dip my head into her neck, laughing.

We probably only have one more minute of alone time as we make our way back to the others. It's mid-afternoon so there's plenty time before the campfire becomes the social hub and the fireworks start going off, but even so I know that I'm going to have to keep my distance.

I just need to think of a way to get Kaleb out of the house for a night.

I shove that thought to the back of my mind and bring up one of my hands so that I can play with her hair. She's got a series of tiny braids plaited amidst her onyx waterfall, so I take the one that's tied with a red ribbon and twirl it around my finger.

"How're your roses?" I ask, leaning down again so that I can kiss her jaw, my groin resting hard and heavy in the arch of her back.

She turns her head slightly so that she can face me and she gives me a sly smile.

"Pink," she says, tone coloured with amusement.

I scrunch up my nose, face flushing with embarrassment. "Uh, yeah, sorry about that, I…" I tug at my metal and then shake the thought away. "I'm a moron. It's all they had. Sorry."

My heart stills in surprise when she reaches her hand up to my face and gently strokes at my stubble. Then my shaft revs to life again.

"No, I love them, they match my room perfectly."

That catches my attention. Baby pink roses… match her room? I run my eyes over her, checking to see that she's still dressed like a little emo, and then my mind goes into hyper-drive as I start mentally detailing her room. I would've bet good money that it was a red and black crypt, metal posters on the wall but with a cool cowgirl twist. Now my body's growing extra hard because I'm picturing the exact opposite.

Pink walls, pink sheets, frilly curtains…

The roses that I got for her right next to her bed.

She smiles as she watches me, reading my every thought.

"Wanna come in my room?" she asks sweetly, but her eyes are twinkling like a demon.

I make a rough unintelligible sound. "Uh, fuck, yeah, I wanna…"

She tinkles out a light laugh and it shoots straight through my heart like an arrow.

I swallow and smile back at her, trying to retain some level of composure.

"You eat your cookie?" I ask, pressing us cheek to cheek.

She nods. "Yeah."

I press both of my hands back down to her belly, rubbing her gently as my muscles swell.

She can sense it. "What is it?" she asks, laughing slightly.

I close my eyes briefly, a heavenly feeling washing over the front of my brain.

I mutter against her neck what I'm feeling but she doesn't quite catch it.

"What?" she asks again, tone still light with amusement.

"I like filling your belly," I repeat.

I like taking care of you. There aren't any women in my life and I know that, once I've got you, I'm gonna take care of you better than anyone else ever could have. I'm never letting anything bad happen to you, ever.

I feel her body grow woozy and I grip her tighter in my arms.

Now it's my turn to breathe out a laugh.

"No, princess. No getting limp again out here, we've gotta-"

I move to the other side of her neck, brushing her hair over her shoulder, little red bow and all, but my stomach plummets when I look down.

Oh shit.

Oh *shit.*

"Kitty." I swallow hard.

Hearing the dread in my voice she twists to look at me, face questioning. "Yeah?" she asks, brow twitching.

I can't take my eyes off her throat. There's a huge, darkening mark right up the side where I was sucking on her and I don't know if I should feel like a terrible piece of shit or if I should allow myself to be turned the hell on.

"What is it?" she probes, more nervous now.

"It's..." I don't know how to say it. Maybe something along the lines of, *I'm an animal, you're softer than a peach, and now you've got my calling card on your neck to show everyone who you belong to.*

Including your brother.

I tug roughly at my hair.

"You're gonna have to – if you don't want Kaleb to know – you're gonna need to..." I meet her scared eyes and press us forehead to forehead, praying that she'll forgive me. "I've covered you in hickeys, baby. I'm so fuckin' sorry."

Her hand flies up to her neck, feeling the side that I just exposed.

I close my eyes, expecting a knee to the balls.

Instead she presses a gentle kiss against my skin.

"I'll cover it with my hair," she whispers. Relief runs down my chest, the dark fog in my mind clearing a little.

I lean down so that I can kiss the purpling area, a mixture of guilt and pleasure pulsing in my groin.

"I'm sorry," I murmur again. They're my new favourite words apparently. I can't seem to stop saying them.

She strokes her fingers through my hair and gives me an encouraging smile.

"I can't wait to see it when we get home," she says,

voiced so hushed that I almost don't catch it.

My eyes fly open.

The twin dimples in her cheeks are out to play and her face is more calm than a summer's evening.

This girl.

I give her a deep appreciative kiss and then step back, jerking my chin at the clearing up ahead, knowing that our alone time is over now.

I watch her turn and walk ahead, one of my hands still running through my hair.

Thank God for this girl.

*

Kitty decides to stay for the whole ordeal which means that, as her self-assigned chauffeur, so do I.

Newly freed of her vocal constraints she spends the whole evening prodding at the campfire kindling and trying out various different songs, naturally capturing the attention of way too many guys. I try not to go too psycho, knowing that if this is her dream then I'm gonna do everything in my power to help her achieve it.

After the food's been shared out Kaleb lumbers my way, eyes glued on his sister because she's gathered a bit of a crowd. He slips a roll-up into his mouth and takes a long pull. I raise my eyebrows when I catch the scent.

"I don't like it," he says on an exhale, eyes narrowed as he watches the scene unfold.

I'm not a big fan of the current set-up either. Tyler's strumming out his acoustic nonsense again because apparently he has a death wish, and Kitty's bikini strings have unfastened, meaning that they're only holding on by a prayer.

My prayer.

I sigh, palm rubbing up my forehead. "Yeah, well." There's not much to say. Not much that he'd probably understand right now either.

He grumbles something that doesn't sound human and I can't help but choke back a laugh.

Kitty Hanson Lu, literally trilingual.

Kaleb Hanson Lu, barely capable of English.

Unfortunately my snicker goes a long way and Tyler glances over to us like an on-duty Doberman.

Great.

He passes his guitar to Kitty and then gets to his feet, stretching luxuriantly right next to her head. My jaw ticks. Kaleb stands to attention.

"What's his deal?" Kaleb asks, his attempt at inconspicuousness about as subtle as a police car. He's scanning Tyler with about as much displeasure as I am.

"Got a crush," I mutter back, hoping to sound more protective brother than jealous boyfriend.

Kaleb cracks his jaw. "Think he'll be a problem?"

You're talking to your biggest problem right now.

I shake my head. "She's a big girl, she knows what's good for her."

Kaleb shoots me an irate look. I give him a grounded palm-up gesture in response.

"Tyler's been your buddy for years. I'm sure if anything was brewing he'd talk to you about it." Which gets me thinking – am *I* supposed to be talking to Kaleb about this? Should I be telling him my intentions?

My faux-composure seems to settle Kaleb and he

nods briefly before pointing his lasers back to Tyler, who's sat back down with a less than pleased expression on his face.

Probably because Kitty's no longer next to him.

"They're setting off the fireworks in a minute."

I startle slightly and then turn around. Kitty's standing between the two of us, a cherub-cute expression glowing on her face. Kaleb pulls her under his arm and smushes a kiss to the top of her head. I try to not feel too jealous, eyes locked in with Kitty as she accepts his display of ownership. I shift closer to her as Kaleb turns to talk to someone on his other side, and I quickly interlace my fingers with the palm that she's splayed out behind her back. I rub her skin gently and watch as her cheeks blush darker.

An echoing pop and then eardrum-shattering canon fire sounds somewhere way ahead, and all of us turn to face the scene, the girls around the fire laughing with shock and someone to our rear turning up the music on their cell.

A cacophony of fireworks – blue, red, and sparkling white – shoot up and explode overhead. The sky's a deep navy, not black, but it's dark enough to make the show crystal clear.

With everyone fully distracted, I step closer to Kitty and give her hand another squeeze.

She looks up at me with wide eyes, the shimmer from above sparkling in her irises.

Soon, princess. I promise.

CHAPTER 19

Kitty

Madden spends the whole of the next two days out on the fields with Kaleb, whilst my body grows more and more agitated. Knowing now that I need to stay in Kaleb's good books so that I can use his guitar at the Barn Bonanza, Madden's been nothing short of angelic.

And whilst he's growing puritanical, I'm on the cusp of requiring an exorcism.

Seeing as he doesn't have long left at the ranch I've decided to take matters into my own hands, in an attempt to karate chop the little angel off of his shoulder.

Today has been so densely humid that a storm is almost definitely on the cards, and I've had to open each window up a crack to encourage some sort of air circulation. Also sensing the change in the weather, Kaleb brought the cattle back inside their shed earlier this evening and he's spent the rest of his on-duty cowboy hours inspecting Madden's handiwork on the barn, followed by showing him around the stables because he's so darn impressed. If Madden wasn't the guitarist in my brother's band I don't doubt for a second that Kaleb would ask Papa to hire him.

The one good thing about their guy-time induced absence is that it's given me girl-time to prepare for my little stint.

Phase one: Eradicate Kaleb.

Phase two: Mesmerise Madden.

First I begin by having the world's hottest shower. Purified by fire, I slip into a special something and then masquerade the whole set with an inconspicuous black hoodie. Fingers wiggling over the amenities crowded around the sink, I pick up Madden's cologne, inhale it like a crack addict, and then spritz it over my jumper in the shape of a cross. *Amen.* I contemplate the bottle for another couple of seconds and then lift up the hem of my hoodie and spritz it under there too.

I chew back my smile. *Let's see if he notices.*

Then I open my freshly purchased makeup bag – a dinky pink thing covered in heart-shaped lollipops – and pull out my vixen essentials. I untwist my mascara, spooly leaving its tube with a suction-laden *pop*, and then I run it upwards over my lashes. I inspect the bottle whilst I hold my lashes in place, the label promising to make them longer and thicker.

Hopefully they won't be the only things getting longer and thicker tonight.

Pleased with my look as the Arachnid Queen, I pat a powder-puff of pink blush at the apples of my cheeks and then compress a lightly shimmered lip balm over my lips. Then I drop my weapons back into the arsenal, zip it up, and survey my handiwork.

Honestly it looks like a five year old has been at my face. Fingers crossed Madden's into the whole Crayola look.

My hair is usually pretty well behaved but since my frisson on the fourth it's become so static that you'd think I'd been chewing electric wires. Maybe it's the humidity, maybe it's my hormones. Maybe it's the chemicals that Madden secretes. Regardless, it's totally fucked, so I don't even bother running a brush through it.

Spritzed, glossed, and secretly dressed to dazzle I steal my stash back to my bedroom and then descend the stairs, my heart going double-time. When I reach the last step I peek around to see if they've come inside yet but, hearing no grunting and sensing no testosterone, I swish into the kitchen to busy myself, biding my time until Phase One can come into play.

I drum my nails against the counter, contemplating my next move as I wait for my chance to kick Kaleb out. I pull open the fridge and scan the bounty. It really has never been so stocked up. My eyes fall to a punnet of strawberries and a thought twitches in my brain.

Strawberries are aphrodisiacs, right? I pull the tub out of the fridge and twist my lips at them.

Sure, what the hell.

I break into the container, rinse the strawberries, and set them on a plate, before reaching into my candy stash and pulling out a bar of chocolate. I break it up into a bowl and then set it over the gas. As my chocolate breaks down its molecular structure I pat the berries dry.

I check on my cauldron again, giving the chocolate a whirl around in the pan, and then I take it off the heat, ready for my dipping.

Then the back door opens.

Hello Phase One.

Kaleb miraculously left his cell in the living room this afternoon and I have been watching with joy as Chastity hounds his messages. At the bonfire the other night I may or may not have slipped in some good words to her and, behold, two days later she's gussied herself up to take the bull by the horns. I try not to think too hard about the fact that the bull is my brother.

I lean down so that I can crouch into one of the bottom cupboards and when I come back out I pull a stocky bundle of sage with me. *Remove my brother from this cabin, o herby bundle.* I lightly torch the top with the gas and then I begin walking it like a witch around the cabin.

Kaleb takes it in.

"What the hell's that?" he asks, gesturing to my flaming torch. Completely oblivious to my princess transformation. God bless brotherly indifference.

"Sage," I say as I waft it past him, reaching up on my tip-toes so that I can purify all the nooks and crannies.

Brow furrowed, Kaleb makes a sceptical noise. Then, on an unfortunately deep inhale, he begins coughing up a lung.

"Jesus Christ!" he chokes out, face turning red.

I watch him with interest as I continue my cabin cleanse.

"Put that out, Kit! I can't fucking breathe."

I slide my eyes over to him. "I bet you can't, demon. That means it's working."

He gives me a growly look but, thinking about his Fender, I decide not to laugh.

"Your phone's been going off by the way," I say, giving him a nice big *hint-hint, nudge-nudge.*

He's still choking but now he's preoccupied with his cell too. His eyes meet mine again briefly, probably wondering if I know who's been messaging him, and then he clomps up the stairs, spluttering slightly as he locks himself in his room.

That went well.

I put out my little fire hazard and then go back to my strawberries, slipping one-handed into my cowgirl boots as I begin the dunking process.

When the backdoor sounds again I don't move a muscle, although my ears are straining like a curious shrew. I pretend to be totally engrossed in my labour as large stomping footsteps make their way over to me.

Bonjour Phase Two.

Madden makes a low grunting sound in the back of his throat. I swirl a strawberry in the chocolate and then place it meticulously on my plate.

I feel the shift in the airflow as he checks up the banister to search for Kaleb, and then he takes another step closer, invading my chocolate strawberry bubble with his heavy boots and masculine scent. Oh Lord. My body grows woozy at his strong scent alone.

Too curious for my own good I glance through my lashes up at him.

My heart flutters dangerously in my chest.

His stern eyes are burning a hole into me, and my cheeks are searing darker than any blush I could have applied. He's assessing my sudden makeover and he doesn't like the implications. When his gaze drops to my hoodie, cropped just beneath my ass, I'm convinced that it's about to burst into flames. God knows I am.

"Going out?" he asks, voice rougher than sandpaper.

I almost snort. *He thinks that I've got a date? After what we did the other day?* I have to turn away from him so that my expression doesn't belie my incredulousness. *What kind of harlot does he think that I am?*

"Nope," I say, dunking another strawberry.

His breathing hitches slightly but he stands his ground. "Someone… someone coming over?"

I roll my eyes. Surely he can't be so pessimistic as to think that he could lose me that quickly?

Sighing, I spin my strawberry by its stem, lifting it up so that the excess chocolate can drip away. "No Madden. I'm staying here. Alone. *All night.*"

He finally gets the hint.

About freaking time.

He instantly positions his body at my rear, dipping his face into my neck as his hands caress my sides. He groans deeply when he inhales my scent.

"You used my cologne," he rasps, rubbing his palms around my thighs. He kisses over the bruise on my neck and I squeeze my legs together, the sensation of his coarse hands against my soft skin too much to bear.

"I don't want to wait any longer, princess," he whispers, jeans grinding into my ass as he rubs himself against me. "But, fuck, Kaleb-"

"I've pulled some strings," I whisper back to him,

my fingers encasing his own as he palms me over my hoodie.

"What?" he asks, his voice barely decipherable as he kisses his way up my neck.

"The other night, around the campfire," I say. "I started talking to that girl he likes, and I made some suggestions."

Madden is no longer computing on the verbal scale, his body taking on an agenda of its own. He's making up for his past few days of chaste demeanour, his hands suddenly desperate to cover every inch of me and his bucking hips ready to do the same.

Just as he starts grazing my ear my phone begins vibrating across the kitchen counter.

I glance at it curiously, more than willing to ignore it.

Then I see the name on the screen.

"Shit!" I hiss, hands grappling for the device.

Madden, sighing, takes a step backwards and I spin around to face him as I fumble for the answer button. Madden adjusts his belt with his thick clumsy fingers, eyes half-mast and trained on my cowgirl boots.

I cross my legs quickly. He closes his eyes, looking pained.

"Yes?" I answer breathlessly. "I mean, hello?"

There's a pause on the other end of the line, then my Papa's loud rumbling chuckle. I must have hit the speakerphone button out of habit when I was accepting the call.

"How's my Pumpkin?" he asks cheerily.

I cringe so deeply my belly cramps.

Madden's eyes shoot to mine, suddenly very interested.

Pumpkin? he mouths at me, smiling with delight.

I frown and turn my back to him, clicking off the speakerphone button. His arms wrap around my belly and he groans lazily into my hair.

Now my stomach's fluttering for other reasons.

I scrunch up my face, determined to get through this conversation smoothly.

"I'm okay Papa."

"Y'all have been AWOL on my cell. Everything running smoothly?"

I nod even though he can't see me. "Everything's perfect Papa. Is Mama there? I haven't spoken to her in a while."

There's the crinkling sound of the cell phone being shared and then my mom's voice comes through the speaker, more honeyed than a waffle.

"Hey Pumpkin. How's things?"

I ignore her question. "Papa's been sending me all your wins, mom. Congratulations, you've done so good."

I can hear her waving me off through the phone.

"That's sweet of you, Pumpkin. We've been missing you over here."

I twist my face because, although I've been missing them too, I've also been enjoying my newfound freedom. Well, freedom of sorts. Incarcerated freedom. At the behest of my brother.

"I miss you too," I say quietly.

Madden presses a small kiss into the side of my neck.

"Don't be gone too long," I add, although I'm not sure who I'm talking to anymore.

Madden stills behind me for a second, and then he

gives me a firm, comforting squeeze.

Mama laughs through the line and says knowingly, "Don't you worry about a thing."

She gives me a quick rundown on her recent successes and then, promising that I'll pass their love on to Kaleb, we hang up a couple Pumpkins later.

When I put my cell back on the counter Madden grazes his teeth up my neck.

"I fucking love your nickname."

I shake my head. "Don't you dare tease me."

He smiles against my cheek, stubble scraping at my skin. "Never," he whispers, hands working their way back down my belly.

The sound of Kaleb's door opening upstairs causes us to fling ourselves apart, Madden crashing backwards into a cupboard door that I'd left open and a chocolate-coated strawberry flying South across the kitchen.

I scuttle to collect it as Kaleb appears on the stairs.

He jerks his chin at Madden as if he hasn't spent the entire day with him.

"You okay if I dip tonight? Got plans."

Even though I'm the mastermind behind Kaleb's exit – special thanks to Chastity – my gears grate as he solely addresses Madden. As if this isn't *my house*. As if I should have *no say* in the matter.

Madden glances over to me, sensing the sibling hostility. I give him a tiny nod and he nods to Kaleb in turn.

Kaleb leaves the cabin without further address, the slam of the front door a nice departing gift.

Then it's just the two of us.

We wait until the Chevy revs to life and then

Madden makes the first move. He walks slowly to the front door and bolts all of the locks, eyes on mine, looking for confirmation.

I glance over to the back door and he goes to bolt that one too.

Then he begins to silently close all of the curtains – the ones around the living room and finally the ones in the kitchen – and then, once the whole place is hidden and sealed, he stands himself in front of me, waiting for my signal.

So I give it to him.

CHAPTER 20

Madden

She drops her hoodie to the floor and I fall down to my knees.

"Oh Jesus."

I splay out my haunches so that I can get a real good look at her and then I wrap my fingers around her hips, chest suddenly heaving.

"You put this on for me?" I ask, slipping a digit beneath the waistband of her panties. If you can even call them that. She's got a barely-there piece of baby pink cotton around her pussy, a matching pink bra that's only just covering her nipples, and in the centre of each there's a tiny pink rose.

I look up at her and swallow, then I roam my hands over to her ass.

I groan, feeling that her cheeks are bare for me.

"Kitty," I say, my voice tormented. I get to my feet and gently turn her around, sucking in a breath when I see her perfect little mounds. I hook two fingers underneath the string that's sliding between the globes of her ass and I pull it away from her, mesmerised by what the hell she's wearing.

"When'd you get this?" I ask, my muscles clenching tight. I run my palms up to her chest and slip my fingers beneath the cotton cups, her body shuddering so hard that she has to hold onto the counter in front of her.

"I ordered it… online… after the roses," she whispers sweetly. Then she begins arching against me as I start rubbing my fingers around her nipples.

"You get this for me?" I ask, thumbs tweaking her lightly.

She sucks in a breath and nods, her head resting backwards against the swell of my pecs.

I kiss the top of her head, too overwhelmed to think straight.

"You didn't need to do this for me, princess. You didn't need to…"

I lose track of my sentence as I pull down her straps, pushing the band to her waist so that I can see her budded pink peaks. I look down over her body and bite into my lip, loving every inch so much that I'm not sure where to begin. She tilts her head farther backwards, brow pinched as she looks up at me, and her expression is so innocent that my cock strains against my pants.

I lean into her neck again and take a deep breath.

"My scent smells so good on you," I murmur, fingers now trailing down to the top of her panties. When I reach the frilly band I run my hands to the centre, and then, when she looks down, watching, I give the pink rose bud a hard little pinch.

She jolts and gasps, her tits bouncing gently.

I grunt and grab a hold of her hips, leashing my fingers through the little ribbons at the sides of her underwear as I rock my crotch roughly against her. Breathing in fast pants, she bends over the countertop and raises herself onto the toes of her cowgirl boots, arching up for me as if she's about to let me take her right here in the middle of the fucking kitchen.

And the animal inside of me is a-fucking-okay with that.

I rip open my belt and shove down the zipper, quickly pushing them to mid-thigh so that I can get to work on my boxers. She glances at me over her shoulder, a waterfall of onyx hair tumbling down her back, and she attempts to lift herself higher when she sees that her hips haven't reached the level of my own. Her slender biceps flex as she wriggles upwards and when her gaze catches mine she gives me a nervous lip-biting smile.

It strikes me right through the gut.

What the *fuck* am I doing?

Enraged by my own lack of self control I give my hair a self-flagellating tug and then, hands encasing her waist, I slip her down from the counter. At first she's surprised. Then she starts protesting. Ignoring her little fight I turn her gently around to face me and then I hold up her body flush against my own.

I haven't even *kissed* her yet today. What the hell was I thinking trying to get into her pants not five seconds after her brother leaves the property?

Kitty doesn't seem to be having this same moral dilemma.

"What're you doing?" she complains, giving me her

spoiled princess pout. "I thought we were gonna-"

I shut her up with a kiss, rough and warm and hard. A promise of what's to come. I move my mouth against her firmly and she quickly melts into me, wrapping her arms around my neck and lacing her fingers through my hair. She tries parting her lips a little, begging me to slip inside, but I can't trust myself to do that without getting past the point of no return. Forcing her lips to stay shut I wrap one arm around her ass, bare and round and softer than sin, and I lift her just enough so that her feet are dangling over the floor. I pull away growling, trying to not get too carried away before I've got her on her mattress, and she strokes her fingers nervously up my jaw.

Then she leans into me again and gives my lip-ring a tiny lick.

Jesus Christ. Hoping that I can get us up the stairs without mounting her halfway, I shift her around to the side of my body, quickly swipe up her crumpled hoodie, and then yank open the fridge door so that I can shove her plate of strawberries inside. Then I turn around to start walking us from the kitchen.

"Meaty," she says quietly, finger jabbing into the swell of my bicep.

I cast her a swift glance, her hands now sliding over my chest.

You haven't seen any meat yet, princess.

When we start ascending the stairs her body bounces gently with every step that I take. I watch her like a predator, jaw setting harder than steel. She's small and smooth and soft all over, and she keeps kicking into my legs with her cowgirl boots. She's trying to rile me the hell up and, for better or worse, it's working.

Sensing my lowering self-control she swishes her hair away from the side of her neck, humming innocently as she shows me her markings.

Shit. My cock thickens drastically, pushing painfully against the band, and I bare my teeth, so hard that I'm almost snarling.

I look away quickly, brow furrowing low.

"No Kitty," I say harshly. "Not like that. Not tonight."

She moans, sweet and sad, and my eyes flutter closed. *I can't wait for her to make that sound when I'm thrusting deep inside of her.*

"I don't wanna make it rough for you on our first time together," I choke out, so aroused that my vision's going blurry. "That's not how it's supposed to be."

She rests her head on the swell of my shoulder, fingers trailing down my abs over my shirt.

Lower, princess. Just a little lower.

"But you'll be leaving soon," she says sadly. "I need you to give me something that I can feel for the next six months."

I get to the top step and look her hard in her eyes. "I can give you something that you'll be feeling for nine."

Her hand pauses at the top of my unbuttoned jeans, her pupils spiralling into blackness and her body growing limp.

I trail my eyes down her torso, the small curves of her shoulders and the extreme synch of her waist, and I walk the last few steps until we're just outside of her bedroom door.

When we reach it there aren't any more words left to say. She brushes the inside of her thigh lightly against my unzipped pants and the swell down there tells her everything that she needs to know.

She squeezes my forearm, silently asking me to release her, so I lower her to the ground and watch as she slowly twists the handle. Positioned right behind her, I cup my hands around her hips and she leans backwards onto me as she pushes the door open.

"I want you to come in," she whispers, head tilted back.

I groan and my hips cant involuntarily as the images of me coming in *her* start to sear their way into my mind. Stomach flexing tight, I lean down and press a kiss to her lips, slowly stroking my hand up the column of her throat.

She shivers against me and I hold her tighter.

Keeping one hand around her neck and the other over her belly I stand fully upright again so that I can survey her bedroom.

It's better than I could have ever imagined.

Her room is tiny and, after just one step inside, it's already half full. It's a clusterfuck of things that were most likely bought for her by other people, in no way, shape or form an accurate representation of who she actually is, and it's probably looked like this since she was five years old.

Doily lace cowgirl curtains and pretty floral bedding, still crumpled from when she rolled out of it this morning. An array of furry little cushions that are both on and off her bed. Wooden walls, wooden bedposts, wooden flooring – the whole damn place is made of wood, which is incredibly fitting all things considered.

Kaleb's Fender, zipped up in its box, is standing ominously in the corner, and a previously lit Sugar Cookie candle sits atop her carved wooden drawers.

Best of all, next to her softly glowing lamp I see the bouquet of baby pink roses that I got for her, taking pride of place on her bedside table.

I drop my gaze, watching her.

She's avoiding my eyes now, twiddling with the ribbons of her bra that's still hanging around her waist. Her long black lashes are casting half-moons beneath her eyes and the apples of her cheeks are burning pink.

I move my fingers over hers so that we can unhook the fastening together and when it slips away from her body I fold it up, propping it on the end of her comforter.

She turns around to face me and I brush my thumb over her flushing cheek.

"Thanks," she says timidly, pointing vaguely to her folded bra.

I raise an eyebrow. Yeah, I'm one altruistic fucker.

Time to give this girl what she wants.

"I've been thinking about taking you in your bedroom since I started coming here in high school," I tell her, my voice deep with need as I back her up against her bed.

She looks up at me nervously, eyes sparkling and wide.

"I used to think about that too," she whispers, her tone quivering. My eyes almost roll into the back of my head. "When you used to sleep next door in Kaleb's room," she continues, fingers shaking a little as she tries to lift the hem of my shirt. "I used to stay up to hear you talk, or sometimes to hear you practicing. The wall planks… the walls are really thin."

Her little revelation makes the cords in my neck tighten. *She used to listen through the walls to try and hear me talk? She used to stay up to listen to me?*

I lift my arm behind my head and, grasping at the neck of my shirt, I rip it off in one quick swoop. Tossing it on the bed I whip my belt through the loops and then I kick off my jeans until I'm only in my boxers.

I watch as Kitty takes it all in, her chest rising and falling fast as she sees what I've got for her.

Tentatively she presses her thumb against the stretched cotton of my underwear and her lips part wide when she feels how solid I am.

"I… I wanna…" she begins, not sure of how to ask for it.

I give my lip-ring a sharp pull. *Yeah, I bet you do.*

But before I can take control, she slips her hand down my boxers, pushing her tits up against my abdomen and panting as she grips my cock.

My brain almost explodes.

"Like this?" she asks breathlessly. She bites into her lip as she squeezes her fist around the thick base of my shaft. She gives it a nervous tug, the gentle, clumsy kind that screams of inexperience, and it's so damn innocent that I have to grit my teeth together to stop myself coming.

I can't speak. I'm still vacuum sealed inside my boxers and the need for expansion room is fucking agony. Exquisite indescribable agony.

Mistaking my stunned silence as a form of indifference she tries a different tactic, sliding her fingers further backwards until she's massaging my sac.

"*Ugh*," I groan loudly, unable to take it anymore. I stumble forwards and in a second she's down on the bed, ass perched perfectly right on the edge. I take my stand between her knees, nudging them wide with my own, and then I take her hands in mine so that she can help free me from my boxers.

Once they're on the floor I kick them away and stand still, my muscles bunched and heaving as I wait for her to tell me what she wants.

I lace my fingers into her hair, tilting her head up to me, and I stroke my thumbs firmly along her jaw.

"Madden," she whimpers, and my cock jerks angrily.

Her eyes widen. My cheekbones burn red.

Yeah, princess. That's what you do to me.

"Madden you're-"

I swallow thickly and give her a curt nod.

"It's just so-"

I nod again, closing my eyes for a moment.

I know, princess. I know.

Suddenly my eyes shoot open, expletives ripping from my chest.

"Kitty, what-" I rasp out hoarsely, heart pounding wildly as I take in the sight.

She's leaning forward between her own spread legs, her cowgirl booties heel-up as she slides my cock slowly into her mouth.

It's involuntary. My hips thrust forward desperate for relief and suddenly I'm halfway in, her hot curious tongue caressing all around me. I grunt, low and tight, bucking further into her as she moans around my tip.

"Kitty, no," I grit out, although my fists are still

clenched in her hair, and my shaft seems to be determined to slide every last inch inside of her. "Not like this," I groan. "We shouldn't be doing this."

I try and pull myself out but she makes a hard determined *suck*, her brow furrowed angrily as if I've pissed her off. I try to raise my eyebrows in question, attempting to understand, but then I'm groaning again as she grazes me with her teeth. She sucks me in tighter and the coil in my abdomen grows heavy, twisting and tensing as she slips up and down.

I grimace as I look down, seeing all of the muscle that she can't fit inside her mouth. For some reason, the fact that she can't do it is even hotter than if she *could*. I wipe one of my hands down my face and then, cautiously gripping my fingers back into her hair, I try and pull her steadily off my cock.

She's not having any of it.

She mumbles something angrily against my swollen tip, and then sucks me back inside with renewed vigour.

Fine. I *do* fucking want this.

I give in to my need to claim, to mark, to fuck, and I push her lips down my length as far as her little mouth can go, withdrawing my shaft in long slow drags and then pushing it gruffly back inside. I spread my feet apart so that my weight is evenly distributed and then I use the thick muscles in my thighs to propel my heavy, quickening pumps.

"*Ugh*, you're a good girl," I grunt, hips thrusting into her rough and sloppy. There are still more than four inches that she can't begin to take but she's enveloped them with her fingers, rubbing and squeezing me the way that I've always wanted. I pull at her hair harder, bucking faster between her lips. When I hit the back of her throat a strangled groan leaves my chest. "You're a good girl, Kitty. You're a good fucking girl."

Eyes locked in with mine and purring sweetly, I realise in this moment that it's now or never. If I don't pull out now I'm gonna come down her throat.

"Kitty," I grit out, trying to still my thrusts. "We gotta… we gotta…"

Knowing that she's never gonna be the one to end this I grip the base of my shaft and then firmly tug until I've slipped it fully out of her mouth. She makes a moan of distress, of emptiness, and I squeeze my eyes shut, needing to block everything out. I'm so hard right now, so ready to come, that I have to restrain Kitty's hands from touching me, the veins up my length bulging angrily with the need to unload.

No, I think to myself, sparks spitting out of my brain. *She's the one who needs to come. Make her come, and* then *you can come.*

I open my eyes again, this time resolute.

I lean down so that I can reach her flushed face and I press a kiss against her lips.

"You're too good to me, Kitty. Never try to look after me first like that again, you hear me?" I ask, pulling away a couple of millimetres so that I can be sure that she's nodding her acquiescence.

She's giving me that huffed pouty look which I assume translates to *no.*

I rub my nose against hers, my hands gently massaging her soft thighs.

"Princess," I murmur, our lips barely touching. "I don't want you to fight me on this one. It's my job to take care of you."

I press my lips to hers and then slowly slant her open, slipping my tongue into her mouth and then rolling it against her gently. I pull it out slightly and then luxuriously sink back in, caressing her nipples with my thumbs as she moans down my throat.

"Okay," she whispers quickly when I move to pull away, her fingers grappling at the back of my neck in a silent plea for me to continue. A cocky grin pulls at the side of my mouth as I slide my tongue back inside of her, teeth tugging at her lip and hands cupping around her throat.

"Good girl," I whisper, the smile unable to leave my voice. "Now lie back for me."

She wriggles her way backwards until she's fully seated on the bed, and then she twists around so that she can get comfy on the pillows.

Which there are about fucking fifty of. I climb on top of her and start tossing them to the floor, and Kitty covers her face with her hands, laughing uncontrollably. They're multiplying like Babushka dolls. I bury my face in her neck because now I'm laughing too.

"Princess and the pea," I murmur, kissing her gently across her collarbone.

"Princess and the pe-*nis*," she says but I cover her mouth with my palm, her smile compressed against my hand and her body shaking with laughter. It's the sexiest thing that I've felt in my entire life and I get that sharp arrow in my chest again, a warning that this is more than lust.

I lift myself up and I crowd my arms around her, loving how right it feels to have her lying here beneath me. Safe. Protected. Hotter than hell.

I dip my head down so that I can take her lips with mine, not waiting this time to fill her up with my tongue. My strokes are long and deep, and I work her until she's slack, her limbs barely able to stay wrapped around me as I slide over and over again in and out of her mouth.

When her pants turn to moans and her hips start grinding desperately against me, I pull slightly away and angle my hips back to hers. I let the length of my shaft knock hard against her belly, a smear of pre-cum rubbing a trail over her skin.

I tangle my fingers in the ribbons at the sides of her panties and tug them away until they're both undone, leaving the cotton gusset to slip down and expose her heat.

A groan rumbles up my throat.

Rose petal pink.

I give my length a few firm tugs.

"You gonna let me take care of you?" I ask gruffly, rubbing her little bud with the head of my shaft.

"Mhm," she says, body splayed like she's already spent.

I watch her pant, her pretty lips parted and swollen from kissing.

"Mhm?" I ask, teasing her a little. I slide my palms beneath her ass, getting ready to ease her backwards so that she can take in the length of me.

She trails her fingers around my biceps, splaying her palms out like she's trying to measure me, but there's a little crease knitting between her brows.

"I'm a little nervous is all," she whispers, so quiet I almost don't catch it.

I still immediately.

Nervous?

She glances up, reading my concerned expression, and she shakes her head, hands now squeezing at my shoulders.

"I'm just not…" She swallows. "I don't really get a lot of opportunities like this, being at the ranch 24/7, you know?"

I blink at her, trying to catch up. I'm not sure if she's saying that she has *no* experience or if she's saying that she has very little, but either way it makes my body hunch over her, more determined than ever to give her the best night of her life.

"Where's my tough girl from the kitchen?" I tease, fitting my tip at her entrance with one hand and gently running my thumb over her cheek with the other.

She crunches her nose up, trying to hide her smile.

God, she's pretty. I draw my fingers through the back of her hair and tell her, "Anything you want, anything you don't want, you just give the order and that's what I'm gonna give you, okay?"

Eyes bright but still squirming a little, she leans up onto her elbows and gives my lip a sharp bite. "Yeah," she whispers, excitement colouring her cheeks. Then she kicks the heel of her boot hard against my thigh, naughtily whispering, "Okay, I'm ready."

My hips buck forward and I plunge right in, her back arching off the bed and thighs spreading as she takes it.

"Madden," she gasps immediately, fingers gripping at my hair.

"That's it, just like that," I whisper, easing out to the tip and then sinking back in a little deeper.

I look down, checking how much more we have left to get inside, and I bite hard at my cheek, seeing how many inches are still to go. *Shit.*

"Princess," I whisper. "I'm gonna have to push a little harder. You think you can take that?" I ask, lifting my chest upwards so that I can watch her face.

Her lips are right in the centre of my pecs and she kisses me sweetly as she nods her head.

Oh *God.* I clasp one hand around the back of her head as I slowly slide back out and then, keeping our eyes locked together, I plunge back inside.

Her face is pinched in pain but she whimpers out a sharp, "*Yes!*"

Holy fuck. I wasn't expecting that. Growling in pleasure, I wrap her hip with my free hand and force her down my length as I pick up the pace of my thrusts.

"This is what you needed, huh?" I ask as she sinks limply into her pillows.

She flutters her pretty eyes at me, not needing to say a word.

"That's what I thought," I grunt. "Such a good girl."

She squeezes her eyes shut, moaning as I thrust her into the mattress.

I reposition myself on my haunches, hands encasing the backs of her knees, and then gripping the ankles of her cowgirl boots I shove her legs over my shoulders. I lower myself back down over her and then start fucking her with deep, slow pumps.

"This is what you want," I say gruffly, my face hardening as my sac slaps loudly against her little ass. "This is what you've been needing, isn't it baby?"

She laps her tongue up the centre of my pecs, moaning dreamily as she tastes my sweat. I slip out of her, hot and wet, and grunt as I push back inside.

"You're a good girl, aren't you?" I grit out, watching as she locks her eyes in with me and starts biting at her bottom lip. "Jesus baby, you're gonna let me fill you up, nice and dirty, aren't you?"

She nods, whimpering, her cowgirl boots crossed over at the back of my neck. My shoulders smack against the backs of her knees and the feel of her soft skin makes every muscle in my body tighten.

I slide out again, possessed by how drenched she is, how perfectly we fit, when a new thought suddenly comes to my head.

"Kitty," I pant quickly, still filling her with sloppy strokes. "Kitty, I'm not wearing a condom," I confess, the realisation not fully registering. I've never taken a woman raw before and the feel of Kitty's pussy is so good she's making me high. Having fantasised about bare-fucking her during every night of my adolescence, condoms hadn't even crossed my mind when we were both ready to go.

Her pussy clenches tight and she moves her hips a little, the soft cheeks of her ass rubbing against me and making me growl.

"Kitty, baby," I plea with her again. For some fucking reason, my thrusts aren't letting up. *I'm going to hell. I'm definitely going to hell.* "I'm clean, I've been tested," I tell her, fingers rubbing at her cheeks to get her attention. "Are… are you on birth control?"

She looks up at me with big baby-doll eyes, a guilty crease toying between her brows.

I raise my eyebrows. Is that a *no?*

She chews on her lip and then starts stroking her hands around my ribcage, avoiding my eyes. I slow my movements because I already know her answer.

We're in purgatory, both shaking in pleasure and pain as we have our silent standoff and try to figure out what to do.

Finally she looks up at me, her hands smoothing over the muscles in my back, and she says nervously, "It's… it's almost my time of the month. Which means that I should have, uh, already ovulated. So… even though I'm bare, it, um, it should be fine. If you… if you come."

I stare down at her flushed face, my eyes burning into her as I try comprehending what she's saying to me.

I'm bare.

She's bare.

And she still wants me to…?

I lift up onto my elbows so that I can look down at her belly, her raised thighs, her perfect little tits. When our gazes meet again I'm so conflicted that I have to dip down and press our foreheads together.

"Kitty…" I groan as her hips grind against me. Ah Jesus, what the hell am I supposed to do?

So desperate for a distraction, anything to prevent me from pulling out of her, I reach up behind my head and rip her cowgirl boots off each of her feet, tossing them onto the floor as I try to calm my breathing. The smooth heels of her feet gently thud against my back and she feels so soft, so sweet, that I bite into her pillow, moaning.

"Please," she whispers up to me, lips moving like silk against my swollen pecs.

I stare down at her, aroused, tortured, and turned the hell on.

She raises her pointer finger and lightly strokes it over my lip-ring. My abs clench tight and my cock jerks inside of her.

Shit. And now she knows that she's got me.

She pushes herself up so that she can lick at the metal, tiny kitten licks that make me grunt like an animal, and slowly I start pushing in and out of her again.

"Fuck, baby," I rasp, letting her play with me and loving every second of it. My strokes are slow and deep and it feels fucking filthy. Knowing that we shouldn't be doing this. Knowing what could happen.

She's so unbelievably slick that I keep on slipping in and out faster than I mean to. I keep my palms firmly on either side of her whilst she toys with me relentlessly, knowing that, when she asks me for it, I'm not gonna be able to stop myself.

She nips her teeth into my bottom lip and pulls it out in a long, languid tug.

I close my eyes and snarl, shoulders hulking and bunching as my whole body coils in preparation. Getting ready for it. Getting ready to give it to her.

I start pumping her a little faster and she begins whimpering against my lips, still holding herself up on one elbow and using her other hand to palm my muscles. *Everywhere.* My shoulders, my biceps, my abdominals… then her exploration pauses until she's reaching right between us, her small palm stroking under me so that she can cup my swinging sac.

"*Ugh*, yeah," I grunt, no longer in control. "That's it, just like that. Keep stroking me, baby. Keep doing that and I'm gonna come for you. I'll come wherever you want."

She falls back against the mattress, hand still rubbing me, and she pulls my mouth down to hers, needing my tongue on her.

"Kiss me?" she asks breathlessly.

Yes ma'am.

I lean down, hunching low, and take her lips with mine. I glide my tongue against hers and she's instantly clenching all around me, thighs splaying further outwards as I wrap my hand around her throat. I keep pumping her, hot and deep, until she finally pulls away gasping, brow arched up to Heaven and limbs so loose that I have to hold her against me with the underside of my forearm.

"That's it," I whisper, her body trembling. "Take what you need. Use it for as long as you need."

She hides her face between my pecs, holding me down against her as she whimpers her way through her orgasm. I pump her right through it until her quivering begins to ease, and then I grasp my hand around her jaw, tilting her up so that I can kiss her again, slow and deep.

I start jerking into her in harder, clumsier thrusts and she tightens her legs around my neck, keeping me in place so that I have to finish inside of her.

"We shouldn't be doing this," I whisper to her, thrusting relentlessly, right on the brink.

"I know," she whispers back. "Don't stop."

Fuck yes. I pull myself up so that I'm raised arms-length over her, and I start pistoning my hips, watching her tits bounce as I get ready to spurt my load.

"You sure?" I ask her, my teeth gritted together.

"*Ah*, please. Yes, Madden, please."

My body clenches, suspended.

Then it unleashes what it needs.

"Good girl," I growl, my body pumping hard. "That's a good girl, taking my load. *Ugh*, taking it just like that."

I thrust into her in loud fast smacks, her lips parted perfectly as I fill her with hot, thick surges. I keep her hips flush against mine until I've pumped out the last of the spill, and then, slowly, I cautiously lay her back against her pillows. She gasps, her body so overly sensitised, and I stroke my hands up her cheeks. Her lashes flutter hazily.

"Kitty," I whisper, encasing her with my biceps so that she's totally protected. Surrounded. Unfuckingtouchable. "Talk to me, princess. Was that okay?"

It was more than okay. It was the greatest fuck that two people have ever had in the whole history of fucking.

But Kitty just blinks up at me, nods a tiny nod, and then purrs a little as she sinks her flushed face back into the pillows.

I try not to get hard again at the realisation that I've fucked the entire English language out of her head. Instead I start stroking at her throat and kissing lightly at her lips. Comatose, she's completely unresponsive, but then she begins to gently trail her heels up the back of my calf.

My body tenses.

Our eyes meet.

And then we're back at it again.

CHAPTER 21

Madden

I woke up at 5am, pride burning through my abdomen as I watched Kitty sleep soundly through her alarm.

One minute. Two minutes. Three. I finally turned it off because it was starting to unscrew my neural wiring but then I scooped her into my arms, kissing my way down her cheeks so that I could wake her slowly.

Now all morning I've been smug as hell knowing that she was so spent after last night that a pneumatic drill couldn't even wake her.

Loose limbed and smiling at me shyly she's attempted to go about her crack of dawn chores the way that she usually would, but she's so energy depleted that she can barely turn a tap open, so I've stayed right behind her awaiting her instructions. They mainly consist of her vaguely pointing to sacks of feed or hay bales that need ripping open, and me hauling whatever she wants right in front of her.

By the time that the animals are fed, cleaned, and

let out to graze, she's all sleepy again. I park it on top of one of the bales from last year's harvest and pull her down onto my thigh so that she can curl up against my chest.

I stroke one palm down her hair and use the other to rub sun lotion onto her legs, trying to ignore the blindingly obvious chafe marks that are peeking out from beneath her shorts. Whatever storm that was supposed to happen last night never came, so the sun's come out with a vengeance, at an insane ninety-plus Fahrenheit.

And it isn't even 8am yet.

Once I'm done creaming up her exposed skin I wrap my hand around her jaw and tilt her chin up so that I can kiss her.

"I wanna give you something," I murmur against her lips, breathing out a laugh when I see her glittering expression. "No, not that," I add, although I definitely *do* want to give her that. "I meant this."

I slip a hand into the front pocket of my jeans, pull out the item, and then press it firmly into the palm of her hand.

When she looks down at it she sucks in a little gasp.

"I can't take this," she says, immediately trying to give it back to me. I half crush her hand trying to stop her from wriggling it free.

"Yes you can. It's not a big deal, I just want you to have it in time for your show."

Her eyebrows pinch severely, fingers still straining to get loose.

"I can't take your pick, Madden. You've had it since you were, like, nine."

"Fifteen," I say, amused. "And it's yours now, so

just take it. It's been lucky for me so I want it to be lucky for you. I want you to win your Barn competition. Yes?" I ask. It's not a big deal, but I'd feel good if she used it when she plays.

"If I take it what are you gonna use? You'll be back on the road in – what? – two, three days?" she says, all sad and concerned.

I skirt my way around answering her question.

"It's not important, baby. I can get another one real easy," I say and then, not wanting any back-chatting, I help her prod the guitar pick into her shorts before pulling her forward and kissing her again.

She exhales prettily, reaching her arms around the back of my neck and opening up for me so that I can stroke her warm and gentle with my tongue.

When one of her hands slides downwards, fingers fumbling with my belt, a chuckle reverberates through my chest and I shake my head. Her body's going to be way too sensitive right now so there's no way that I can give her what she wants.

Do I feel slightly guilty for filling her up like I did last night, over and over again?

Yes.

But was that guilt enough to stop me from doing it to her again this morning, another three times?

Hm.

"No princess," I laugh. "We're just kissing."

She palms at the front of my jeans, no clue of her own limits.

"I wanna do more than just kiss. Before Kaleb comes home," she adds, and hell if that reminder doesn't excite me like a motherfucker.

Uh, *yeah* I want another round of forbidden fucking

before the guy who's meant to be my *best friend* can catch on to what I've been doing with his little sister. The hot pool in my abs starts pulsing dangerously, keen to let the fire spread down low.

I turn my head away from her, jaw clenching as I try to steel my resolve.

"No, Kitty. Not right now," I say, so worked up that my fingers are starting to rip the straw from the bundle beneath us.

She's looking up at me, eyes all twinkly, so I'm refusing to meet her gaze. She's a little demon and she knows it.

When I finally glance down at her she has a small smile on her lips.

I pull my other hand away from her, propping that one behind me too in order to prevent my temptation from mounting any further.

"You tryna get us caught, or something?" I ask, unable to stop my eyes raking her up and down. Jesus, she's cute in the mornings. She's wearing her usual black tank and black shorts combo but her cheeks are flushed pink and her hair's a little static.

And her freaking *boots*…

"Maybe," she whispers shyly, biting back a dimply grin.

My eyebrows skyrocket.

Maybe?!

My fingers bite into the hay at my back, every muscle in my body clenched so that I don't do anything stupid. Like actually fuck her right here in broad daylight.

"I've never had a… a quickie," she continues, face blushing even brighter than before.

I tilt my head back, groaning, and she leans up to kiss at my Adam's apple. God help me. I scrape a hand down my face and then harness it back in the straw, wishing that I could stop the hardening that's currently happening in my pants.

Instead I ask thickly, "What else have you never had before?"

Expecting her to take my question rhetorically I almost spurt on the spot when she presses her lips against my ear and whispers nervously, "I've never… I've never had cum in my mouth."

My eyes shoot open, the blood in my head pounding loudly.

"You've never had…?" I can't get the words out but it doesn't matter because she doesn't let me anyway. She lifts herself onto her knees and starts biting at my lips, chaste and sweet and never ending.

The fact that no man's ever been lucky enough to do that with her, to go that far with her, the fact that that first is there for the taking… I move one of my arms between us so that I can lift her knees over my thighs, splaying her out so that she can straddle me like the sexy cowgirl that she is.

Who am I to deprive her of a morning rodeo?

Just as I go to run my hands down the cute dimples in her back, ready to get my palms all over the round globes of her ass, the sound of tires crunching gravel shoots onto the scene and suddenly she's jumping right off of me, hands quickly smoothing over her hair as she whips around the side of the cabin to see who the hell's just pulled up.

My chest is heaving and I've got so much whiplash that I can't catch my breath. Frustrated and setting harder than concrete, I grind my fists back into the straw and dip my head low as I count to ten.

One, two…

"Hey Pumpkin!"

My head snaps up, immediately on high alert.

It's not her brother.

It's so much worse.

I tentatively stand up, wincing as I adjust my straining hard-on through my jeans, begging it to calm down. Then, following her tracks, I begin to make my way around to the front of the ranch.

I grip my hand in the back of my hair and sigh.

Kitty's parents are back early.

*

Everything was fine until Kaleb got home.

Other than Kitty's initial huff about them sending her brother down here to guard her in their absence – some job he's been doing – the three of them were all smiles and sweet talk from the second that they dismounted their vehicle. Her mom gave me a curious once-over when she saw me leaning by the porch, arms folded, but after a friendly *hello* she got to taking her prized horses from their attached transportation cubby and leading them back to the stable.

Her dad on the other hand was more keen to get to know.

I helped him carry their luggage into the cabin and then, once their truck was all emptied, he stopped me in their kitchen with a scrutinising look on his face.

He jerked his chin at me to shut the front door, implying that our conversation was not for the ears of his wife or daughter.

Eyeing the pistol in his hand, I moved like a fucking army squadron.

"Any incidents?" he asked as soon as the door was closed.

Other than me bare-fucking your daughter? No incidents other than that, sir.

I swallowed, guilty as shit. His eye ticked like a time-bomb.

"No, sir," I said, squaring my shoulders and folding my arms behind my back. Said a silent prayer that his upstairs corridor wouldn't be reeking of sex right now.

"You sure?"

I tried not to bite at my lip-ring, fearing that drawing his attention to it might make him rip it right out of my face.

"Yes, sir."

"And you're the one who's done that stuff to my barn?"

I winced, hoping that "that stuff" was a rare Hardy Hanson compliment.

"Yes, sir."

He nodded slowly, eyeing me up and down whilst leaning against the counter and running his palm up his chin. We were both in desperate need of a shave. I couldn't help but wonder if his woman liked the feel of it on her as much as mine did.

After a beat he sighed and then jerked his thumb at the back door.

"You did a fine job, kid. Now get outta here for a bit."

He didn't have to tell me twice.

I spent the rest of the morning checking the

inventory pages in their admin folder, making notes of the items they were running low on, mainly just to keep out of everyone's way whilst they had their reunion. Knowing that Kitty was probably en route to telling them about her upcoming Barn Bonanza I figured that doing any chores to alleviate her burden would be worth my while.

I chuck the folder back onto the shelf and step into the midday sunlight just as Kaleb puts the Chevy in park. He scopes his parents' car and I watch his face blanch behind the front window. Good luck, pal.

When he dismounts the truck he runs over to me. I can't deny, after my potential close shave with Papa Hanson this morning, I'm now cool as a cucumber.

"Bro," Kaleb says, gesturing his hand to his parents' truck.

I cringe. He really should not be calling me that after the night that I've just had with his sister.

"Hey man," I say tensely, trying to prevent any further familial nicknames.

"My parents are back?"

We both glance over to their car. I don't bother giving him an answer, seeing as it's pretty fucking obvious.

"They're gonna murder me," he says.

I can't argue with him on that.

Sensing his son like a bloodhound, Hardy strides out through the back door. He glances at me, most likely not wanting to air his dirty laundry in front of an outsider, and then, looking back at his son, Hardy points his arm to the side of the cabin.

"Get over here, kid," Hardy orders.

Kaleb slunks forward, head bowed. He's not much

shorter than his dad, but Hardy's presence is unlike anything I've ever seen. Kaleb walks over to him like he's about to get a military bollocking.

He's right, and there's no way that I should be watching this.

I walk over to the fence by the field that the cattle are in, trying to give them their privacy, but Hardy's hushed scolding hangs in the thick July air.

"You call this taking care of her?" Hardy whispers, followed by another sound. Maybe a bucket being accidentally knocked over, or his patience snapping in two.

Kaleb mumbles something. Whatever he said, Hardy didn't like it.

"What the hell does that mean? You were meant to be spending your time here, *with* Kit. I told you to keep my girl safe."

Kaleb raises his voice and says, "She's alive ain't she?"

"That's one smart mouth you've got there, kid. You a comedian now?"

I wince. I'm so uncomfortable right now that when Kitty's aggressive little goat comes over and starts bashing into my legs again, I let it.

"You had *one* job, Kaleb, and it was only to last three weeks. Stay at the ranch, spend some time with your sister – have two people keeping an eye on things instead of having all of this on her shoulders. And you couldn't do that? For your *sister*? What were you doing last night, huh? Go on, tell your old man."

Dead air. I don't blame him.

Hardy exhales. I can practically see him shaking his head in that *kids these days* type of way.

"That's what I thought," Hardy says quietly. "So whilst you were out on the town doing who knows what with who knows who, your sister was working here all alone with barely any protection. In fact, *another man* had to do your job for you because you were so preoccupied."

He lowers his voice but I still catch every word.

"If that friend of yours hadn't been here to keep an eye on things last night, to make sure that no-one and no-thing got to Kit, and if something bad had happened, you would've been kissin' goodbye to this music career of yours and earning your keep like your father does. You're an adult man Kaleb, but family should always come first."

He sighs, his muted tone laced with disappointment.

"Kit can look after herself, I know, but I expected a little more consideration from the brother who hasn't seen her in two years. You're right, everything *has* been fine, but even so… I'm not impressed."

I hear the sound of heavy shuffling and then, after a moment's consideration, Hardy adds on, "And get that goddamned paddling pool out of my yard!"

I press my fist against my mouth, head spinning with everything that I just heard.

When I turn around I see that they've both gone back inside the cabin. Kaleb's probably going to be on house arrest for the rest of the century.

I look out over the pastures as I think over Hardy's words – his desire to keep Kitty safe and his opinions about his kids working off-ranch – and I wonder what repercussions it'll have on Kitty when she finally admits to her dad that her brother's career of being a full-time singer is exactly what she wants too.

CHAPTER 22

Kitty

I have no intentions of telling my parents that I signed up for the Barn Bonanza.

First of all, the chances of winning are slim, so there's no need for me to rile them up when it might not lead to anything anyway.

Second of all, if I *did* win, the sponsorship and recording opportunities are local, so it's not as if I would be giving up my position on the ranch. It would be like taking on a part-time job that could potentially lead to something bigger whilst maintaining my status as Golden Child.

Plus, I don't even know if I would want a music career that's *that* big. I would be more than happy doing what Kaleb's band has done, touring their way across other small towns in the country with their loyal base of listeners and an expedient little income, thank you kindly.

But to hell with my intentions apparently, because

the Universe has other plans.

I'm in the stable with my mom, braiding the horse's hair after a scrub down, when I make my first mistake.

It's ten degrees past volcanic and my hair's clinging to my neck like a scarf so I dig around in the pocket of my shorts, wondering if I've got a saving grace scrunchie in there, when I remember that I can't expose my neck to my mom *anyway*. I squeeze my eyes together and think of how I'm going to be able to keep my hair down and simultaneously survive in this heat, when I pull my fingers out of my shorts and Madden's guitar pick flies out with them.

Mama's eyes slide over to where it's fallen between us, right beneath the horse's belly, surveying it with a vaguely interested expression. Then she lifts her eyes to me, both curious and expectant.

"It's a guitar pick," I say way too quickly.

She smiles at me over the back of the horse, smoothing a hand through the hair that she hasn't braided yet. "Mm-hm," she says, meaning: *go on*.

"Uh, Kaleb said that I could use his old Fender. Because it's in his room. And he isn't using it."

"That's nice of him," she says, expression calm. "And what are you using it for, exactly?"

"Um…" I look around the stable, trying to find a good enough lie.

My mom sighs, then rests her arms on the horse's back and lays her head down between her elbows.

Undeniably she's my spitting image, and when she looks into my eyes I feel like she's hypnotising her way into my brain. Hopefully she can't see *everything* that I'm hiding from her.

I must look Death Row guilty because she gives me

a consoling smile and says, "What's going on in that noggin of yours, Pumpkin?"

I stop braiding the horse's hair and start braiding my own. Then I give my noggin a little rub around the temples, trying to ease the ache in my brain.

"Don't be mad at me?" I ask nervously, looking up at her, unsure.

She shakes her head, still smiling encouragingly. "Go on, Pumpkin. It can't be that bad."

I swallow and look away, feeling guilty for what I'm about to admit. Telling her about wanting to pursue a career separate to the ranch makes me feel unbelievably disloyal. Maybe people who aren't small towners won't understand the extreme importance of familial fidelity, but in a place like this sticking by your blood is rule number one.

"There's this competition in a few days' time and I want to compete in it. It's a music competition for locals who want the opportunity to get a trial run in the local recording studio, plus a sponsorship."

I scrunch up my nose, trying to make the stinging in my eyes die down. I keep my gaze on my glossy toenails, peeking out of my flip-flops.

"I can sing really good, mom, and I think that I could do it. The money would be a good nudge in my bank account, and working with a local studio means that I won't have to leave the ranch. I don't want to leave you and Papa, but I think that it's time that I give some of my own dreams a try." I wince, cringing at myself a little. Then I shake my head and add, "So the guitar pick is so that I can play Kaleb's Fender when I'm onstage, seeing that the show's totally acoustic – like, all the music's live, so no stereo background stuff is allowed. I practiced a little in town when Kaleb was watching over things, and I think that I could do a half-decent job of it."

I shrug and then look up at her.

"So, yeah. That's that."

My mom blinks at me, expression neutral. I shuffle on the spot, nervously awaiting what she's about to say.

Then she presses her chin into her hand, laughing lightly as she shakes her head.

"Oh, Pumpkin," she says soothingly. "Why do you look so scared? That's wonderful news, I don't know why you'd be keepin' it from me."

She rounds the horse so that she can wrap her arms around me, pulling me in for a comforting hug. My lips round in surprise and then I cautiously hug her back, still anxious because I wasn't expecting such a good response.

When she pulls away she's giving me a pitying look.

"Pumpkin, I know that we run a tight game around here but that doesn't mean that your Papa and I would ever hold you back from an opportunity like this. We let Kaleb do his thing, didn't we? Of course the same applies for you. I know we advised you about stopping that Management course you were doing, but that's 'cause we saw how freaking miserable you were. This talent show, this competition or what-have-you, it sounds absolutely perfect. You'll get your salary from the ranch and, if you win your show, we can let you switch to part-time. I just want what's best for you, Kit, please never fear being candid with me."

I blink at her, bedazzled. Then I nod, because I'm too stunned to speak.

She leans down to get the guitar pick. Inspects it before she hands it back to me.

"What a lovely pick," she says casually as I slip it back into my pocket. "What does the 'M' on it stand for?"

I still.

Oh dear. I blow out my cheeks and say the first word that comes to mind.

"Uh… music."

She breathes a laugh. "I'm convinced. And your sheets are out on the line because…?"

"Mom!" I say, mortified. I guess she *can* read my mind.

She runs a hand over the plaits I've given the horse, scrunching her nose up because she really is my freaking twin.

"Your brother was out for the night, his best friend can't take his eyes off you, and you've washed your bedding for the first time in a century. I'm no detective, but even I can put two and two together," she says, looking almost as embarrassed as I feel. When she looks up at me she holds her palms up, pleading her innocence. "I'm not interfering, but this might be tricky when he goes on tour with Kaleb again. And this is going to be weird for your brother – not that it's any of his business, but he's probably going to feel betrayed by the both of you. If this is that serious, that is," she adds, eyeing me with interest.

When my cheeks burn even brighter she exhales deeply and mutters, "Which I guess that it is."

I shake my head, feeling the need to defend myself. "We're just friends, he's gonna be away too much for this to become… something. Anything." My stomach sinks as the words leave my mouth.

My mom raises an eyebrow at me, her face sceptical. "Those his words?" she asks.

I shake my head.

She gives me a knowing look. "Didn't think that they would be. You seen the way that he's been watching you?"

When I shift around uncomfortably she wafts her hand through the air, letting our conversation disperse into secret molecular wisps.

"Never mind, forget that I said anything. It's between you and him, and I trust you with your choices."

Then she says something that I wasn't expecting.

"I'll talk to your Papa about your talent show and I promise he'll be as on board as I am."

My head snaps up. "You don't have to do that," I say, both grateful and terrified.

She pats my shoulder consolingly. "He'll be fine with it, Pumpkin, you're his sweet little girl. Don't you worry about a thing."

*

Madden's hands slide up my belly until he's cupping my chest, palms squeezing gently as he pushes against me from behind.

We're in the kitchen over the counter and I'm chopping vegetables for this evening's salad bowl. My parents are wrangling the animals back into the barn and Kaleb's in his room strumming out slow sad rock songs, meaning that Madden and I are risking a couple minutes of solitude to get a little closer than we should.

His crotch rubs against the back of my shorts and I lean further forward, feeling lightheaded.

"Princess," he murmurs hoarsely, his palm rubbing around my neck. He leans his head forward and starts kissing over my hickey.

I place the knife down because I'm finding it hard to concentrate right now.

He squeezes my throat lightly and a small gasp leaves my lips.

"I'm glad that your parents took the news about the music competition so well," he says quietly, the thick fronts of his thighs pressing firmly into the backs of my own.

Yes, I told him about what happened with Mama. No, I don't want to be thinking about my parents right now.

I turn so that I can look at him and his face is set, dark and hard. I trace my fingers tentatively up his stubble and a low growl rumbles in his chest.

He dips down to kiss me and he slides his tongue against mine, spreading an ache through the peaks of my breasts.

"I want you now," he says gruffly, hands gripping and squeezing everywhere.

I shake my head. "Everyone's here," I say pleadingly. "We'll have to think of some other place, some other time."

He makes another deep noise, and his jaw flexes. "You're my woman, Kitty. They're gonna have to get used to me sooner or later."

I make a little scoffing sound. His irises blaze red.

"Oh come on," I whisper, rolling my eyes in

amusement. "I'm hardly your *woman*. You're gonna be on the road in a matter of days and then it'll be like none of this ever happened." Then, really gambling with my life, I give him a little punch in the chest and add on the word, "*Friend*."

His mouth crushes down on mine and I immediately gasp, inadvertently opening wide for him so that his tongue can slide back inside. He rolls it against me in long, lush strokes until I'm aching so badly that I'm rubbing my heat against his thigh.

He pulls away growling, and then looks down so that he can see what I'm doing. He grasps his hands more firmly around my ass and uses his strength to help me grind harder.

My eyes roll backwards and the warmth in my belly spreads and pounds.

"Oh shit," he grunts, and his voice is so deep that my legs slip wider. "Use me, princess. I want you to use me every day. I swear, the second you let me get a ring on your finger I'm gonna claim you as my wife."

I whimper, too loud, and leash my fingers into his hair. It's so warm, and soft, and thick, and my body grows more limp by the second.

I try and lift myself up in an attempt to kiss his lips when there's a loud knocking to our right and Madden stumbles backwards, all the way to the other side of the kitchen. Sadly, it's a small kitchen, so really it's not far enough. I look at the two feet of emptiness now between us. Just enough space for Jesus.

Not enough space for Papa.

His head was turned away from us, probably, horrifyingly, having heard our little show. My stomach crunches painfully in embarrassment. Madden's standing more erect than an Army General.

When Papa turns to face us he does not look happy.

"Funny. I was just talking to your Mama about this fandango. Didn't expect to walk in on it in *my kitchen* though."

He's looking pointedly at Madden, eyes razor sharp.

"Luckily for you, I heard your nice bit of sweet-talking over there. You mean what you said?" he asks, deep shadows casting under his eyes. God I wish that he didn't carry that pistol all the time.

Madden nods his head. I'm so overwhelmed that I don't even know what they're talking about.

"What's that?" Papa barks.

"Yes, sir," Madden replies immediately.

Papa points his finger at him, thick and weathered. The kind of finger that could gouge out an eye or two. He scans Madden up and down like he's trying to decrypt his DNA. He doesn't seem to hate what he sees but his voice is still low and authoritative when he says, "If I find that you're lying to me, or to my little girl, and you haul ass like a punk…"

His fingers shimmer around his gun. Madden nods in understanding.

My brain ping pongs around my skull, not sure about what's just happened.

Papa turns the pointer on me. I try not to look away in humiliation.

"No screwing in my kitchen. I don't care how old you are."

Then he spins around and leaves, the front door slamming closed, followed by thunderous steps down the porch.

I immediately hide my face in my hands.

"Hey." Madden's voice is hushed as he wraps his arms around me, big warm palms rubbing up and down my back.

I shove him away.

"What the hell are you doing?" I hiss, gesturing wildly to the direction that my dad just walked. "No touching! He's probably gonna ground me for life!"

Madden smiles sceptically, dilating my rage.

"He can't ground you, Kitty. You're an adult woman."

"On *his* property!" I whisper back at him. "Under *his* roof!"

I'm frazzled with anger. Why is it so hard for people to comprehend tight familial relationships? Bully for them if their parents set them free when they were a teen, but not everyone can sever that leash quite so easily.

"Princess-" he begins but I push at his chest when he tries to envelop me again.

"No 'princess'," I snap, at as low a volume as I can.

He narrows his eyes but still manages to swaddle me between his biceps. I put up a weak fight, too distracted by the breadth of his chest to care about the conversation that just went down, and I try not to purr when his heady male scent starts penetrating my bloodstream.

"Did we not just listen to the same conversation?" he asks, his tone hard and firm.

"Yes," I nip. "Papa said no funny business. You're lucky that you got away without a castration."

Madden rolls his shoulders, unleashing another tide of pheromones. Half of my brain has turned to cotton candy mush.

Clenching his teeth he growls quietly against my ear, "He just said that I can make you my wife."

I blink, startled, as he bites at my lobe.

Uh, what?

I shake my head, confused.

"At no point did he say that," I argue, although with Madden slipping his knee back between my thighs my willpower's draining faster than a tractor guzzles oil.

"He asked if I meant what I said about putting a ring on your finger. I told him yes." Madden pulls back, thumbs stroking firmly up my jaw, possessive, in need. "He's saying that, when the time's right, I can have you."

Still miffed about being caught I whisper back to him, "I'm not *his* to give away."

Madden cocks an un-amused smirk at me. We're both angry now.

"True," he says, backing my ass into the counter. "You've always belonged to me."

I knee him away from me and then slide my knife off the counter.

He raises a brow. "You flirting with me?" he asks.

I walk backwards from the kitchen, weapon by my side, a silent message saying *do not touch*.

He follows me anyway.

"Band's playing at the bar in town tonight. Get ready."

I snort. "I'm staying here tonight. With my *Papa*."

His eyes blaze. He doesn't like sharing.

"I didn't ask. I'm *telling* you that you're going."

"And *I* didn't ask. I'm telling you that I'm *not*

going."

"Yeah?" he asks, voice sinisterly calm.

"Mm-hm," I say, cautiously placing my weapon on a side table as I intend to sprint up the stairs in less than three Mississippi's.

I don't even get to Mississippi number two.

"Right," he grunts, before slamming a shoulder into my belly and tipping me upside down over his shoulder.

I squeak like a chew-toy as he strides us into the guest room, locking the door behind him and then throwing me down onto his bed. He quickly rounds it so that he can shut the curtains and, in a second, he's back in front of me again.

Holy shit does it smell like him in here. His crumpled sheets gather around me and my body arches from the feel of them alone.

Luckily I still have one remaining brain cell and I hoist myself up onto an elbow as he chucks my flip flops over his shoulder.

"The hell do you think you're doing?" I ask, eyebrow arched to the High Heavens. "You don't think everyone will have heard all of that?"

He spreads out his knees, settling between my thighs.

Uh…?

"Kaleb's preoccupied with his pity party and your parents are still outside," he says, ripping down my shorts. He's so eager that the zip snarls and the button pings somewhere across the room.

Good God.

He looks up at me, black fringe falling devilishly over his eyes, and he says gruffly, "I'm going down on you 'til you tell me that you're gonna come."

My mouth pops open. I don't miss his innuendo.

"Madden, don't be stupid – *ah*!"

One second I'm hissing at him and the next I'm covering my mouth with my hands as he licks a warm, wet stripe right up my centre. My body bucks off the bed and he releases a pleasured grunt.

"You just tell me the words," he whispers hoarsely, stubble scraping up my inner thighs. "Tell me that you'll come."

My thighs squeeze around his head and he lets out a deep, masculine rumble, dipping back down so that he can kiss and suck some more. His tongue slowly laps me in long eager slides, and my fingers find their way into his hair, so warm and so soft.

No more words leave my mouth until I'm whispering that I'm gonna come.

CHAPTER 23

Madden

I shoot my dad a text as soon as I turn off the engine, my SUV pulling up right next to the Chevy in the reserved parking spaces outside of the bar in the town square.

If all was to go as was planned before we first pulled up at Kaleb's parents' ranch, we were supposed to be getting back on the road this weekend – which is now also the weekend of Kitty's barn competition. I haven't managed to see my dad since I got back in Phoenix Falls and, no matter how uncomfortable being back at our old house makes me feel, I know that I've got to make the visit.

It's not as if we don't get along. My dad's a suffer-in-silence tough guy and he helped shape me into sterner stuff, but I know that once I step foot in that house all of those feelings, all those memories of my mom, all of the insecurities about holding onto what I love and then having it taken away… they'll all come flooding back.

My fingers work the screen. I let him know that I'm thinking of dropping by the house tomorrow morning before his shift starts up at the county police dept, and then I slip my phone back into my pocket, knowing that he checks his cell about once every century so I'll be here all night if I try waiting for a reply.

Then I look out to my left through the driver's side window, straight into Kaleb's passenger side.

Sensing my eyes, Kitty glances through the window back at me. Gives me a scowly once-over. Then turns her face back to the windshield.

After Kaleb's bollocking about being AWOL he's had his tail between his legs, and from the goodness of his heart he told Kitty to ride with him in the Chevy. I couldn't exactly stop him without prematurely unveiling my fucking affair with his sister so instead I kept my mouth shut tight and then tailed his car like a cop, all the way from the ranch to the lot.

I hear Kaleb's car die down as he shuts off the engine and then I get out of my door just as he gets out of his, reaching back inside so that I can pull out my guitar case.

Kitty remains in her seat, a secret war raging behind her eyes.

"You know, I'm kind of stoked to see the guys," Kaleb says, jerking his chin to the car next to mine, the vehicle belonging to our bassist. "It's been a fucking minute."

I nod even though I couldn't care less. The band's group chat aside, I haven't texted the guys at all, and although it'll be fun to play this gig in town, I'm not exactly thrilled with the idea of getting back to touring

– or, more specifically, leaving Kitty.

I lock up the Jeep whilst Kaleb dips back into the Chevy, asking Kitty to move her ass.

I crack my neck from side to side, less than happy with his tone.

When I turn back to face him he gives me an irritated shrug, gesturing to Kitty's unmoved ass.

I bite back a smirk and hold out a hand, palm up.

"You go on and set up the stuff backstage, I'll lock up," I say, like I'm doing him a favour.

He tosses me the keys with no hesitation and heads to the bar's side door without a second glance.

I wait until he's inside before I pull open Kitty's door.

Our cars are big, broad, and submerged in darkness thanks to the lack of invasive street lighting. The space between the Wrangler and the Chevy, especially with Kitty's door wide open, is as private as a confessional.

I lean back against the side of my door, legs outstretched as I wait for her to get out. She's got her cowgirl boots on her feet, her knees under her chin, and her two braids from earlier dangling down over her chest. She's wearing a miniscule dungaree dress that I've never seen her in before and there's a baby pink handkerchief tied around her neck, a cutesy veil to inconspicuously hide the marks there.

I drum my fingers on the top of her open door. She looks away in the opposite direction.

"Silent treatment?" I ask, a little incredulous.

She's really gonna act like I didn't have my tongue between her legs not two hours ago?

Sensing that she's still embarrassed about what happened with her dad, I crouch down between the cars and smooth my palm behind her knee. I'm never gonna get over how soft her skin is. I caress my hands against her soothingly, trying to placate her like a gentleman.

"It's for the best that he knows," I say, hoping to God that I'm not reinvigorating her fury. "All we need now is for the right moment to tell Kaleb, and then-"

"What's the point?" she asks suddenly. "You're going to be gone in a few days."

I sigh. *Shit.* So that's what this is about.

"I hate goodbyes," she adds quietly, and a knife twists in my chest.

"Princess, it doesn't have to be goodbye-"

She waves me off, rolling her eyes. "Yes it does, *rockstar*, that's how it is if you're on the road."

I press my forehead into the side of her thigh as I soak in the fact that she obviously wants our secret situation to continue, to *grow.*

If that's what she wants then like hell am I going to be the one to end it.

I lift my head, looking up at her from my position on the blacktop, and I watch as she rubs her palms flat over her knees.

My eyes trail down her braid and I bite at my lip-ring, wanting another taste of her so badly that my abs physically hurt.

"Look at me, baby," I whisper, ducking my head so that I can catch her eyes. They're shimmery and wet and it makes my muscles clench in pain. I reach my arm up so that I can grip at her chin and stop the little wobble in her bottom lip. "I'm not going anywhere," I promise her, entwining my other hand with hers.

She's so small and warm and I fucking hate seeing

her like this.

"Come on, tough girl," I say gruffly, standing to my feet and tugging her out of the Chevy.

She reluctantly dismounts, but she doesn't close the door behind her, instead keeping us hidden behind it like a shield. She presses her forehead against my chest and I swell like the freaking Hulk. Christ, nothing gets me going like knowing my girl needs a little affection.

I cast a quick glance at the side door to the bar, checking that we're unwatched, and then I let my hands run down her back, rounding my palms over her ass through her denim mini dress.

My breathing starts hitching because she's turned me into a nymphomaniac and, feeling the tensing of my muscles all around her, she looks up at me through her lashes as she cups her hand under my groin.

A strangled groan leaves my chest and her eyelashes flutter closed.

"Yeah, princess," I murmur hoarsely. "I'm always ready when I'm with you."

She breathes a little moan that makes me want to take her in the back of my car.

"We don't have much time," she says, her mind spiralling as she thinks about the band leaving for tour. "And we can't do anything at the ranch."

"After the show," I say quickly, my hips canting against her palm because she's massaging me like a demon. "I'll bring you backstage."

I dip down because I'm about to kiss her when I hear the bar door swing open. My head snaps in the direction of the sound and I breathe a sigh of relief when I see that it's just our drummer. Kitty's face is hidden in the shadows but there's no doubt that he'll know that I'm out here with someone.

I raise my hand to signal one minute and he gives me a thumbs up before heading back inside.

Once he leaves I close up the Chevy, slipping the keys into the pouch at the front of Kitty's dungaree dress, and then I haul her by her hand to the front door of the bar.

"Anyone you know gonna be here tonight?" I ask her, not wanting to leave her on her own whilst we perform.

"I texted River," she says, and I exhale with relief. I've never been so happy to hear that little tyrant's name in my whole life.

"Is she bringing Tate?" I ask, hopeful.

"He's bringing her," Kitty replies, because River is still sans license.

I nod as I push open the door, immediately scouring the room for Tate and his miniature fiancé.

Funnily enough, Chase is here, so I give him a quick handshake before I go and scout out Kitty's accompaniments.

Standing at least four inches above the growing crowd Tate Coleson is not a hard guy to find. They're right at the back, hidden away in the most private area, and that suits me just fine seeing as I'm about to make them guard-dog my girlfriend.

I stride my way over to him even though he hasn't spotted me yet, too distracted running his hands all around River's belly and neck.

River, who is about ten inches smaller than everyone else, manages to see me right away, and she whispers something to Tate that gets him to raise his head, looking for me.

When he catches my eye he gives me a jerk of his chin, although I know that he'd much rather us leave them be, so that he can rub up his woman for the rest of the night.

"Hey man," I say, pulling Kitty in front of me by her shoulders like a piece of cargo. I raise my eyebrows at him, silently asking *look after this one for me, will you?*

He sighs and runs a hand through his hair. His fiancé pulls Kitty into her arms and their bellies press together.

Tate instantly looks down at them, jaw ticking hard when he sees what's happening. Tate, unsurprisingly, is not a sharer, least of all when it comes to his precious bespectacled bounty. He flashes his eyes to me, unimpressed by the girl-on-girl show, as if to say *this is your problem, sort it out.*

"Uh…" I say thickly, not exactly sure where to put my hands. I settle for under Kitty's armpits, lifting her backwards away from Tate's fiancé. "None of that, Kitty. Don't want y'all making an alien or something."

I give her a parting squeeze on the shoulder and then, feeling Tate's death stare boring into my soul, I turn around and haul ass, suddenly keen to get backstage and away from Tate's twitching knuckles.

When I get backstage I'm no longer so pleased.

Kaleb, Kyle the bassist, and Dustin the drummer are all here but tuning his strings with a smug look on his face is also my best friend Tyler. His guitar glints at me and my brain short-circuits.

What, from the bottom of my heart, the fuck?

I'm so stumped that I'm standing stock still right in front of them, too surprised – no, too *mortified* – to even bother saying hello.

Kaleb sees my reaction and nods at me as if to say *I've got this under control.* I raise an eyebrow. So he's really taking the whole "keep your enemies closer" thing to heart, huh? Cannot say that I'm on the same moral high ground.

"Sup," Tyler says finally, his eyes narrowed in pleasure.

Fucking sadist. I'm like one petty remark away from jumping this guy.

"Uh-huh," I say back to him, about as friendly as a punch in the jaw.

I try to diffuse the tension by asking the guys that we haven't seen during the break what they've been up to, what with not living in Phoenix Falls and therefore basically being extraterrestrials. Tyler keeps his eyes on me the whole time, and I charitably restrain myself from smashing his guitar over his head.

When the woman running the bar comes into our backstage nook to ask if we're ready, Kyle, Dustin, and Tyler head up through the thick red curtain to plug in and strum out some crowd-stirring intros.

I turn around to look at Kaleb, although he's almost completely obscured by the backstage darkness, and I hiss out, "The fuck is going on?"

Kaleb raises his palms, trying to placate me. Naturally, I'm suddenly even angrier.

"Let me explain," he says, voice hushed.

Please do.

"Tyler expressed some interest in rejoining and I thought that it might be good to keep a closer eye on him – work out his intentions, see if I'm sweating for no good reason."

"Rejoining?" I grit out, my teeth clenched together.

Rejoining over my dead body.

Kaleb leans in closer, like he's about to give me nuclear codes.

"He actually thinks that she's got her eyes on someone else, and I think he'll tell me who if I get all buddied up to him."

Steam pours out of my ears. *I bet he fucking will.*

"Right," I say stiffly. I can't exactly argue with the band's lead singer when, without him, there would be no band, so I just nod my head again and mutter out another, "Right."

"Let's get out there," he says, slapping me on the back and brushing Tyler under the carpet.

There's no point arguing my case when I can see Kaleb's logic. If I was him, maybe I'd even do the same.

But I'm *not* him. *I'm* his worst nightmare.

I follow him out onto the stage and the cheers and clinks and rowdy crowd noises instantly aid the dulling of my frustrations. With Tyler. With Kaleb. With myself.

I look down at my guitar, suddenly remembering that I'm now without a pick, and I half-laugh half-groan as I realise that my fingers are about to get ripped to shreds.

But I don't even care anymore, which is a dangerous feeling to have. There's only one thing that I care about.

I stroke out my first chord, the stage lights turn low, and when I look to the back of the crowd, she's all that I see.

CHAPTER 24

Kitty

Almost two hours later when the final note is struck, the guys untangle themselves from the wiring and step down off the stage into the adoring arms of Phoenix Falls' leather-clad rock scene, ruddy-cheeked and pumped up on loud music and alcohol.

Except for Madden. Madden stays on the stage.

He unleashes his guitar strap from over his shoulder and pulls his cell from the thigh pocket of his jeans, the thick muscles underneath casting stark shadows across the denim. He steps backwards, away from the low sheathing of warm red lighting, and he catches my eye from across the room. He subtly holds up his phone, before quickly moving his thumb across the screen and then pressing it to his ear.

Guessing that's my signal, I unlink myself from River's elbow, allowing her to become instantly swaddled by her man-mountain fiancé, and I retrieve my own cell from the pouch of my dungaree dress, smiling like a munchkin when I see Madden's name on the screen.

Feeling devious, I answer the call with a nonchalant, "Hello, who is it?"

I see Madden's mouth tick upwards when my voice hits his ear.

"Your boyfriend," he says brusquely, rolling his shoulders as he leans against the side of the stage.

I give him a look of mock-confusion. "I'm sorry, I think you must have the wrong number."

I hear a low growl reverberate through the line. Then he replies, "Hilarious. You should come backstage so that I can show you how funny I think you are."

I squeeze my legs together as I hide my naughty smile, butterflies fluttering in my belly and my limbs tingling excitedly.

"*Ooooh*," I say tauntingly. "What are you gonna do?"

I grin as he shifts his belt uncomfortably, growing agitated as he watches me from afar. I press my back against the wall and twiddle precociously with my braid.

"Uh…" he rasps, glancing around to check that no-one's clocked us. Of course they haven't. No one else here is sober. When his gaze meets mine again a deep flush is staining his cheeks, working its way across his tan neck. "I could do that thing we did the second time, where-"

"How do I get backstage?" I say quickly, the warm pool in my belly suddenly overflowing.

"Follow where I go. When you dip behind the curtain there's a door back here and it leads to the corridor behind the bar counter. There's some offshoot storage rooms and…" he trails off, eyes looking in the direction of the backstage area. Then he winces and runs a hand down the stubble on his jaw, looking pained.

"I know it's fucking seedy," he says gruffly, shaking his head. "I can try and think of someplace else. Maybe I could drive us somewhere, or-"

I shake my head, looking him hard in the eyes.

"Start walking," I say curtly.

"Yes ma'am," he replies.

I shut off my phone and start making my way to the other side of the room, Madden watching me for a moment and then ducking behind the makeshift curtain, away from prying eyes.

I slink into the shadows until I'm just in front of the stage and then I nimbly skirt around the side until I'm peeling back the edge of the curtain and stepping behind it. I can see that his gear is bagged up but it's too dark to make out anything else so I quickly look around for the door and then, seeing it slightly ajar, I quietly step through it.

The corridor is small and narrow and lit by two old wall sconces, a grate-covered window at the end of it showing nothing but blackness from the night outside. A series of storage room doors line the left wall at uneven intervals.

It looks all the more small and narrow when six foot four Madden Montgomery is in the centre of it, his two hundred and thirty pound frame brushing both sides of the walls.

His dark tan skin is glinting with sweat and his chest is heaving more than I realised from the back of the room. I guess two hours of arm-pumping under the heated spotlights will do that to a man.

As soon as I close the door behind me he strides my way, sliding the metal bolt at the top of the frame and then gripping his hands behind my thighs so that he can lift me off the ground.

"Oof!" I breathe out as he squeezes his way down the corridor.

When he reaches the storage room at the end of the line he kicks its partially opened door wider and then forces his way through it. Once we're inside he shoves it closed with the hard swell of his shoulder, removing one of his hands from my skin so that he can twist the key in the lock.

It's a beer bottle holding cell, with the back wall entirely made up of surplus stock. There's a small table lining the right corner, most likely where someone writes down the accounts, and there's a small bulb overhead, sunset orange, providing us with a grand total of one watt of light.

I smooth my fingers into Madden's hair – hot, thick, and damp – and he groans like he's being tortured as he pins my hips against the door.

"No cameras, right?" I ask, quickly scanning the corners of the room.

He breathes out a laugh, shaking his head. "I've learned my lesson, princess."

He wraps a hand around my jaw and suddenly crushes us together, a low growl in his throat as he moves his lips against mine. I slide my hands down his neck and shoulders, my body entranced by the hot slickness of his skin.

"You're drenched," I whisper against him, my

fingers sliding up his black shirt so that I can feel his thick abs.

He swallows hard and pulls away, looking down at his soaked clothing as if he's only seeing it for the first time.

"Shit," he mutters, his breathing still ragged. "I didn't even… I didn't realise. I'm sorry, princess, I should get a shower first."

I shake my head adamantly, forcing him to meet my eyes.

"No, that's not what I meant," I explain breathlessly, hands desperately tugging up his top. I get a low-lit preview of his abdomen and my thighs squeeze around his thickly-muscled middle. "I love it. I love your sweat."

He tilts his head back, groaning, and then rips his shirt off from the back of his neck. He tosses it onto the table behind him and then stands still for my perusal.

Dark, swollen, meaty. I palm my hands across the breadth of his chest, thanking God that he spent his teenage summers hauling boulders on construction sites. He's obviously kept up the weight work and Lord does it look good on him.

"*Huge*," is the only word that I can whisper out, my eyes trailing across his heaving pectorals. I tentatively move my fingers until I'm caressing his happy trail.

"*Jesus*," he grunts, hips jerking involuntarily. He bucks me against the door and I let out a little moan. His hands grip their way from my thighs to my ass.

When his fingers reach beneath the bottom of my dress he pauses for a moment as if he's puzzled. His palms roam around for another few seconds and then his eyes flash up to mine, a hungry glint shimmering beneath them.

"No panties?" he asks quietly, his jaw flexing hard.

I let my silence answer his question.

Then his gaze drops to my dungaree straps, face almost setting into a sneer when he realises that there are no bra ribbons peeking out from under there either.

"No… no underwear," he murmurs slowly, his body swelling against mine.

I nod my head and he sets me down. No more nimble fingers – after two hours on stage his movements are rough and impatient, and he shoves my dungaree straps off my shoulders without grace or delicacy.

It's a micro mini dress that's supposed to be tight and fitted, but I'm a micro mini person so it doesn't exactly work the same for me. As soon as the straps slip down the whole dress drops to the floor, leaving me bare in nothing but my neckerchief and cowgirl boots.

Madden undoes his belt.

"Holy fuck," he grunts, crouching down so that he can pull off my boots.

The second that he sees my white pop-socks he shoves his fist into his mouth and bites down hard.

"Can we leave those on?" he asks desperately, his eyes on their cute lacy trim as he stands upright again.

I bite my lip and nod, sliding my soft inner thigh back up to the side of his bare ribcage.

He snarls instinctively, then tugs hard at his lip-ring, two fingers tucking beneath the cloth around my neck so that he can pull it loose. He pockets it in the back of his jeans and then shoves his pants down to his knees, spreading his legs wide so that he's in a strong position to take me.

My eyes lower to his groin and I feel my body grow drowsy at the sight of his muscle. It's thick and extended, the fat domed head glistening with pre-cum.

"Oh my God," I whimper quietly, my belly muscles clenching with need.

He pulls my face up to his, both of his hands gripping at my jaw, and when our lips finally meet he slides his tongue against my own. I claw my fingers into his hair and press my chest flush against his, my body writhing in agony as his tongue works me until I'm soaked.

"God, you're fucking sweet," he says hoarsely when he finally pulls away. I'm already moaning in pain and he hasn't even started yet. With one hand massaging my ass he uses the other to present himself to me, firmly tossing at his length and then cupping his palm beneath his sac.

I can't even keep myself upright anymore. I let my back press into the wooden door panel, too weak to keep it together.

"Want lube?" he asks, his voice a low scrape.

"You… you have lube?" I ask back, too puzzled by his question to give him the actual accurate answer. In other words: *I definitely do not need any fucking lube.*

He looks away almost nervously, cheeks flushing as he tries to answer.

"Uh, not exactly," he rumbles quietly, brow creasing as he decides whether or not to tell me what he means.

I raise an eyebrow, too turned on for

comprehension.

"I meant that I could, uh…" he trails off uncertainly.

He pauses momentarily. Then he shows me.

He looks me straight in the eyes as he raises his right hand and then, after a second's hesitation, he spits clean into his palm, immediately dropping it back to his length and fisting it all over himself.

"Holy sh-!"

"You should do it," he says breathlessly, the veins in his bicep bulging as he prepares his shaft for me. "You should spit on it," he clarifies, his face almost grimacing with arousal.

"I can't," I say helplessly, one minute away from melting to the floor.

"I want you to," he growls, still giving himself long, hard tugs.

"Madden," I say pleadingly, just needing him to soothe this ache, this emptiness.

Hearing his name seems to snap something in place and he nods apologetically, dipping down again to kiss me.

"I'm sorry, I shouldn't have… I shouldn't have asked that," he whispers as he hoists me up, arms encasing me protectively, and he positions himself against my entrance.

I squirm in agitation as soon as his smooth tip touches my heat, and he grips at the back of my neck, trying to keep me in place.

"You said you'd never had a quickie," he says, looking down at me from above. I peer up at him and nod, tingling with anticipation.

His length, his *girth*. My body clenches before he's

even put it in.

He lets out a low grumble as he aligns us just right and then he says, "I'm gonna give that to you," his palms both moving to the sides of my hips.

"Okay," I whisper up to him, lips moving softly against his sweat-covered chest.

Then his hips are thrusting upwards, his hands are shoving me down, and his entire solid length plunges straight inside of me.

My nipples pinch in shock and I let out a whimper, keeping my sounds muffled as I press my face against his pecs.

"I'm gonna sort you out," he grunts, his strong hips pumping fast. "Get this pussy nice and full."

My eyes roll into the back of my head as he slides himself in and out of me, quicker than ever before.

He rubs his palms down from my hips so that they're positioned behind my knees, and then he shoves them both backwards so that they're pinned against the wall.

My body splays open and he clenches his jaw as he slides in deeper.

I can't comprehend how strong every inch of his body must be – his thick forearms, his large thighs – to keep me in place like this right now, but the hard set of his face shows me that I'm his sole mission, the only thing in his mind as he relieves himself after his show.

I wrap my arms around his neck and softly nip and graze at his throat. He presses himself closer to me, his hips bucking faster.

"You've gone all limp, baby," he grunts, his feet spreading wider as he ruts in from a new angle.

There's no arguing with that.

I try to cling onto him harder, to give him something back, but he shakes his head and kisses the top of my hair.

"No, it's okay, you don't need to do that," he says quickly. "It's my job, princess. It's my job to sort you out."

I clench tight around him and a strangled sound leaves his chest.

He suddenly pulls me from the door, clutching me roughly to his body as he turns around, surveying the rest of the cupboard. As soon as his eyes land on the little table he swipes his forearm across the paperwork, whipping them onto the floor. Then he tilts me down onto the emptied surface, repositioning himself so that he's standing upright between my thighs and my body is spread beneath him.

His palms massage my breasts as he pounds me into the wood.

"There you go, princess," he says gruffly.

I let out a little mewl.

"You're almost there now, aren't you? Almost ready to soak me."

My calves cross behind his back, pressing him down onto me, and a snarl rips from his chest. He heaves his elbows down onto either side of my head, pumping into me harder as my nipples brush against him.

"Give it to me, princess," he rasps, face sneering. "Give me your orgasm and I'll let you take my load."

The tightness inside of me snaps. My thighs fall backwards and my spine arches up, my body only kept in place because of Madden's hands holding me there.

He finishes me as fast as he can, his chest heaving

as he watches me take him, and then he lets out a deep sigh, spreading my thighs wider.

My gaze falls to where we're joined and I feel his hands on me tighten. His hips are barely moving as he slowly slides himself in and out, inches of thick muscle glistening in the low lighting.

He leans down so that he can kiss his way across my forehead, too much taller than me at this angle to be able to reach my lips. He groans in pain when I nibble love bites into his throat.

His palms cup my cheeks and he looks down into my eyes. The veil of lust has almost completely lifted and there's something much more potent shimmering beneath the surface.

"I need to come," he whispers, and his deep timbre makes little flames lick their way up my core.

I nod my head, begging him to do what we both know he shouldn't. My period's due so it shouldn't be too much of a gamble, but in the heat of the moment it's a gamble that I'm willing to take.

"Inside of you?" he asks quietly, slipping back and forth a little faster now.

"Yes," I whisper. Then add, "Please."

That does it for him.

On the sound of my plea his hips jerk forward, hard and uncontrolled, and with a low animal growl he thrusts his spend into me.

"Milk it," he snarls, and my body tightens in shock, encouraging him to give me all that he can. His large palms find my ankles and he pins them down against the table. "Such a good girl," he grunts, releasing himself, warm and thick. "You take it so good."

He pumps my body a few more times and then,

with a final rough jerk, he exhales slowly and presses us forehead to forehead.

"I don't wanna pull out," he whispers as he begins the painful process of leaving my heat.

I whimper in protest despite knowing that he has to, and he groans loudly when he's fully extracted. He immediately cups a palm over my sex, keeping me warm.

"Keep your hips up like this," he murmurs, as he kicks himself free of his jeans and boxers.

At first I don't understand what he's doing but when he slides his underwear over my pop-socks I finally get it.

His eyes meet mine almost shyly, his face flushed and drenched with sweat, more from the after-party than the actual show.

"Gotta put these on you so that it doesn't all..." His face is blushing and he bites roughly at his lip-ring. *Drip out* are the words that he's looking for.

Once I'm fully dressed he kisses at me sweetly, then tugs his jeans over his hips, carefully sliding up the zipper. He reties the scarf around my neck and then strokes at my jaw, my plaits.

He slips his tongue into my mouth even as we're leaving the store room, my head tilted backwards as he rolls gently against me.

"I could go again," he murmurs quietly as we leave the corridor.

I stumble over my boots at the thought of another round.

He presses his face into my hair, laughing at my reaction, and then gives my breasts one final squeeze before he falls back, letting me go on without him.

I turn around and see an unidentifiable expression hardening his features, his eyes narrowed.

"This is the part where we're supposed to get into the shower, make you all warm and clean, and then go back to bed and just…" He shrugs. "Hold you for the rest of the night."

I don't know how to respond to that without screaming that that's exactly what I want. I don't want this to be a secret anymore – I *never* wanted this to be a secret. But in order to stay in Kaleb's good books whilst simultaneously not getting too attached to Madden before he gets back on the road, this is the way that it has to be.

Sensing our emotional synergy, he leans forward to give me one last kiss, light and gentle. Then he buries his face into my neck and takes a shoulder swelling inhale.

I stroke the thick muscles in his back and he shudders beneath my fingers.

"What do I smell like?" I whisper, putting a smile in my voice to try and keep this moment from getting heavy.

"Like you're *mine*," he murmurs back, before pressing a firm kiss into my collarbone.

I reluctantly pull away and step backwards until I'm touching the curtain.

"I'll see you back at the ranch," he promises, gesturing behind him to his kit.

For the last time, he doesn't add, because we both know that he's leaving on Friday.

I nod anyway, then walk away.

I already accepted this fate.

*

Kaleb spent the post-show wind-down rekindling his spark with Chastity, so I make my way over to Tate's truck to say goodnight to River before we all leave. When I step outside of the bar I feel the gentle tap of rain droplets, so I look up to the sky sensing that the storm that's been brewing is en route to letting loose.

River is sat in the passenger seat, feet dangling over the blacktop, whilst Tate hunches through the car doorframe, pressing kisses over her cheeks and attempting to strap her in. When River catches my eyes over Tate's shoulders she gives me a mischievous smile.

"Passenger princess," I say to River when Tate removes himself from the car interior, not sparing me a glance as he rounds the front so that he can get into the driver's side.

"Yeah," she replies naughtily, pulling her knees up so that she can curl on the seat like a cat.

"Must be nice," I say, gesturing vaguely behind me in the direction of the Chevy, parked somewhere on the other side of the lot. "I'm cruising with my brother. I'm lucky if I'm a survivor."

River laughs and then glances behind me, trying to catch a glimpse of our pretty blue truck. I squint my eyes skyward as the pellets begin coming down harder, fat cold raindrops hitting off my cheeks and exposed shoulders.

I shudder slightly at the feel of the cold, foreign to me now after so many weeks of scorching heat.

When I look back down to River, about to say my goodbye, I notice that she's suddenly frowning, leaning up onto her knees as she tunes into something that's going on across the lot.

"What's going on over there?" she asks, pushing her glasses further up her nose. Tate gently un-straps her so that the belt doesn't cut into her chest.

I glance over to where she's looking, hearing the low sounds of an escalating spat. I snort and shake my head.

"Probably two idiots about to fight," I say, re-braiding the end of my plait.

River throws me a serious look that makes me still my fingers and then jabs her thumb towards the scene, eyebrows climbing higher by the second.

"Isn't that *your* idiot?" she asks, her eyes shooting back to the growing noise.

Now it's my turn to frown.

What?

Unsure of what she's talking about I stand on my tip-toes to try and catch a glimpse of where the hushed growls and grunts are coming from.

As soon as I do catch a glimpse, I'm no longer interested in fixing up my hair. I'm running as quickly as I can to the other end of the lot.

Oh shit.

CHAPTER 25

Madden

One minute earlier

Once I pack up all of my gear I trudge my way through the quickly emptying bar, out of the front door, and then straight over to the Wrangler. I unlock it so that I can set my guitar down in the back and then I turn to the truck next to me, brow furrowing as to why it's still here.

Shouldn't Kaleb have taken Kitty home by now?

I look at the pitch black sky, not liking the turn that the weather has taken.

Rain on the roads when Kitty's being driven home…

I look around the lot, jam-packed as the patrons descend, picking up taxis or generally milling around, but I don't see Kaleb anywhere. I try and remember if he was meeting up with anyone after the show but my head is too scrambled for recollections, having just obliterated every thought out of my head after the hottest fuck of all time.

I shift my belt, already feeling the need to take her again.

I'm just opening up my driver's side door when I hear a voice behind me.

"Nice neck, man."

I turn around and look at Tyler, his expression glib as hell.

Here we fucking go.

"What?" I ask him, trying to keep my own face neutral. It's kind of hard to do when your eyes are turning red.

"Your neck," he says, over-enunciating each word. "I bet it matches Kaleb's sister's real nice."

I squeeze my fists behind my back, begging myself to not bite the bait.

Kitty's been wearing a scarf all night so I know that he hasn't seen her neck, but I sigh internally as I realise that I never bothered to check my own.

Tyler continues. He really shouldn't.

"You come out here black and blue like you've been shacking up with a vampire, and Kit's in our crowd with her neck all hidden?"

I try not to laugh when he says *our crowd.*

Who does he think he is? Jimi Hendrix?

"With all due respect, which is none, I'm sure that it's just a coincidence," I say curtly, trying to kill this conversation in its tracks.

Tyler pulls out his CPR pads and replies, "A coincidence the size of Quebec."

Stay calm, Montgomery.

"Drop it, man," I say steadily, although I'm twitching to let loose on this guy.

He gives me an unfriendly smile. I give him one back.

"It's a little cruel if you ask me," he says, putting on the whole Patron Saint act. "Fucking her brains out before you leave without a trace-"

I slam my door shut and squeeze my nails into the palms of my hands.

"Your wiring twisted or something?" I ask, jaw ticking like a time-bomb. "I said drop it."

He shoves his way into the gap between the SUV and the Chevy, getting right in my face. Obviously he has a screw loose. I gauge that he's over two hundred pounds but my muscles swell in the knowledge that I'm about to crush him like a grape.

"Couldn't keep it in your pants for three fuckin' weeks, huh?" he snarls, his own hands twitching violently at his sides.

Okay, so he must have seen us go backstage. But he's not Kaleb, so his knowing anything doesn't mean shit to me.

I try not to smirk when he presses his gym-hardened chest up against my own. Guys like him with their designer weights… try hauling metal on a construction site, asshole.

"You tryna dance, sweetheart?" I ask when he pushes me up against my own door.

And I thought that *I* had anger issues. This guy has even less of a right to get pissed over Kitty than I do, and he's vibrating like he's about to detonate.

"You're one cocky bastard," he grits out, and suddenly I'm not laughing anymore.

Getting called a bastard when you've only get one parent left… an ice cold chill runs down my sternum as the increasing raindrops lash at my skin.

"What did you just call me?" I ask, finally pushing back on him, serial killer calm.

"I said that you're-"

"Madden, don't!"

My head snaps up at the sound of Kitty's voice and I see her running towards me from the other side of the lot, the blur of the rain obscuring her small body.

I instantly hold my hands up in surrender, letting her know that if she doesn't want me scrapping then I'm not about to continue, and I feel the change in the air as Tyler similarly accepts defeat.

No point fighting over a chick if she doesn't actually want you to.

I shove past him and start striding towards her, actually completely thankful that she just nipped that shit-show in the bud. I want her in my arms. I want her in my bed.

The rain splashes up my jeans as I storm my way forwards, a new idea, a new future, suddenly flashing in my mind crystal clear.

I'm about twenty feet away from her when I hear the sound of skidding tires.

A huge truck, lifted as hell, swerves its way around the bend in the lot, plummeting down the blacktop like it's trying to go back to the fucking future.

It's Chase's car.

And it's heading right for Kitty.

"Baby, move!" I bellow, hurtling towards her. I see the exact moment that understanding dawns on her face.

She spins on her heels, sees the truck a second away, and then throws her body down sideways in an attempt to miss its bumper.

The driver, seeing the impending collision, spins the wheel drastically, and runs a wide uncontrolled U turn, the tires completely skewed.

I stay on my spot, panting, having only scraped the turn of the truck by the skin of my teeth.

And then my eyes find Kitty on the ground and I'm on her in less than three seconds.

"Kitty!" I say breathlessly, knees wet as soon as they meet the rain-coated road. I quickly scan her body, an erratic pulse in her neck and her hands impaled with dirty gravel.

She breathes out a shaky exhale and then whispers, "It missed me. I'm fine."

A wash of relief sheathes my throbbing brain.

I wrap my arms around her, burrowing my face in her hair and shielding her from the rain.

My worst fucking nightmare. My worst fucking nightmare almost came to life right in front of me.

A surge of emotion swells in my chest, the memories of losing my mom suddenly unlocked. The way that it felt to have the person you love the most taken away from you without a goodbye. The fears of cars and driving that it took me years to finally overcome…

It could have happened all over again.

I press a series of hard kisses onto her small warm shoulder, easing her body off the blacktop and setting her gently onto my thigh.

She turns her head slowly to face me and my eyes immediately fall to the top of her cheek. A series of angry red scrapes glimmer with blood in the moonlight.

My rage goes stratospheric.

"That fucker," I growl out, hauling us both upwards so that I can get my hands around Chase's neck.

"Madden, I'm fine," she says quietly, stroking at my arms like she's consoling *me.*

I run a hand down my face. *Calm the hell down.* If I hadn't been about to fight Tyler in the first place, none of this would have ever happened.

I nod at her, although I'm seriously considering turning Chase into a Slushie beneath the bonnet of his car, and I lift Kitty up to kiss her, holding her gently against my chest as the rain streaks between us.

"We should take you to hospital," I murmur, wincing when I catch a look at her grazes again. "Oh baby," I whisper, stroking my fingers around the area.

She shakes her head. "We can disinfect it at the ranch. I'll be fine. It's all fine."

I move us safely to the curb and then kiss her again, longer and deeper. For a second I think that she's pushing at my chest, telling me to get off of her, but maybe my head's going crazy, so I keep kissing her anyway. I run my hands over her thighs, so fucking happy that she's right here, but she taps fervently at me again and this time I do pull away.

Her eyes are wide open, raindrops hanging like little crystals in her criss-crossed bottom lashes.

"What is it?" I pant, trying to read her expression. "Did you change your mind? You need me to take you to the hospital?"

She shakes her head and her eyes slide over my shoulder.

I know that it's him before I even see him.

Not now. Please not now.

"Kaleb," I begin, turning slowly around, gently dismounting his sister from her straddle around my waist.

His face is the darkest shade of red that I've ever seen.

"She was running, and there was a car, and she had to jump out of the way-"

"Why're you holding her like that, man?" Kaleb asks, his brow low and his eyes sharper than a knife's edge. He takes a step closer. "What the hell do you think that you're doing?"

"Let me explain-"

"Don't tell me that there's something going on, man. Don't tell me that you've been messing around with her."

I feel Kitty hide herself behind me, her little paws clinging to the shirt at my back.

"I'm not messing around with her, Kaleb, it's not like that-"

"*It* shouldn't be like *anything*," he bellows, arms slicing through the air. "She's my *sister*. You're my *best friend*. You think I can work with you everyday if I know that you wanna get with her? Or, worse, if you've actually *been* with her?" He drops his face into his hands, his angry façade crumbling. "Please tell me that you haven't been with her."

I keep my mouth shut.

"You know what, don't tell me. Just promise me that you'll stop this. We're going back on the road in *two days*. I don't want this to ever be brought up again."

I'm confused by his speedy dismissal, his desire to brush it under the carpet, and I'm thinking that he's taking the news pretty well until Kitty peeps out from around my back and his face sets into steel.

"You can kiss the Fender goodbye," he snaps, jabbing his pointer towards her.

"But Kaleb, my show-!" she begins, voice pitched high with suspended tears. Kaleb shakes his head, looking stone cold betrayed.

"My best friend? Really Kit? Couldn't get someone of your own?"

"Kaleb-"

"And now you think that you can be a little rockstar? Trying to impress *my* friends?"

Sibling rivalries aren't something that I understand having never had any siblings of my own, but what I'm gathering from the tension radiating from Kaleb is that the concept of sharing does not exist here.

"Kaleb," I say, aware that I'm probably overstepping a boundary. "If anyone should be punished for keeping this from you, it should be me. Don't take this out on her, man. She hasn't done anything wrong."

Kaleb continues talking as if I haven't said a word.

"Drive yourself home Kit. I'm not hitting the ranch tonight."

He turns on his heel, rain water spraying up his calves, but then he hesitates for a moment and spins back around.

"And you?" he says, turning his lasers to me. "I want your ass off the ranch by tomorrow morning. When we're back on the road, we never speak of this again."

I'm too stunned to speak. Never in a million years would I have thought that in this situation Kaleb would turn on *Kitty* rather than me.

Kaleb thunders away, and I spot Chastity waiting for him with a group of her friends.

I turn to talk to Kitty but she brushes straight past me.

"Kitty," I say quietly, trying to chase after her without getting her brother's attention again. "Kitty, I'm sorry, I can fix this."

She throws me a look and then starts sprinting to the Chevy, too distraught to care anymore.

CHAPTER 26

Madden

I tail her like I'm trying to give her a ticket the whole way back to the ranch, throwing myself out of the door the second that the car's in park and chasing her up the porch steps like I'm trying to fulfil an SAS operative.

Damn is she fast.

"I know that it's my fault, Kitty," I pant, taking the stairs two at a time whilst she sprints ahead like the Duracell bunny. "If I hadn't been careless like that then you wouldn't have been in harm's way tonight, and then I wouldn't have been all over you in public, and then Kaleb wouldn't have confiscated his guitar-"

"Meaning that I can't do my *show*, Madden! My *one* ticket to get me off of this ranch, slow but steady, and now it's gone!"

She throws her hands up to her face, scrubbing away too many tears for me to handle, so I lean down to try and scoop her up before she can get through the front door. She swats me away like a fly.

"We had *two days* to go – only *two days*! And now you're going to be back on the road, all buddy-buddy, and I'm going to be stuck here with no contest to go to, nothing to show for myself, nothing of my own, and nothing to make *me* happy."

Fuck, I'm such an asshole. I tug hard at my hair, trying to think of a way around this.

The only solution that I come up with is her singing a-cappella, but half the point of the talent competition is showcasing layers of musical talent. Which she has. In fucking buckets. It would be an insult to even say it so I keep my mouth shut, racking my brain for another avenue.

Too slow. She yanks open the door and bolts straight up the stairs.

I'm about to start mounting after her when her mom appears at the gallery balcony. Sees Kitty's tears, the blood on her cheek.

Gives me a look that says I'm about to be vaporised.

Kitty slams her bedroom door shut and her mom starts descending the stairs, her eyes swinging over the railing towards the pistol mounted on the wall.

Fair enough. I raise my hands in surrender for the second time tonight.

"I swear," I start, shaking my head from side to side. "I swear that it's not what it looks like."

"If you laid a hand on my girl," she whispers, eyes slicing me up like salami, "you'll be leaving this property a couple muscles lighter."

I don't fucking doubt it. I nod in understanding.

"There was a car accident – no, an *almost* car

accident," I correct myself, then saying a quick *thank you* prayer to God. I shake my head, trying to clear the mist from my brain. "She was running over to me, it was streaking with rain, and this fucking lampshade with a licence-"

"Watch your mouth."

"Sorry, ma'am. I mean, this guy who can't tell his elbow from his earlobe spun out into the lot and Kitty had to throw herself down to avoid being hit. She..." I try not to let that painful bubble in my chest swell too high up my throat, an uncomfortable stinging feeling prickling behind my eyes. "She cut her cheek during the fall, but she didn't let me check it out..."

Marie's expression wavers a little, less enraged now that she knows that we didn't just have a domestic. A perplexity still remains as she tries to work out the reason for Kitty's anger.

I raise my hand, gesturing in the direction of Kitty's bedroom door, and then, keeping my voice low, I say, "Kaleb found out about..."

Shit. Does *Marie* know? I can't freaking remember. I know that Hardy knows, but I don't exactly want to give Marie any more ammo for wanting to hack off my balls tonight.

Fuck it. Hardy will have told her.

"Kaleb found out about my... *seeing* your daughter," I say, not sure of the best alternate verb for *incessantly fucking*. "And he won't let Kitty use his guitar for her show anymore. Which means-"

Marie holds her palm up, nodding. She knows what it means.

It means that Kitty's get-out plan is scuppered and it's all my fucking fault.

"I want to talk to her," I say, eyes on the upstairs corridor, but Marie shakes her head.

"I should talk to her first, try and calm her down a bit. Perhaps in the morning you can…"

A new realisation dawns on the both of us. I can't stay here tonight.

Kaleb and I were only supposed to stay here until this Friday, but with the predicament that I've just put her daughter in, I have no right to stay under the Hanson Lu roof.

Where can I crash for a couple of nights?

I turn to look out of the window. My Wrangler shudders in the rain.

Great.

"I'll come and collect my stuff in the morning," I say, not wanting to even step inside the guest room tonight. I have well and truly outstayed my welcome.

Marie nods, a surprisingly compassionate look on her face.

She really is the mirror image of her daughter.

I look at her for one hard moment and then turn myself around, heading back out into the night.

*

I tap my thumbs on the steering wheel, my eyes glued to the bungalow in front of me.

My dad never sold it after my mom died. I mean, there was no need to down-size – it's a *bungalow* for crying out loud – but even with the constant reminders of her, he decided to never close that door.

I chew at my lip-ring, unsure about whether I admire or pity him for that. Maybe both.

It's almost six in the morning and I know that he'll be up with the cawing crows, so I begrudgingly heave my aching body out of the Jeep and I start trudging my way up to the front door.

After all of these weeks of warmth my body is now freaking freezing, the sweat from last night's show clinging to me like sticky ice water, and my car's battery en route to death after power-blasting the heating system during the midnight storm.

I pound my fist on the door. A large shadow appears behind the frosted window.

"Dad?" I call out loudly, aware that we hadn't properly arranged a catch-up before my show last night.

He pulls open the door. I'm met with eyes not unlike my own.

He tilts his head behind him, offering me to come inside.

I nod in response and kick my shoes off before I enter.

The second that I step foot inside I'm sucker-punched with the memory of my mom. The embossed wallpaper, the framed family photos, even that freaking buttery-citrus scent. Glass shards pierce the backs of my eyes but I squeeze the pain aside as I duck under the door frame and into the kitchen.

My dad does the same. We are two tall dudes.

His brain is clearly on the same pathway as mine.

"Too tall for this place," he grumbles, sliding his chair out from under the little table with a loud scrape and then spreading his thighs ten metres apart. He pulls his plate closer to his body and stuffs a wedge of bagel into his mouth.

I check the label on the jelly next to his plate.

Peach. Nice.

"Well, sit down," he says, pronouncing it *siddown* with his deep officer drawl.

I sit and he grabs a spare glass, shoving it across the tabletop for me to pour some orange juice into.

My heart tightens in my chest. *Why didn't I visit him sooner?*

I breathe out a sharp exhale. He squares his shoulders like I'm about to give him the name of his next inmate.

I let out a grunt of discomfort. Then, thinking that I should start light, I ask, "How're things?"

He rolls his eyes as if my two year disappearance act didn't even happen, just as at ease with me now as he was when I was a full-time resident. "You're twitchin' kid. To answer your Q, same old same old. But let's cut the crap, and tell me what's on your mind."

Thank God we both hate small-talk.

"There's this girl," I say, dropping my head into my hands.

I swear I hear him chuckle lightly. The room suddenly grows ten shades lighter.

"What about her?" he asks.

I lift my head and watch as he toys distractedly with the little spoon in the sugar bowl.

Jesus Christ, I remember the day that my mom bought that thing. It's a vintage ceramic affair covered in birds and ribbons, and when she took it to the till I thought that it was so ugly that I cried.

Seeing it right now I've never been happier.

"She's my best friend's sister," I say, keeping my eyes on the bowl.

He lets out a low whistle.

Yeah. I know.

"She like you back?" he asks, his stare warm on my face.

I hesitate, then nod.

"And it's the brother who don't want y'all together?" he continues, Detective Montgomery over here.

I nod again.

Then he surprises me by saying, "Well, what's his freaking problem? You like her, she likes you, and I know I raised you to treat your woman good. Why the hell's he throwing his toys out of the pram?"

I bury my face harder into my hands, squeezing my eyes shut. "Sibling rivalry? Jealousy? Ownership? I don't know, dad, I'm not a psychologist."

He gives me a sceptical look and mumbles, "Kinda sound like one to me."

I breathe out a laugh and meet his stare, looking away quickly because he is one intimidating guy.

"I work with her brother – he's the lead singer in our band. And the weird thing is that he's taking this whole thing out on her instead of me. Plus, I'm meant to be leaving town this weekend, meaning that this whole thing with her will be getting put on pause anyway…"

My dad remains silent for so long that I finally have to look at him again. His eyebrows are raised high and there's a disbelieving curve to his lip.

It takes me a moment, but then I finally understand.

Why the hell would I put my relationship with Kitty on pause?

Why, when I finally can have her, and when I can maybe help her achieve her *dreams, would I ever leave her again?*

I slap my hand on the table, ideas exploding in my mind like meteorites.

"I've gotta do some things. I'll be back after your shift, Pops."

I see his mouth curve into a smile and then I race from the house, straight to my car. My head is whirring with the names of the people who I need to get in touch with, but I try and compartmentalise all of that so that I can focus on the task at hand.

I have a lot of calls to make this morning, to a lot of people who won't be expecting to hear from me.

When I get back to the ranch, Marie's outside the barn, her head turned in my direction as soon as I dismount the SUV.

"Morning, ma'am. Is Kitty up?" I ask, breathless and pumped up on adrenaline.

She frowns slightly, her tone cautious. "She's sleeping in today. You're not going to try and talk to her, are you?"

I shake my head. "No, ma'am, I'm here to collect my things."

Well, *most* of my things.

When she gives me the go-ahead to let myself inside I tread fast but quietly to the guest room. I shove all of my stuff into my bag and then throw it straight into the back of my car, going quick so that Kitty can't catch me in the act.

She's not going to fight me on this one.

Once my bag is down I look at the item laid next to it, allowing myself to feel a wash of nostalgia and finality before I pick it up. I stride silently into the cabin and up to the corridor outside of Kitty's bedroom.

I hover outside of her door for a moment, wishing that I could tell her that I've found a way out for us, but I decide that I can wait for the right moment, once she's ready and it's all sunk in.

I hold up a scrap of paper against the wall and then scribble out a quick note, saying all that needs to be said.

Then I lay my guitar outside of her room and place the note on top.

All that it says is "*what's mine is yours*".

CHAPTER 27

Madden

I grind the heel of my work boot into the gravel at the back of the crowd, fists clenched over the top of a discarded silver blockade used to keep the Barn Bonanza audience in some sort of order. My eyes are trained on the stage, a makeshift wooden construction standing in front of the large barn, situated at the rear of the colonial hotel. I scan the building briefly, awash with memories from when I was still a teenager, just before I went away for our tour.

It's the building where Kitty had her prom two years ago, an event that she basically carved out solo with her bare hands. Out of a sibling loyalty that her brother doesn't share, Kitty had hired our band to be the performers of the night, letting us take the stage for the first time in a venue that wasn't a bar or a warehouse or somewhere covered in ten years' worth of grime.

It was cool and I loved every second, but my

favourite part of being there took place *after* we dismounted the stage.

Over the years Kitty had been begrudgingly tolerant of me whilst I became best friends with her brother but more than anything I was still a nuisance. When we were at high school together I couldn't spot her in the corridor without trying to get her to engage with me, to humour me, to let me spend ten freaking seconds with her. I tried to join her fifty-thousand committees and I made sure as hell that I was in her eye-line, taking part in every sport that was available on our campus.

But it was once I'd graduated and Kitty was at her farewell-to-high-school dig that she finally spared me a minute. She finally let me talk to her, to take away a few bricks from that wall she'd built up, to show her that I'm more than just her brother's best friend.

Luckily for me, it turned out that maybe she wasn't so impassive about me after all.

We kissed. A lot. And it was enough for me to know that she was exactly what I wanted.

So why the hell would I give that up now?

When the current act finishes the host announces from the side the name of the next performer.

I take in a deep inhale when I hear Kitty's name.

I wasn't sure if she'd even be competing today so showing up was kind of a gamble, but deep in my gut I trusted that she would accept what I'd given to her and do this for herself.

I received multiple texts along the lines of "*Is this your guitar?!*" with Kitty stressing about how I could let her use it when the band would be out of town by the time of her competition.

And the band is. I just didn't go with them.

I shake away the past few days and re-focus on what's happening on the stage.

Like two-way traffic the most recent performer heads back behind the barn and then, walking towards the audience, Kitty suddenly appears.

I shove my hands into the front pockets of my jeans, soaking her in like syrup on a waffle. She's wearing a little floral dress that's puffed up like a dandelion cloud, chiffony pink and dotted with flowers. She's going for the farmer's daughter look, the pure home-grown American Dream, and I'm hooked. There's a brown cowboy hat atop her head, her usual cowgirl boots slipped over her feet, and then, best of all, a shiny black guitar slung over her shoulder.

The guitar that I gave to her.

My body swells with pride.

She takes her place behind the microphone, plugs in the guitar, and then starts twiddling with the stand, attempting to wind it down to Kitty-height. It takes a good ten seconds for it to reach her tiny level. Then she lets out a little cough and does a quick "*one, two, one, two*".

She flicks up the brim of her hat and reveals her sparkling eyes, glittering wildly in the early evening glow.

Then she strums out the first chord, a warm sharp *twang*, and parts her lips to begin her song.

My heart swells in my chest when I register what she's singing and I bite hard against my lip-ring to try and keep my emotions in check. She's singing *Make Your Own Kind Of Music* by The Mamas and The Papas, and it's so fitting that my body almost can't take it.

This freaking girl.

As I watch her I realise that she's got a small daisy shaped plaster on the tip of her cheek, something that I hadn't noticed when her hat was tipped low. It's inconspicuous enough to look like one of those cutesy kids tattoos that chicks sometimes dot themselves with in the summer, but I know that she's using it to cover up the graze on her cheek.

A waft of red mist sheathes my mind for a moment.

The only thing stopping me from pulling up to Chase's apartment and knocking him into next Sunday is the fact that, one, Kitty told me not to, and, two, she really liked that cookie that he made, so I don't want to deep-fry her favourite baker in case she gets a craving again.

I pull myself from the fog. I have something much better to focus on right now.

I stare at her, captivated, until the very last note, goose-bumps prickling my arms and my chest rising and falling fast, in awe of the talent that the whole audience has just laid witness to. The crowd erupts into claps and cheers, not aware that behind her beautiful performance there were a million obstacles and moments of doubt that very nearly almost prevented this from happening.

The second that she dismounts the stage and starts walking away from the panel I immediately kick myself into sixth gear, heading straight for her.

She moves with delicate steps, like a weight has lifted from her body after taking the leap, after giving herself this opportunity, and she hides herself away from the rest of the competitors, ducking inside of the barn instead of behind it. I keep my tread light because

I don't want to shock her and I watch for a moment as she kicks gently at a stray piece of hay. Presumably this barn is now solely used for events because it smells pine-fresh and there are fairy lights strung around the beams.

She's got her back to me but I can tell that she's looking down at her guitar, fingers gliding tentatively over the polished surface.

I lean a shoulder against the doorframe, crossing my ankles as I tap a knuckle against the wood.

She spins around, eyes wide, a kaleidoscope of emotions flashing across her face.

"Hey princess," I say, my mouth lifting at the corners. "You sounded beautiful out there."

Her eyebrows lift higher, irises all shimmery.

"You're supposed to be on tour," she breathes out, scanning me up and down like she can't believe that I'm really here.

I decided not to let her know what was going to go down when she was texting me, because there was no way in hell that I was going to let her try and talk me out of it.

"The band left this morning," I say. "I sent a replacement."

"A replacement?" she asks and her brow twitches in confusion. It's gratifying as hell that she can't remember which person could possibly take my old spot in the band.

It looks like Tyler came in useful after all.

"Yeah," I say, pushing my body off the wall and taking a step forward. Just a small step, because I'm not sure if she's still miffed at me about ripping the band-aid with Kaleb. "And I got in touch with Jace, an old boss of mine, so that I could secure a job back in town."

I swallow, really nervous now, because I have no idea if she actually still wants me.

"I'm staying in Phoenix Falls," I say, "so that we can pick up where we left off. Maybe we can start spending some more time together – if you'd like to, I mean. For as long or as little as you'd like. I'm not saying that you have to spend your whole life with me–"

She closes the space between us, the guitar nudging against my abdomen.

The twinkly smile on her face makes my chest heave and swell.

"Madden," she whispers, stretching up onto her tip-toes. "I would spend all of my nine lives with you."

My heart explodes, and I grab her face and kiss her.

She gasps into my mouth as I hold us firmly together, sliding my tongue gently against hers as she strokes at my neck, one-handed.

I pull away and she laughs as her cowboy hat is damn near falling off her head. I set it down with her guitar on the large wooden worktop, and she places my old pick on the top of the pile like a cherry on a cake.

I bring her into my arms again and move her over to the tabletop, letting her clamber onto it as I stand between her thighs.

"Nice location too," I say, grinning kind of cocky because this barn at this hotel is where I kissed her for the first time.

She runs her fingers up my forearms, looking sweetly into my eyes.

"Back where it all began," she smiles, crossing her calves behind my back.

I shake my head, smiling back at her. "Baby," I say. "I was in love with you way before your prom night."

She gasps at my admission. I nip it in the bud with another kiss.

When the kiss grows deeper I pull away breathing hard, aware that we can't take this any further before the competition is actually over.

She senses my hesitance and raises an eyebrow, whispering, "You don't want to, ya know… in the barn?"

Be a gentleman. Be. A. Gentleman.

When I don't respond she gives me a naughty look. "I would've thought that you'd feel right at home."

Oof. Don't hold back, baby.

I swallow hard, thinking back to my little incident in her parent's barn.

"When this is all over," I say thickly. "Once your name is called out, I promise I'll take you somewhere so we can… *ya know.*"

Yeah, I don't doubt that she's gonna win. And even if she didn't, I know that those scouts are gonna be on her more desperately than vultures on a steak.

She smiles up at me, that naughty glint still in her eyes, but she nods and acquiesces.

I kiss her again and envelop her in my arms.

She fits me better than my guitar ever did.

EPILOGUE

Madden

Seven months later – February

I ease the four-wheeler up onto the curb outside of the bungalow, tires moving slow-mo through the deep frosting of snow, and then I shut the engine off, turning to look at my girlfriend next to me.

On the top half she's wearing a giant white puffer jacket with a thick fluff-trimmed hood, pulled up over her head to make her look like a furry angel. On the bottom half, all that I'm seeing are her long bare legs and a pair of white cowgirl boots. Her knees are tucked up under her chin and she's happily stuffing her mouth with marshmallow after marshmallow.

You know how hard it is to find vegetarian heart-shaped marshmallows? Really hard. In fact, it's so hard that I had to order them online five weeks ago to ensure that they'd arrive in time for Valentine's Day.

I reach across to gently twiddle with her long soft

hair and she taps her feet against her seat, humming with contentment.

"You have one hell of a sweet tooth," I say, smiling as she tears into marshmallow number fifteen.

She slides her eyes over to me, giving me a devious smile of her own. "There's *something* salty that I like," she replies, and my neck burns volcanic.

Jesus. I look away from her as my face flushes red, pretending to concentrate on un-strapping both of our seatbelts, but really I'm trying to recover from the image that she just put in my head.

Incited by her own naughtiness, she suddenly reaches into her candy pouch and tries to shove a marshmallow into my mouth. I keep my lips firmly shut, disallowing the invasion, and then I take hold of her wrist and remove it from my face, wiping at my chin with my other hand to try and brush off the sugar dusting.

I pluck the marshmallow from her pincers and hold it in front of her lips for the taking.

She gobbles it straight from my fingers like Fantastic Mr Fox.

I laugh, shake my head, and then I let myself out of the driver's side door, moving around to the passenger side so that I can free my little demon.

When I open the door, she's unmoved and still munching.

I lean under the car roof and scoop her straight out, hoisting her up into my arms and shoving the door closed with the back of my bicep.

"Come on, Puss in Boots," I say, eyes trailing down her exposed skin, all the way to her waggling toes. The thick February snowfall is radiating a glittering icy chill and a series of tiny goose-bumps are puckering up her soft thighs.

She gives me a hard kiss on the cheek, purring when my scruff scrapes over her.

"I wanna give you your present before we start making the dinner for my dad," I say, shifting her weight onto one arm so that I can fish for my key in my back pocket.

Since deciding to stay in Phoenix Falls my relationship with my dad has been one of my top priorities, making up for the time that I was away and incommunicado, hence why we're spending our first Valentine's here, making him dinner and then maybe going to see a movie. Then, obviously, I'm going to steal Kitty for myself.

I never claimed to be a saint.

"A present?" she asks, beaming up at me. She stuffs the almost-empty marshmallow bag into her pocket, suddenly keen to give me her full attention.

I laugh. "Yeah, a present. It's Valentine's Day, baby. You thought that I was gonna let you go without?"

She scrunches up her nose, and gives me a shy smile.

Yeah, like hell she thought that I'd let her go without. With a nickname like *princess* what else would she expect?

I unlock the front door and push it open, kicking off my boots before walking up to my old bedroom, still in the same shape that it was when I was fifteen.

It wasn't difficult for me to decide what to buy for her. After winning the Barn Bonanza in July and signing a local contract before the New Year, I knew that it was time to get her fully equipped for a year of studio sessions and potential touring.

When Kaleb realised how serious I was about his sister – after I gave my position to Tyler and took a break from the band so that I could stay in town with Kitty – he started coming to terms with the idea of us being together. So much so that he's been texting me repeatedly, offering me to get back on the road with the guys.

I knew that he was finally *really* okay with Kitty and I being a couple when he suggested that she could tour with us.

My chest swells at the idea.

I kick open my door and then set Kitty down, facing the bed.

She lets out a squeal when she sees the large guitar-shaped case resting on the comforter.

She spins around to face me, her eyes sparkling with excitement.

"I hope it's a puppy!" she says, and then she laughs and yelps when I bury my face in her neck, biting at her ear.

"I'm kidding, I'm kidding!" she cries, squirming as I tug at her skin, but I can tell that she's loving it because she's holding me in place by my hair, arching her throat upwards so that I can get better access.

I pull away, breathing hard, and then jerk my chin behind her again.

"Open it," I say, trying to hide my nerves. I hope to God that I haven't totally misread her.

I don't need to tell her twice. She whips around, hood thrown backwards because she's moving faster than the speed of light, and in one quick swoop she unzips the guitar bag, pulls the top to the side, and reveals the guitar within.

She steps backwards into my arms, fingers covering her warming cheeks. I unfasten her jacket and rub my hands over her stomach.

"Like it?" I ask, resting my chin in the crook of her neck. She shivers when my stubble stabs into her.

"Yeah," she whispers, eyes roaming all over it.

It's her first real guitar that's actually fully hers. Not a second hand gift or a rental from her brother. It's new, it's electric…

And it's rose petal pink.

She turns around, all shy now, and lifts herself up so that she can kiss at my lips. I smile as she pecks at me, heat pooling in my abs, and I let my hands push her coat off her shoulders, exposing her little white dress.

I pull away, tugging at my lip-ring, and my eyes trail down her body, stopping when I get to her boots and crouching down so that I can take them off.

She sits down on the edge of my bed, holding each ankle up for me so that I can slide her shoes off of her.

I grunt when I see what she's got on underneath. Those little freaking pop-socks. I run my palm down my jaw, wondering if we have time for a round in here before we start making dinner for when my dad comes home.

Reading my thoughts, she pulls the straps of her dress off her shoulders, rolling it down to her waist and exposing an eye-popping push-up bra that has me lunging for her chest, ripping down the cup so that I can take her in my mouth.

"*Ah*," she whispers quietly, fingers lacing through my hair. I lick and suck at her until she's moaning and then I pull her dress fully away from her body.

This is *my* Valentine's Day gift.

I tower over her, standing between her legs, and I pull my wallet from my pocket so that I can take out a condom.

Yeah, I'm not a total animal.

She rolls her eyes and tries to steal the foil packet from my hand with her toes.

I laugh as I release my belt, shoving down my jeans and rolling on the condom. I pull my shirt off over my head and press my torso firmly down against hers. My fingers slide down over her cotton-covered heat and then I gently tug two digits beneath the gusset, pulling it to the side.

"You want me to become a Papa or something?" I tease her, aware of how huffy she gets when I make us use protection.

"Maybe," she bites back, looking me hard in the eyes.

My abs clench tight and my cock jerks, slapping hard against her soft inner thigh.

"Don't say things like that," I whisper, aligning myself up with her. "You'll make me wanna take it off."

She squeezes her thighs around my back. "That's the whole point."

I grunt, grip my hands around her hips, and then thrust the whole way inside. She arches off the bed and makes the prettiest sound that I've ever heard.

I slip it in and out slowly, wanting to take my time with her, and I rub a hand over her breasts, caressing her nipples and making her whimper.

She leashes her fingers into my hair and pulls my

face down to hers.

"I love you, princess," I murmur and she clenches involuntarily around me. A whine leaves her throat and my balls immediately ache, growing heavier with the need to unload.

"I love you, too," she whispers, and then she starts pressing kisses into my lip-ring.

I smile as she licks at me, and I close my eyes in pure contentment.

That's my girl.

A NOTE FROM THE AUTHOR

Dear reader,

I hope that you enjoyed reading *Where It All Began*!

I knew as soon as I introduced Kitty and Madden's characters in *Where We Left Off* that they were destined to be together. Their love story is so sweet, and it makes me so happy to be able to give them their happily ever after.

Now, as a special thank you to the readers who loved my first novel, *Where We Left Off*, I am excited to share an exclusive bonus chapter, dedicated to all of the amazing people who fell in love with River and Tate's story.

This is for you.

Chronologically, this bonus chapter takes place just after Chapter 12 in Where It All Began.

BONUS CHAPTER

River

My flip-flops slap against the porch steps as I walk up to the front door of the cabin. By the time that I reach the handle I've created a little puddle right behind me, the light from the warm-tone wall sconces catching and reflecting against it.

I pull open the door and clip-clop inside.

The Hanson Lu cabin is a gorgeous open-plan wooden extravaganza, so as soon as I'm in the doorway I can see the living area to my left, the kitchen to my right, and, up the wooden staircase, the whole of the upper-level gallery corridor. The only room which is slightly shielded is the guest bedroom at the back of the bottom floor.

It's no matter though. Tate hears me come in straight away.

As soon as I've closed the door behind me Tate makes his way from our room for the night, a towel in one hand roughly scrubbing at his hair, darkened with dampness from his shower. A dimple appears in my cheek as I soak in the fact that he's mine.

I twiddle with the large diamond on my left hand and the other dimple appears.

Everyone knows that I'm his too.

I have my hands bundled into tight little fists underneath my body-enveloping towel, keeping it in place around my shoulders to mid-thigh. I use my cloaked upper-arm to nudge my glasses back up my nose and Tate gives me a heart-stopping grin as he strides over to me. I smile back at him and he throws his towel around his neck, clasping his hands behind my back, and then hoisting me up using the strength of his forearms. He bounces me slightly against his chest and then ducks down to kiss me.

Butterflies flutter in my belly and I waggle my feet happily above the floor.

"I need to get a shower," I whisper, as his mouth begins exploring my sun-kissed cheeks and the sensitive edge of my jaw.

He nips at me lightly and my body clenches.

"The hot-tub water," I say by way of explanation.

His hands have remained above-towel, but I can sense his growing urgency. It's in the Southern region, and it's heading quickly North.

"I should wash off the hot-tub water, and then we can go to bed."

"I can come up there with you."

The man will not be defeated.

"Tate," I laugh as he rocks into me against the front door. "I'll be ten minutes. In fact, no – I'll only be five."

He pulls away from me slightly so that he can look

into my eyes, that sparkly look burning behind his sugar-crystal irises. The midsummer heat is radiating from the large planes of his body, and his tan looks even darker now that the sun has finally set. After a moment of consideration he rubs his nose against mine and then gently sets me down.

He hasn't let go of me though. His arms are still compressing me against his abs.

"Five minutes," I repeat.

He watches me carefully from above. Then, "Five minutes," he murmurs, reluctantly acquiescing.

I wriggle out of his arms and then, after kicking off my flip-flops, I skedaddle up the steps, peeping over my shoulder when I reach the top.

Tate's left hand is holding onto the ball at the bottom of the banister, tapping at it with his thumb as he watches me.

I smile.

I then proceed to have the fastest shower that anyone has ever had, dipping my hand into the toiletry bag that we've had with us whilst being on the road for Tate's most recent motorbike competition, and pulling out all of the amenities that will get me squeaky clean.

And, more importantly, smelling good enough to eat.

Once I dry off my cookie-scented skin I slip my glasses back up my nose, my diamond on my ring finger, and I pick up my soggy new bikini, holding it loosely over my fingers as I make my way back downstairs. I imagine that Kit will be staying outside with Madden for a while, meaning that Tate and I will be alone in the cabin, but I remain huddled under my towel to prevent a peep-show, just in case.

When I get to our room I slowly toe the door open and then, once inside, I bump it shut with my butt. I toss my bikini atop the carrier bag that it came in and, without looking up at Tate, I turn slightly so that I can lock our door.

I can feel his energy darken the second that the bolt is secured.

I glance up at him and I see that he's folding my Sunday dress. I tossed it on top of his bag like a discarded napkin when I headed out for my hot-tub evening and, being so fond of it, he probably doesn't want it getting permanently wrinkly. My eyes sweep over the soft baby pink gingham in his large tan hands and the contrast is so extreme that I feel a pleasurable warmth pool in my body.

He finishes folding it and places it on the top of the pile.

Then he moves around to the other side of the bed and yanks the curtains shut.

I move a little bit closer to the bed, still shrouded in my towel, and Tate tosses his shirt onto the comforter as he rounds the mattress to get back to me, instantly distracting me with his thick hard build. The large tattoo on his bicep flexes as he strides my way, his veins pumped from the strenuous summer that he's had with his dad's joinery company, but still twitching with energy that he's yet to spend.

On *me.*

I keep the towel gripped around my shoulders as Tate heaves me from the floor, sitting us down on the bed so that I'm straddling his lap. His mouth finds mine the second that the startled *ah* leaves my lips, and he kisses me firmly as his hands run over the fabric covering my back.

"Hi," I whisper quietly when he pulls away for a second. He's looking at where our groins are compressed, carefully shifting his belt buckle so that it doesn't press into my bare skin too hard.

His eyes flash up to mine and in the next second I feel his smile against my lips, kissing at me with a solid and steady rhythm until I'm panting against his mouth, desperate to remove my fingers from the towel so that I can run them through his dark hair.

"Hey baby," he whispers back, both of his hands now stroking my neck. His hips are rolling relentlessly upwards, causing me to squirm and grind in his lap.

I decide to risk it all, switching my clutch on the towel from both of my fists down to one, and with my newly freed hand I begin fumbling at his belt buckle.

Tate pulls away with a groan, leaning backwards so that he can watch what I'm doing.

I'm not exactly putting on the most graceful show. Instead my fingers are tugging at the metal like a lion cub attempting to tear into a steak.

His chest reverberates slightly, a chuckle rumbling up the thick column of his throat, and he removes his hands from my neck so that he can release the leather tongue of his belt from its confines. Once he pulls it open he leaves it dangling from the loops of his jeans, his fingers having already moved onto the more important task of working on his zipper.

I lift up onto my knees so that he can shove the denim down his thighs, and then I settle myself back into his lap, the only barriers that are left now being my towel-shawl and his cotton underwear.

The concrete shaft in his boxers has me seeing stars

when it presses against me.

Tate can tell. He grips his hands back around my throat before kissing me long and hard.

When I have fully melted against his warm chest he murmurs, "Are we…" He takes a deep breath, then swallows. "Do you want to… here? In someone else's house?"

I have lost control of ninety-nine percent of my body. The one remaining percent is my brain.

Like a child I feign innocence, looking up at him with twinkly eyes and whispering back, "Do I want to what?"

He grins down at me, playing along with my impishness.

"I'm being serious," he murmurs, although he's still smiling. "Do you wanna have sex in someone else's house or would you rather we hold off it tonight?"

Tate and I aren't often in a situation wherein we're spending the night in a place that isn't "ours". During my first year at college he spent most of his non-working hours hauling his truck to my campus and keeping me company in my tiny dorm, and over this summer so far we've spent the majority of our time at Silver Lake, bar the instances when we've been on the road for Tate's comps.

I didn't exactly have intentions of us doing it at the Hanson Lu ranch tonight but when I was being pressure-cooked in the hot-tub with Kit she did vaguely allude to the high potentiality that Tate and I may want to be intimate. I naturally turned strawberry-patch pink but she told me that she would be okay with it, especially if we were being discreet.

And we *are* currently in the cabin alone.

I twist my lips to the side and then glance at the wooden cabinet next to the bed. The almost empty box of condoms that Tate had packed for whilst we were away for his comp is perched in the centre, illuminated by the night-lamp in a magical golden glow.

When I look back at Tate I can see that he's noticed what I've clocked, his cheekbones flushing crimson at his own eagerness.

My heart flutters at the sight.

I lean quickly forwards, capturing his mouth with mine, and he moans like I've just answered his prayers. His kisses me back full force and his hands finally rip the towel away from my body.

He doesn't pull away to look at my newly exposed skin – instead he compresses his warm palms firmly against my back and then squishes me tight against his chest. When my nipples brush against his muscles he grunts and moves his hands to my hips, grinding me over his arousal with a strong grip and a fast pace.

I pull away gasping and he finally allows himself to look down at me. He bares his teeth slightly when he takes in my small curves and he lifts a hand so that he can palm at my breast.

"*Tate*," I whisper as he makes us switch positions, pushing me down into the centre of the pillows and settling his large body between my thighs.

"You looked so pretty in your new bikini, baby," he murmurs as he works his way down to my chest. I lock my hands in his hair when his tongue meets my nipple, my back arching off the bed as he swirls and caresses me.

"I'll… I'll wear it for you. At the lake," I gasp out

quietly as he starts sucking on me. He makes a deep pleasured sound and I wrap my thighs around his solid middle.

He looks up at me through his lashes, his bright eyes so dazzling that I forget how to breathe. Finally he gently removes me from his mouth, kissing my little peak sweetly before settling himself higher up my body, his hips now almost flush against mine. I squirm as his thick length presses against the top of my inner thigh and he has to look away from me, his jaw hardening, in order to maintain his composure.

When he turns his face back to mine, gently pressing kisses across my forehead as his right hand reaches for the box on the dresser, I remember the thought that had crossed my mind earlier.

No time like the present.

"I was thinking about getting a belly-button piercing," I whisper to him as his hand retrieves the foil package. His eyes flash to mine immediately, his irises burning. I don't miss the fact that he almost dropped the condom.

He blinks down at me as if he's trying to raid my mind. I smile up at him, pressing my nipples against his warm muscles.

He sucks in a sharp breath through his teeth and then lifts up an inch so that he can look at my belly. I remove my hands from him so that I can drum my fingers around it. He instantly smiles, his cheeks flushing when he looks up at me again.

"You want that?" he asks, the arm that he isn't leaning against moving between our bodies. I move my hands back to his hair and he splays his palm over my tummy.

"I thought that *you* might want that," I explain, a happy warmth spreading in my chest as he rubs his thumb into me. "Because, you know…"

I trail off. Because he *does* know.

Tate has always loved the idea of making a family together, but when I reapplied for college during my year out after high school we made a sort of deal.

The plan was simple.

I go to college. I graduate.

Then Tate takes me down the aisle and spends our honeymoon pumping me pregnant.

I don't use birth control pills and Tate has used condoms for our entire relationship but, once I'm his wife, he wants us both to be bare.

Tate bites at his bottom lip, his hand pressing firmer into my belly.

"You're so sweet, baby," he whispers, and his fingers start moving a little lower.

When he reaches my clit he begins rubbing circles into me, and I writhe underneath him, moaning in need.

"Baby," he rasps, his hips rocking against me as he watches. "You don't have to do that for me. It'd be so pretty, I know, but the thought of someone touching you there, to stick a needle in…" He winces slightly, then shakes his head. "Unless you want it for you, you don't need to do that for me. I fucking love your belly, baby. I love you exactly as you are."

I start to pant as he rubs his fingers against me harder, and he groans as he pleasures me, his hips bucking faster.

"I need to…" he whispers, his eyes flashing to the condom on the quilt beside us.

I nod my head adamantly, because I need him to do that too.

He quickly frees himself of his underwear and then he grabs the foil packet, shoving it between his teeth and then tearing it open. I make a small nervous humming sound, sliding my glasses further up my nose with my left hand, and Tate's eyes catch onto the diamond that he bought for me, his gaze blazing like an inferno as he rolls the condom down his length.

"Hold onto me," he commands when his eyes move back to mine.

I wrap my arms tight around his neck and he groans as he moves himself into position, my body tiny underneath his.

His pectorals are large and swollen, his biceps crowding over my head as he moves his hips to mine. Then he reaches down between us so that he can align his arousal against my heat.

I clutch him tighter, my body already clenching. He looks down at me with a dark heated gaze and then slowly drags his tip up my clit.

The warmth in my belly overflows and I swallow back a whimper. He's so large and strong and I can't wait to be full of him.

"Please," I ask breathlessly, tightening my thighs around him so that there's no room for misunderstandings.

He catches my drift.

Holding the base of his shaft he begins to push against me, letting out a low growl when his tip breaches my entrance. I arch and wriggle and it drives Tate crazy. He slams the rest of his length inside of me, stopping as soon as he's filled me to the hilt. He dips his forehead down so that he can look at me, gauging my reaction.

"Sorry," he whispers, his chest heaving in eager pants. "I didn't mean to… to…"

I press my body upwards into his muscled abdomen, instantly distracting him from the verbal realm. He looks down at my small compressed cleavage and slides himself out, pushing back in slowly as he sets his pace. His movements are unhurried but each stroke hits me deep, and my belly contracts as he fills me up.

My eyelashes flutter and my brow pinches at the feel, the size, and the scent of him. He smells warm and *male*, and I have to remind myself to maintain my grip in order to prevent myself from melting on the mattress.

Tate takes one of my hands from around his neck and interlocks our fingers against the pillow. He squeezes our hands together and then his hold suddenly becomes more firm, as he begins using it for leverage as he increases his rhythm. He slips in and out faster and faster, his eyes raking down my torso and grunting as he watches me bounce.

I free my other hand from his hair, at first stroking up the stubble on his neck and jaw, and then eventually placing it over my stomach. When Tate looks down at me, his eyes molten, I whisper up to him, "I can feel you here." I delicately touch my lower abdomen. "In my belly."

"Baby," he groans, his own brow arched in pain and pleasure. "No talking like that, baby. You know how talking like that makes me get."

I do know, and the effect on his movements is

immediate. He's thrusting harder and faster, the hand that was holding mine now gripping at my breast, before sliding behind my knee and pushing it backwards against the mattress. I claw my fingers into the meaty muscles of his back and a low rumble leaves his chest, his eyes avoiding mine as he tries to stay calm, to not finish just yet.

"I loved watching you win your race this week," I murmur, my fingers trailing up to the back of his neck. "You make me so proud," I continue quietly, swallowing thickly when his gaze flashes to mine.

"River," he warns, his damp fringe making his eyes look even darker. He moves my knee back to his waist and then slips his hand down to my clit.

I arch off the bed as he tries to caress me, his size and strength making gentleness out of the question. He tries to make his thrusts less rough but he looks like he's in agony.

"It's okay," I whisper quickly. "Don't stop, please. *Please.*"

"You sure?" he grits out, his muscles bunched and vibrating.

I take a deep breath and nod. "Please," I say again.

He gives me what I want.

Tate's hand slides up to my inner thigh, pushing me wide to accommodate his thrusts, and he pumps me rough and deep. My nails bite into his back and he grunts in pleasure, his sac slapping loudly against my skin as he pounds me into the quilt.

"Fuck, baby," he groans, his palm massaging my thigh against the mattress. "I can't get enough of you."

His eyes trail up from my tummy, back to my chest, and lightning flashes behind his irises.

"As soon as you finish I need your tits in my mouth again, baby."

I moan and squirm but he holds me in place, pumping me to the brink so that I can finally reach my orgasm.

I squeeze my eyes shut and I hear his breathing grow ragged, his thrusts growing sloppy as he watches me about to come undone.

"I'm almost…" I start to whisper, but as soon as his fingers begin rubbing my nipple I'm suddenly already there, my head falling back into the pillows and a series of quiet whimpers leaving my chest.

Tate rolls into me, hard and heavy, his arms keeping me in place as I pant and writhe. I peep up at him as my orgasm ripples through my body and he's watching me with the sexiest look that I've ever seen. There's a solid determination in his eyes, along with his own rugged lust, but above all he's watching me with care and patience, one hand now cupping my jaw as he works me past my peak.

"Baby," he murmurs when my movements gradually subside.

He strokes his thumb across my bottom lip and, although I have barely one ounce of strength left in my body, I press a tiny kiss against his skin.

He swallows hard and then slowly slides out to the tip, checks my reaction, and then pushes back in.

"*Mm*," I hum, attempting to wrap my arms over his hulking shoulders.

"This okay?" he asks, as he begins slipping in and out of me again.

My eyes almost roll into the back of my head.

"It's more than okay," I whisper, and he grits his

teeth, stifling a groan.

"We could… I could…" I bite my lip as I watch him increase his speed, losing himself in me as he works himself to the brink.

I caress his biceps with my hands and he tilts his head Heavenward, the thick column of his throat making my brain go fuzzy.

"I can roll over," I whisper up to him, wanting to give him an orgasm that's as strong as the one he gave me.

He dips his head down, his eyes heated and hazy.

"What, baby?" he murmurs, his thrusts never letting up.

I massage my fingers into his shoulder muscles, suddenly nervous about being so forward.

"I can… roll onto my belly," I say again, my cheeks getting warmer. I look shyly up at him, comprehension dawning on his features. "Or on my hands and knees."

"Jesus Christ," he says hoarsely, no longer in control of his movements. His brow is pinched in agony as he slams his hips into mine, and he shakes his head when he meets my eyes. "You're too good, baby," he groans. "You're too fucking good to me."

I tighten my legs around his body as he passes the point of his climax, thrusting hard and from every angle that he can, in order to fully relieve himself of his aching spend. He keeps his eyes on my face as he pumps himself through it, and I move one of his hands to my breast so that he can grope me as I bounce. He grunts, low and tight, his palm rubbing and squeezing as he unloads his spill.

I stroke at the large planes of his back as he finishes, his chest heaving, and then he lowers his body onto mine, compressing me into the bed.

I lean up to kiss at his neck and a contented rumble sounds in his throat.

"You're too good," he mumbles again, the hand that was massaging my chest now tangling in my hair.

I snuggle into the crook of his elbow, his swollen bicep engorging against my cheek, and I sigh out a sort of purr.

He moves slightly so that he can duck down and kiss my forehead. Butterflies flutter excitedly in my belly.

"Gonna be a while 'til I can get you down the aisle," he murmurs quietly, his eyes on mine when I peek up to look at him.

"I could always drop out," I murmur back.

He groans and smushes his face into the pillow, a muffled sound of pain sounding above my head. I try not to smile, but I freaking love how much he wants to make me his wife.

"You know I'd never ask you to do that," he says quietly when he turns his face back down to me. "I want you to finish your degree. If that's what you want," he adds.

I give him a tiny secretive smile, knowing exactly what is currently being unsaid.

Tate would be the happiest man on the planet if I dropped out of college and married him this summer, but he's being a gentleman about it so that I can quench my need to satiate my mom, as well as prove to myself how capable I am.

Plus, Mitch would love to see me graduate.

And, of course, we should maybe wait a little longer until we finally get me pregnant.

"You know I'd rather drop out," I say, my pointer finger drawing a heart over his chest. "And I know you'd rather that too," I mumble, my brow dipping at the thought of how long we'll have to stay restrained for.

His cheek ticks up and he tilts my head so that I'm looking into his eyes again.

"I know," he says quietly, his irises glowing with adoration. I purse my lips, sulking, and a chuckle rumbles in his chest.

He carefully shifts his body so that he can tenderly pull out of me, groaning when we're no longer joined, and then he compresses his torso against mine, allowing me to nuzzle into his warm skin. He dips down so that he can meet my lips, and then kisses me chastely until I'm no longer frowning.

Tate pulls back so that he can look down at me and then he finally murmurs, "You're worth the wait."

ACKNOWLEDGEMENTS

Thank you to my mother, who raised me a reader, and who is always the first person to read my books.

And to my father, who said that I should write about whatever I wanted to – that's exactly what I did.

Finally, I would like to say a humungous ginormous THANK YOU to you, my amazing readers, whom I love so dearly.

Your kind messages make every season feel like summer.

Love always,
Sapphire

ABOUT THE AUTHOR

Sapphire is a romance writer, specializing in contemporary new adult love stories. She has a First Class Honors degree in English Literature and Education Studies from Durham University, and she graduated from Cambridge University as a Master of Philosophy.

Where It All Began is an interconnected standalone book, and it is the second book in the Phoenix Falls Series. The first book in the series is *Where We Left Off*, which is a coming-of-age enemies to lovers romance.

Where We Left Off and *Where It All Began* are the first books that Sapphire has ever written, both of which she wrote and published in the space of one year.

If you are looking for books that will give you butterflies, you have come to the right place.

Author website: www.sapphireauthor.com
TikTok and Instagram: @sapphiresbookshelf
Pinterest: @sapphireauthor

Made in United States
Troutdale, OR
10/06/2023